COLD QUARRY

A Frank Pavlicek Mystery

D1711775

Praise for the Pavlicek series:

"A breath of fresh air in the field of private eye fiction."
—*NY Times* bestselling author Jeffery Deaver

One of "Ten Rising Stars in Crime Fiction" feature
—*Publishers Weekly*

"A great read." —*Library Journal*

"Fast-paced, twisty, and complex." —*Booklist*

"A book this good, and this original, helps remind
me why started reading mysteries in the fist place."
—Edgar Award-winning author Steve Hamilton

COLD QUARRY

A Frank Pavlicek Mystery

ANDY STRAKA

PUBLISHED BY:
LLW Media

ISBN 978-0-9848438-0-0
Copyright 2010 by Andy Straka
All rights reserved.

First published by Signet, an imprint of New American Library, a division of Penguin Putnam Inc.

NOTE
This is a work of fiction. Names, characters, places, and incidents either are the product of the author's imagination or are used fictitiously, and any resemblance to actual persons, living or dead, business establishments, events, or locales is entirely coincidental.

Cover design e-book edition: Mayapriya Long, Bookwrights

ACKNOWLEDGMENTS

Thanks are especially due to Genny Ostertag, my editor at NAL, whose suggestions, as always, have helped turn this into a much better book. And to my agent, Sheree Bykofsky, for her continued guidance and support.

Author Deborah Prum, former NSIS Agent Bob Brackett, and falconer Lee Chichester kindly offered their expert input on the manuscript as well. I'd also like to thank Ed Clark of the Wildlife Center of Virginia for his ideas; Officer Mike Pridemore and the Charleston, West Virginia Police Department for letting me ride along on patrol; Joan McClanahan, Nitro city recorder, and Bryan Casto of the Nitro Fire Department for pointing me in the right direction and supplying information about the history of the town; and Doug Gellman of Blue Ridge Mountain Sports for providing information about handheld GPS systems.

Last but not least, my family deserves the greatest thanks for putting up with the long hours and preoccupation of a novelist husband and father. Writing may be a solitary pursuit, but it is never performed in a vacuum. Their love and support make it all worthwhile.

AUTHOR'S NOTE

Charleston area residents will observe that I have taken a few minor liberties with West Virginia geography, and with a few locations, in particular through the creation of the fictional KBCX television station and Balthazar Hotel. As always, all names, characters, places, and incidents are either the product of the author's imagination or are used fictitiously, and any resemblance to actual persons, living or dead, business establishments, events, or locales is entirely coincidental.

For Bernice Lucille Presnell Straka,
and Orville and Blanche Presnell,
who never forgot the mountain South.

Prologue

There is a light that sharpens the hunt during darkest
winter, a delicate radiance belonging as much to the earth as
to the sky. After dawn, it clings to the trees like some
corporeal messenger. Remember the stark reality of cold
possibilities, it says, black memory, the frozen echoes of
hollowed-out veins beneath the ground.

The old man remembered.

"Ee-lo-y-lo-y-lo," he cried. Neither the earth nor the sky
offered an answer; Elo was gone.

The man faced the gathering of a gray emptiness above,
straining for a glimpse of his falcon, but saw nothing: no dot
above the horizon swelling with approaching speed; no
twirling air dance to materialize on the wind. There'd been
no response to his whistle either. His gyrperegrine must
have jumped the ridge, caught sight of a mallard maybe on
the state-land pond on the far side of the slope. The faint
telemetry signal from his receiver appeared to be coming
from there.

Other sounds seem to come to him on the wind.
Footfalls? Motors? Or just a distant highway? For a few
moments, the old man had the distinct impression he was
being watched. Something to do with Elo? Something to do
with the illness that had affected his bird not so long ago?

No, he decided, pushing the thought from his mind.
This time, at least, he was dealing with nothing more than a
falcon off on a lark.

He pictured the duck again, high wheeling as it took to
the air over the pond. In his mind's eye, he watched Elo
overtake the slower-flying bird. The falcon, falling in its
lightning stoop, would have jackhammered the bigger bird
with its talons, ending the mallard's life instantly, then
would have broken away to recover from the force of the
strike, before swooping down again to gather in its prey
from the air.

The falconer was sorry he might have missed the show. Not sorry to have missed the killing part, because he'd seen enough of it in the past, but sorry to have missed the culmination of the bird's graceful exit from his stoop. Sorry his sixty-seven-year-old hip, the one he'd injured in Korea, had begun to bother him again. Sorry because he understood whenever you allowed a captive falcon to fly free, if the wrong circumstance developed, the bird's bond to you could break without warning. It had happened to him before.

"C'mon, Chester, ya idiot. Let's get it goin'," he said out loud to himself.

He willed himself uphill through a stand of burdocks that stuck to his clothing, fighting against the weariness, ignoring the troublesome doubt that the prostate cancer he had already beaten once might be attempting to book a return engagement.

There was snow today along the ridgelines running back from the river. Not much, just a dusting. Damn hard drought. The pond beyond the slope might be dried up or frozen, in which case there would be no ducks there, only dry yellow reeds stuck like frozen hair to its icy surface.

This was not the terrain for a longwing hunter. They'd started a half mile away where the forest had been cleared and opened to an adjoining acreage of pasture. Here, the trees closed in, cutting his bird's line of sight.

With a grunt he crested the hill and stepped up into a cold slap of wind. He took in the scene on the other side.

More forest. A sharp-topped rock of a hill rising into the distance above a slushy brown puddle, a pitiful excuse for a pond. He put his hand to his brow and scanned the sky and the tree line once more, looking for Elo, but all he saw were a pair of mourning doves, dropping to alight in a distant bracken.

B-deep, b-de-e-ep.

Good news. The signal from the telemetry receiver sounded loud and clear. Wherever Elo had gotten himself to it must be on this side of the hill. The old man tweaked the dial on the unit then held the yagi aloft like a personal television antenna to see if he could get an exact bearing.

There, straight into the trees toward the peak. With a gloved hand he wedged the receiver beneath his arm, pulled his whistle to his mouth, and blew a haunting note.

The wind gusted as if in response, but still no sign of his bird.

"Ee-lo-y-lo-y-lo. ..." he bellowed at the top of his voice and waited.

Nothing.

He sat still, scanning the trees and listening. Then he noticed a flash of silver white, boulders and fallen spruce beyond a bank. The stream, or at least what remained of it. He stumbled down the rocky slope, stopping for a moment to break off a length of fallen limb to use as a walking stick. The air was thick with the smell of pine and moss.

As he approached, he saw that the streambed here was wide, but the water itself flowed only in a narrow channel, meandering among the stones. At the rivulet's edge there was soft sand, mud, and foam. An accumulation of encrusted debris from the last heavy rains of some time ago swelled up against the banks. Downstream showed more evidence of drought, small pools of standing water, chalk-yellow stone. He stepped gingerly along the streamside, clambering over another fallen tree trunk, and almost stepped on the first of the tracks.

It clearly belonged to his falcon, he saw, crooked in the talon and toes spread wide apart. Except something was wrong. The bird appeared to be moving in an irregular zigzag, dragging its own weight in an unnatural fashion.

The signal was stronger than ever. The stream ahead curved around a stand of high grass, and when he stepped beyond this obstacle, the old man noticed something on the ground beside the water. As through a lens coming into focus, he recognized the white underbelly, black bandit hooding.

It was Elo, lying on his side.

He rushed to his downed falcon. The peregrine was still

alive, trying to move his legs, but appeared incapacitated, his whole body shuddering and a wing flopping haphazardly. The old man tried to get the bird's attention, but Elo's ancient eyes appeared fixated on the sky. Had his raptor been attacked by another predator? He bent over and examined the body and wings for signs of injury, perhaps a broken bone or a bleeding wound, but found nothing. No, these were some of the same symptoms Elo had exhibited before, only worse. Much worse.

"Bastards. ... We better get you straight to Doc Winston again, young soul."

He unbuttoned his hunting vest, lifted Elo and cradled him in the crook of his arm as he stood to go. A large branch breaking in the woods nearby startled him.

"Afraid it's a little too late for that," a familiar voice said. "Took you long enough, old man."

The falconer turned. "Wha—what's going on?"

"What can I say? You were right. ... Sorry we have to do it this way."

1

The ski-masked man balanced the business end of the twelve-gauge Mossberg Persuader against my temple with a shaky hand. Of equal concern, he appeared to lack the hard-won experience that might discourage him from pulling the trigger.

"You sure you want to do this?" I asked. "Seems like you're overreacting."

"Shut up, dick-wad," he said.

Did I also happen to mention his limited vocabulary? That and the dark green swath of cloth covering his head and face had almost convinced me of the futility of attempting to reason further with the guy. With his free hand, he was digging in my coat pocket for my truck keys, but that was the least of my worries.

"Let's just think about this now —"

"I said shut the fuck up!"

A few snowflakes twirled like bits of ash among the branches overhead. This peaceful winter mountain scene, I thought for one dark moment, must have made for a quiet place to die. But steam flaring from the nose and mouth holes in the assailant's mask snapped me back to reality. Though he juggled the keys once he had hold of them, the dark barrel didn't move from my face. I was as concerned he might shoot me by accident as I was about his shooting me on purpose.

Ironic, because it was a supposed accident that had brought me up here to this spot in the first place.

Chester Carew had been a friend and fellow falconer, a lifetime West Virginian from Nitro, an old factory town of about seven thousand souls just downriver from Charleston. Three days before, someone had put a round from a high-powered rifle straight between Chester's shoulder blades not far from where we were standing. The cops, I'd been told, were calling it a hunting accident, an errant shot from some yet-to-be-identified drunk or stoned poacher. I thought they were probably right—neither I nor my friend Jake Toronto, Chester's falconry sponsor, had ever been able to talk the hard-headed old cuss into wearing blaze orange in the woods during deer season when he should have known better.

But just to satisfy my own curiosity, and since Chester's funeral wasn't due to begin for another three hours, I'd gotten directions from Toronto, who'd otherwise been circumspect about the whole business so far, and had taken a ride up here to this patch of ridge and fallen scrub oak to have a look around.

"This isn't even your land," I said, hoping to distract the gunman. Funny how a piece of weaponry like his could alter the equation between two people.

"Never said it was."

The acreage was posted and technically now belonged to Carew's estate until it passed through all the vagaries of probate to the old man's widow. The police had left vehicle tracks the size of tractor treads and a shredded trail of crime scene tape to lead me toward where Carew's body had been found. Mr. Ski Mask had popped into view just as soon as I, unarmed and not expecting him, topped a small knoll near the actual scene. At first, I thought he might be one of a group of teens out playing paint ball or something. Until I laid eyes on the shotgun he leveled in my direction, that is. He was obviously not too keen about me being here.

"All right, mister. Turn around and start walking. And keep your hands in the air."

"Why? So you can shoot me in the back the way you did Chester Carew?"

"I said shut up! I didn't shoot nobody. But I'm about to shoot you if you don't get yourself moving." The accent was thickly Southern. The voice sounded young—I guessed early twenties—and scared. I wondered what of.

"Okay. Okay." I started to turn.

"Wait a minute."

What now?

"Let me see your wallet."

"You want to rob me too, is that it?"

"Let me see your friggin' wallet," he demanded.

I pulled it out and handed it to him.

He flipped it open and looked at my license. "From Virginia," he read. "Frank Pavlicek. ... Oh, Jesus. You're a goddamned private investigator."

I stared at him and shrugged.

"Shit," he said. He repeated it four times. "What am I going to do with you?"

"If you decide to shoot me, they'll find you. You'll leave a lot of traces of your presence."

"Shut up," he said. "You hear?" He swung the barrel of the gun away for an instant; then he brought it back hard against the side of my mouth.

The blow from the cold steel felt like being struck with a heavy chunk of ice. My tongue tasted blood and my lip seemed to have suddenly caught fire.

"Now turn around and get moving!"

"All right." I nodded vigorously. I guess I'd pushed him about as far as I could. "You didn't have to do that."

Turning, I felt the shotgun drop completely away from my face and heard the thump of my wallet and the jingle of my keys as he flung them off into the woods. It was the brief mistake I'd been waiting for.

I kept on turning to spin a complete three-sixty, squatting toward the ground as I did and driving forward into his lower body. I must've had thirty or forty pounds on the guy and I was lucky; he'd instinctively pointed the gun toward the sky as he'd tossed the keys. He gasped and let out a sound like a bull snorting when I hit him. The Mossberg went sailing from his grasp. It also discharged into the treetops with a thundering boom while we tumbled together in a heap to the muddy ground.

Keeping ahold of him, however, proved to be like trying to wrestle a wriggling trout. I opted for going after the gun. Maybe that was *my* mistake. The young man recovered quickly and leapt to his feet. As he did, I noticed he'd torn the shoulder of his fatigues in the fall. A colorful tattoo, a firebird it looked like to me, winked out for a second before he shifted the ripped material back across his upper arm. Then he panicked. Simply gave up on the weapon and ran. He was already about twenty yards down the ridge by the time I was able to grab the gun. His dark boots flying over fallen logs made thumping noises like a deer pounding through the trees.

I let him go. Plenty of tracks to follow, as long as it didn't rain later. I'd also seen the mark on his shoulder and I hoped there might be some latent prints on the weapon. I fished a tissue from the now-muddy pocket of my town jacket and pressed it against my lip to stop the bleeding. The front of my cord pants were soaked and spotted with mud as well.

I reached into my coat pocket the way my attacker had and felt for my cell phone to dial 911—maybe I could get somebody on this idiot's tail before he got too far. Only one problem. It wasn't there. Had I left it in the truck? No, I remembered stuffing it into my pocket as I entered the woods. I hadn't realized it, but the masked man must have taken it along with my keys. Wonderful.

I looked over the weapon. This was no recreational duck hunter's gun. A sleek black *über*-modified model, similar to the military version, it held at least five more three-inch shells in the magazine ready to pump into the chamber.

I spent the next fifteen minutes rummaging around in the brush before I finally came up with my wallet and my key ring snagged around an exposed rhododendron root. No such luck with the phone, however. Maybe the guy still had it with him. It would most likely end up in a trash can somewhere.

I followed the masked man's tracks until they ended at the highway about three-quarters of a mile from where I had parked my truck. So he must've had a vehicle too. Or maybe someone had been waiting for him. Either way, he had to have been in one heck of a hurry to get out of there because I found his second mistake lying in plain sight on the shoulder of the road.

It was a handheld global positioning receiver, a Magellan Sport Trak Pro, built especially for climbers and hikers. Scuffed with dirt but brand-new from the looks of it. Was the guy worried about getting lost?

A slick shotgun and now this shiny new piece of hardware in trade for my cell phone — seemed like a better than even exchange as far as I was concerned.

Something told me this was going to be one heck of a funeral.

2

"Father, Son, and Holy Spirit, we now commend ..."
    The pastor talked on, but his words soon faded into the background of a staccato whoosh of wings. Two red-tails and one broad-wing hawk selected for the release leapt from their respective falconer's gloves. They shot away above the headstones, maybe the oddest and most beautiful version of a twenty-one-gun salute I'd ever seen.
    To his credit, the pastor got the message of the birds' sudden premature departure and hastily concluded his sermon. Chester Carew may have been one of the most fervent followers of Jesus I had ever known, but he'd never been one for long preaching.
    His final resting place was a tidy affair, an orderly arrangement of a dozen or so tombstones on the heights overlooking the factory bottomland below. In Nitro, the pulse of the Kanawha River was never far away. In St. Albans, Institute, Dunbar, South Charleston, and Kanawha City — most of the industrial towns surrounding the state capital — the river flowed in wide snaking arcs past chemical plants, boat landings, and fine river houses. Here, at the metro area's farthest reaches, it did much the same; except that not being blessed with a modern chemical facility, the old factory buildings down along the shore were mostly either dead or dying. The main evidence of industrial activity came from the gargantuan trio of steam stacks of the John Amos power plant belching out their smoky product in the distance beyond the rising girders of the I-64 bridge. Much closer in, around the casket, fresh-cut flowers held out their blossoms bravely against the cold.
    "That was really nice," Marcia D'Angelo whispered in my ear.
    She meant the hawks. For a moment, I'd almost forgotten about her leaning against me with her arm wrapped in mine. Marsh was a class act. She'd met Chester

Carew the year before and said she wanted to drive out for the funeral. She was also my former girlfriend. We were ultimately incompatible, she'd decided, which had started me wondering whether any two human beings were ever really compatible. My ex-wife had used the same logic on me for different reasons years before.

On my other side, my daughter, Nicole, also had an arm looped within mine. My best friend, Jake Toronto, stood several yards in front of us at the edge of the small crowd, a frail old man leaning heavily against his shoulder. All in all, a sad reunion for a sad occasion.

"You okay?" Marcia asked. She kept her tone low.

I nodded. "You?"

"Fine. I hate funerals."

Chester's wife, Betty, and his young son, Jason, moved into position beside the casket. The pastor began speaking to them about something no one else could hear.

"Are you going to get involved with this ... Chester's shooting, I mean?" Marcia asked.

"I guess I'm already involved."

After returning to my truck, I'd driven down to Dutch Hollow Park to find a pay phone and called the Kanawha County Sheriff's Department. By the time I'd finished talking to the two deputies who'd shown and turned the shotgun over to them (I decided to hang on to the GPS unit), it was nearly time for the funeral to begin. I'd brushed off my coat as best I could, found a change of pants in my overnight bag, and rushed to the church. Marcia had shaken her head. "You look awful," Nicole had said. Jake had waited patiently to hear what happened. After I explained about the man in the woods, they'd helped me get cleaned up further so as to be at least halfway presentable for the service.

"Do you have to be involved?" she asked.

"Yes."

Marcia nodded. I could sense her disapproval but she said nothing. We'd all driven in separately the night before and were staying at a motel at the Cross Lanes exit off the interstate, a Sleep Inn just over the hill from an industry that *was* thriving: a thousand-slot "racino," as its promoters liked to call it, complete with a greyhound racing track and video poker. Apparently, suckers spring eternal, even here in the shoulder of the Appalachian Bible belt.

A particular numbness settled into the pit of my stomach. It was the same as I'd felt at my own father's funeral a decade before. All the conversations I'd had with Chester over the past three or four years, mostly about falconry, but about other things as well, came flooding back to me.

If you've lived in West Virginia your whole life and have any brains about you, Carew once said, you learn to endure the hillbilly comments and inbreeding jokes about Appalachia with a certain amount of defiance and pride. I'd heard the jokes ever since I'd lived in Virginia. *What's the state flower of West Virginia? A satellite dish.* You get the idea. In New York, we used to assume the same sort of superiority over New Jersey or Upstate. I've been told they say the same thing in St. Louis about Arkansas. Why do you suppose we do that, Carew had asked, run down somebody else's home turf in order to elevate our own?

I stared across the blue tarp surrounding the casket at Betty Carew. Her face was stoic as she listened to the pastor's words, the wind catching wisps of her white hair and winding them about like tendrils, though her eyes betrayed a hurt the likes of which I could only imagine. She and Chester had been together for what, thirty years? Beside her, the boy shifted his weight awkwardly from one foot to the other as he continued holding on to her hand. He was seven or eight years old and was adopted, but besides that I knew little about him.

The wind rose again and several of the three or four dozen other mourners in attendance shivered against the damp air. More than half were falconer friends from Virginia, West Virginia, Pennsylvania, and Ohio, but the rest were people from Chester and Betty's church or people he'd known from his work at the chemical plant in Institute. Chester had lived in the Kanawha Valley his entire life. This was home ground for him and he had loved it. At least the local earth had seen fit to return the favor and had not been too frozen to delay the interment.

When the ceremony ended, the assembled mourners began to file from the cemetery, navigating the narrow walkway along the edge of the bluff back toward their cars. Marcia, Nicole, and I went over to Toronto and the old man at his side.

"Marcia, Nicky, I don't think either of you have ever met Jake's father."

Felipe Baldovino—he and Toronto's mother had never married—listed hard to port into the wind, using his son's ample arm as support. He was shorter than Toronto and much thinner, except for a bloated belly. Across his wizened face he bore a perpetually surprised expression, the result of thick gray eyebrows curving upward. Today he wore a threadbare black overcoat with a tall gray fedora atop his head that must have been a holdover from the sixties.

"A pleasure to meet you young ladies," Felipe said. His voice was firm despite his frailty and the cold.

"It's a pleasure to meet *you*," Marcia said.

"Me too," said my daughter.

"I'm only sorry it had to be on such a sad occasion. Chester was a good man. A very good man. And my son here … well, I suppose you all know how he felt about him."

He looked at my mouth. "Frank, what happened to your face?"

Marcia and Nicole had managed to help me stop the bleeding from the corner of my Up, but when I'd looked in the mirror in the church bathroom, I also saw a nice little bruise blossoming there. I exchanged glances with Toronto. He'd been the one who'd called to tell me about Chester's death a few days before, but his expression, or lack thereof, gave nothing away.

"Let's just say I had a bad encounter with a pine tree," I said.

"Did you come all the way down from New York, Mr. Baldovino?" Marcia asked. She was the only one of us, besides Felipe, dressed appropriately for mourning: a long black wool overcoat, black pants and fashionable low-heel black shoes. From me she knew how Felipe had lived in Queens while his son had grown up mostly without a father on the streets of the Bronx and Yonkers. Felipe had worked for years as a longshoreman. He had also, according to Toronto, nearly drank himself to death, chased just about anything in a skirt and, although he'd never physically struck Toronto's mother, had inflicted unimaginable mental anguish on the woman he refused to make his wife. Seems Felipe, at the time, had had this little problem of a wife and five children over in Queens.

I was surprised a few years before when Toronto had told me he was going up to New York one weekend to visit his father. But by then his mother had already been dead for more than a decade, the old man wasn't in the best of health, and maybe Toronto had wanted, if not to forgive him, at least to allow the remaining years of his father's life to include some form of relationship with his estranged son.

"No, no. Didn't Jake tell you? I own a cabin maybe thirty, forty miles from here," Felipe said. "A few of us got together and bought it to go hunting way back when I was still working the docks. Now I'm the only one left. We didn't pay but a couple hundred dollars for it. Just a battered old place ... like me, eh?" He chuckled to himself. " 'Course that was pretty good dough back then."

"You still come down here to hunt?" Marcia asked. She knew he meant deer hunting.

"Nah." He waved his hand. "I come down for a few weeks every now and then just to check on the place. That's how I got to know Chester. Didn't think I'd ever be attending his funeral though while I was here."

No one said anything for a few moments.

"That was a nice touch with the release," I said to Jake. "Whose idea was it?"

"Mine," he said. "I got Mark Bigelow and Lonnie Richards to set it up. They run that rehab operation and breeding facility down toward Beckley."

"I didn't know Chester all that well, but from what I remember and what Frank has told me, it seems to me it's exactly what he would have wanted," Marcia said.

Toronto nodded. "Still remember the day Chester called and asked me to be his sponsor ... like I could teach *him* anything."

His father poked him in the arm. "Hey, I told him you were my son. He said he checked you out with all those other hawk people and they said you was the best."

"Hawk people" was how Felipe referred to anyone having anything to do with falconry. He said he couldn't see why anyone would waste time chasing a bird around the woods when you could a lot more easily just grab a box of shells and a thirty-ought-six and go.

A wiry man with dark red hair and a goatee came walking over to us. "Hey ... Jake, Frank, you guys got a couple of seconds?"

Toronto and I turned to look at him. Damon Farraday was a plumber from across the river in St. Albans who was a recent apprentice of Chester's. He'd probably spent more time with the old guy in the past few months than anyone besides the new widow.

"Geez, Frank, what happened to your mouth?"

I repeated the pine tree story.

"That's too bad. Listen," he said, "I'd really like to talk with you guys."

"Yeah?" Toronto said.

I was afraid Farraday might want to talk about what would happen to Chester's remaining two birds, which seemed a bit untimely given the fact that he wasn't even cold yet in the ground.

But instead he said, "I suppose you guys have heard I'm the one found Chester the other day."

"Right. We know."

I hadn't, in fact, but obviously Toronto had known so I said nothing.

"I'd really like to talk with you guys about it. I mean, you two used to be cops, right? And nothin' like that's ever happened to me before."

"You must've already talked to the police, didn't you?"

"Yeah, but you guys knew Chester, and I want to get your take on it. I got some ideas of my own about who mighta killed him."

"Oh, yeah? You think we got time for that, Frank?"

I guessed my gunman had been about the same age as Farraday; not as tall, however.

"Plus, Betty wanted me to ask if you two will be stopping by the house before you leave town," Farraday said. "There'll be a bunch of folks and food and stuff, but, Frank ... she especially says she'd like to talk with you."

I glanced back at Marcia and Nicole and at the remnants of mud on my clothes. I also felt the inside of my swollen lip with my tongue. "Be happy to talk with her," I said.

Another mourner, a woman, came along in front of us. She was of medium build, wore her wavy blond hair in a short bob, and was dressed from head to toe in the chocolate-brown uniform of a West Virginia conservation agent, a forty-caliber Smith & Wesson handgun holstered to her side. Farraday introduced her. Her name was Gwen Hallston.

"So you must be the famous Jake Toronto." She looked Toronto up and down. "Heard a lot about you from Chester."

"Mmm. ..." Toronto said.

She said she had had a great deal of respect and admiration for the old falconer.

"He'll be missed, that' for sure," I said.

"You going by the house now?" Farraday asked her.

"No. I've got to head down to Cabin Creek for a meeting."

"Can I ask you something?" I said.

"Of course."

"What's your opinion of how Chester died? You buy into this hunter theory?"

She shrugged. "We get our share of hunting deaths, that's true. Except, of course, it's usually the people carrying the guns."

I nodded.

"The shooter could've been lost or might've been poaching. He could've thought he was firing at a deer or a bear, maybe even a wild boar. Or it could've just been some yahoo with a rifle stoned out of his mind. Had a guy last year said he thought he was trying to take down an elk. He said that after he'd blown apart someone's backyard birdfeeder with his black-powder rifle. We get a few of those kinds too."

"Are you saying the person might not have known they were on Chester's land?"

"Exactly. Those posted signs deteriorate. Chester hadn't kept them maintained."

"You must know a lot of the deer hunters around here. Any particular suspects come to mind?"

She laughed, scratching her arm. "Most of the hunters around here are pretty responsible. ... Something like this? Drive down the road and flip a coin. You might as well start searching every vehicle."

"Okay," I said.

She eyed me thoughtfully for a moment. "You don't mind me asking, Mr. Pavlicek, what's your interest in all this?"

"I knew Chester from falconry. Jake here was also my sponsor when I started."

"I see. ..."

"Frank's a private investigator," Farraday interjected.

"No kidding?" She raised her eyebrows toward me. "Don't get involved in shooting cases too often though, do you?"

"Not when I can help it," I said.

"You got any ideas, you best share them with the sheriff's department."

"Sure. Thanks."

She said it had been nice meeting us and moved on.

Marcia and Nicole had come abreast of us. "Hey," I said. "You folks up for stopping by the Carews' house first, maybe grabbing something to eat, before we hit the road?"

"I thought you were all going to head straight home, and—" Marcia stopped in midsentence, obviously remembering our earlier words and realizing that my getting socked in the face with a shotgun barrel was going to have to make a serious dent in our plans.

"Damon wants to talk with Jake and me about Chester's shooting," I said. "And Betty wants to see us too."

"Oh," she said.

We all walked together for a few more paces, then Marcia and I peeled off from the group for a moment to stand awkwardly by her car. She seemed distracted.

"You see," she said softly. There was anger tinged with hurt in her voice. "This is why you and I can't be together."

"Really? Why is that?"

"Because I can't even show up at a funeral for a friend of yours without you getting punched in the jaw and involved in some kind of trouble."

I said nothing because she was right, at least about the getting in trouble part.

"I think I'll just head on back to Charlottesville," she said. "It's a long drive and I've got a class to teach in the morning. Please pass on my sympathies to Chester's widow and son."

It was one of those times I didn't know what to say. Didn't know how to act or what she needed or didn't need from me. I didn't want her to leave but she seemed determined.

"It was really nice of you to come, Marsh," I heard myself saying. "Even though you hate funerals."

She kissed me on the cheek, unlocked her car, and opened the door. I turned so that no one else would see my face while I watched her climb in, start the engine, and drive away.

3

Toronto and I rode with Damon Farraday in his old Scout.
Nicole followed in my truck. The Scout was one of the
ugliest buckets of bolts I'd ever seen, stained a permanent
shade of rust. I got stuck in the back. My head hurt.

Toronto had left his own mode of transport, a brand-
new silver-and-black Harley-Davidson V-Rod most other
people wouldn't be caught dead driving in the middle of
winter, back in the Carews' barn. Felipe said he wasn't
interested in going to the gathering at the house, so Toronto
had walked his father to his vehicle before saying good-bye.

The land around Nitro looked dry and distressed.
Farraday maneuvered down a steep hill, negotiating a
hairpin turn. He looked uneasy himself. He glanced first at
Toronto, then back at me. "Never thought I'd have to be the
one to go finding somebody dead like that," he said.

"Most people don't." I kept my tone neutral. "What
happened?"

He glanced across at Toronto. "Well, Jake here already
knows some of this. ... I was working on a residential job
down in South Charleston when I got a message from my
office saying Betty was trying to get ahold of me. I called her
up and she told me Chester hadn't come back yet from his
early-morning hunt. He was supposed to be going to his
regular doctor's appointment, but he hadn't shown up back
at the house and she was starting to worry about him. Asked
if I'd go up there and make sure he was all right."

"So you did. ... What'd you find?"

"I found his Suburban parked down at the start of the
dirt road leading up to his land. Didn't look like nothing was
wrong."

"Then what?"

"Well, you heard he had Elo with him, didn't you, and
that the bird is still missing?"

I nodded.

"I know Chester's two favorite fields and a couple of ponds where he likes to take Elo. I checked those first."

"But you didn't find him."

"No."

"So what did you do?"

"It was after noon by then. I was starting to get worried myself. I saw a couple of turkey vultures circling around high up along the ridgeline so I decided to head on up there. ... Took me awhile."

"And is that where you found him?"

"Along the streambed. About dried up with the drought."

"Jake told me he'd been shot in the back."

"Yeah. I ain't never seen that kind of thing before."

"How was he lying on the ground?"

"He was on his stomach." Farraday paused for a moment, almost as if he were looking at the scene all over again. "His arms were spread out wide. Face was turned toward the ground."

"You could tell he was dead?"

"Yeah. I felt his neck for a pulse and didn't feel anything. I turned him over, blood all over his clothes, but there was nothing to do 'cept call the cops."

"They came right away?"

"I called on my cell phone. Took 'em about a half hour to get up there."

"No sign of the bird?"

"No, sir. That's what I did while I waited for the sheriff's department to show up. Chester had his yagi and receiver with him. I picked them up and tried to see if I could get a reading on the bird, but there wasn't a thing. Not even a signal."

"But the unit was still working?"

"Yeah."

"Where is it now?"

He shrugged. "Deputies took it, I suppose."

The talk of telemetry and tracking made me think of the GPS unit I'd found earlier belonging to my assailant.

"What do you think happened to Elo?" I asked.

"I don't know, but I'm especially worried about what happened to that bird."

"Why is that?"

"Ain't you heard?" Farraday looked at Toronto. "Didn't you tell him?"

"Tell me what?" I looked over at my former partner. Toronto's activities over the past year had been even more mysterious than usual. We hadn't talked much. I'd been busy working under a new subcontracting arrangement with a northern Virginia investigative agency, helping with a mountain of background checks on both existing and prospective government employees. Nicole, who'd been working for me part-time ever since she'd been a student at UVA, was now trying it out full-time since she was on winter break from her senior year. We were becoming a pretty good team.

But Toronto often seemed preoccupied with his own brand of increased business, the extent of which I could only imagine. He maintained a number of contacts from his time spent in the military before we'd worked together on the force in New York. At least twice in recent months he'd said he had to leave the country for a couple of weeks, although to where he wouldn't say. The second time, he'd brought his two birds over to Chester's place in Nitro for safekeeping.

He spoke without looking at me. "Chester told Farraday here that Elo had been sick. Some sort of illness and partial paralysis. The vet ran a bunch of tests, but wasn't sure what was wrong with him. Sent some kind of labs out for further analysis. Chester called me about it too."

"But Chester was out hunting with Elo when he was killed," I said. "He recovered?"

"Yeah. Elo got better," Farraday said. "Chester said he thought he was going to be all right."

I thought about that and what it might have to do with my own encounter in the woods. How many people walked around the woods like that toting a military-style shotgun? Did the guy in the mask have something to do with

Chester's murder and Elo's disappearance?

"Maybe the bird just raked out on him," I said.

"Maybe."

"What's the vet's name?"

"I don't know where he took him. You, Jake?"

Toronto said, "He told me he took him down to see Dr. Winston. Winston's a local vet, not an expert on raptors, but he's treated Chester's birds and a handful of others for a few years now, so I suppose he knows what he's doing. I've met him on a couple of occasions with Chester. Seems like a good man."

The Scout rumbled over a rough patch of road, causing my forehead to scrape against the ceiling, doing wonders for my throbbing cheek.

"Sorry about that," Farraday said. "Got to get the shocks looked at one of these years."

We had been heading down First Avenue along the railroad tracks straight into Nitro. What was left of the WWI boomtown created specifically for the manufacture of gunpowder were the hulking foundations and shells of the former Explosive Plant C, row upon row of orderly streets populated by mostly bungalow-style houses, a throwback to the days when massive barracks housed the thousands of workers, and a washed-out business district spotted by decaying buildings. We turned left and drove past the firehouse. Another quick left brought us past a giant American flag festooning a proud little city hall across the street from the headquarters of the Nitro Police Department.

"So why did you think Chester even called you guys in the first place?" I asked.

"He'd given me permission to hunt up there if I ever wanted—not that I was planning to since it's so far from my place—and he wanted to warn me about a potential problem," Toronto said. "He thought there might be something in the air or the water up there, maybe something that was affecting the game population too. Seemed pretty worried about it."

"Yeah," Farraday chimed in. "He told me the same kind

of thing. Let me go hunting on his land sometimes with my redtail, Tawny, and he knew I'd been over there in that same area a couple of days before. He wanted to know if Tawny was showing any symptoms too."

"Did she?"

"Nope. She's been fine, far as I can tell."

"So maybe Elo just happened to come into contact with something that made him ill. Maybe he ingested some kind of pesticide or something."

"Maybe," Toronto said.

"When did all this happen?"

"About ten days ago."

"The lab results come back yet?"

Toronto shrugged. "Not that I know of. ... Damon?"

Farraday was busy wrestling with his gearshift at the moment. He stared straight ahead.

"Damon?"

"Oh, sorry. What were you asking?"

"Lab results. You know if anything more has come in on Elo?"

"Uh-uh. I ain't heard a thing."

I put my hand up against the ceiling to steady myself in the seat. "Damon, you said you had an idea about who might've killed Chester."

"Yup. I do. I mean I ain't no cop or anything, but if I was, I'd sure be looking at these two."

"What two are you talking about?"

"I first ran into 'em when I was hunting up there on Chester's land a few weeks ago. Had ourselves a conversation. Two guys, seemed about my age, both carrying shotguns."

"Poachers?"

"I ain't sure. Didn't look like no hunters to me."

"What did they look like?"

"That's just it. I couldn't really tell 'cause they was dressed in camo and masks."

A ball of apprehension materialized in the pit of my stomach. "What did they say to you?"

"They wanted to know what I was doing up there. I had Tawny with me and I told 'em, and naturally, I asked the same about them."

"And?"

"They said they was lost."

"Lost."

"That's right."

"You tell the sheriff's department about all this?"

"Yes, sir."

The Scout rumbled a bit as we rounded another curve.

"Hey. If it was one of these dudes shot Chester, why don't we just get after 'em?" Farraday asked. "Cops probably won't do nothing about it."

"Let's not go off half-cocked until we know what we're talking about," I said.

"I'll tell you one thing. Whoever killed Chester is gonna pay if I have anything to say about it," Farraday said.

4

The Carew place was a smallish Victorian relic that had seen
better days. The exterior siding, though not quite peeling,
was painted a dull shade of what might have once been
yellow. The foundation planting lay listless in the cold. More
than a dozen other vehicles lined the driveway and spilled
onto the lawn.

Toronto and I were sitting in the cab of my pickup. He
had pulled me aside while Farraday went with Nicole into
the house and said simply, "We gotta talk."

Both my back and my aching head rejoiced at finally
being able to peel myself out of the back of Farraday's Scout.

"What's going on?"

"There's more to this story," he said. "I didn't want to
spill in front of anybody else."

"Tell me," I said.

"There was something else eating at Chester besides Elo
getting sick."

"Yeah?"

"He took me to a couple of meetings to see if I could
help him sort things out."

"Sort what out? What kind of meetings?"

"Ever hear of a group calling themselves the Stonewall
Rangers Brigade?"

"Sounds like a bad name for a country-and-western
band."

"Well, this is no musical group. They're active around
this area. I'd guess you'd call them a militia for want of a
better term. Named themselves after a unit from the Civil
War."

"You're talking about a bunch of fools with rifles." My
masked attacker was beginning to come into clearer focus.

"Yeah. Except these people aren't exactly fools—at least
some of them aren't anyway. They're full of white
supremacist crap, and they seem pretty serious about it."

"I thought most of their kind went underground after the whole McVeigh execution and all that."

"Apparently not—not around here at least."

"Okay, but what's any of this got to do with Carew? You say he took you to a couple of meetings? I find it hard to imagine Chester having anything to do with white supremacists," I said.

"Me either, but here's what happened. A few of them started showing up on his land out there where you were today. Since he was the only one hunting or doing anything on that acreage, they wanted to know if Chester would give them permission to use part of his land for some of their" — he mocked quotation marks with his fingers—"training exercises, as they called them."

"So what, Chester let them on his land?"

"No. At least he said he told them no at first, but they kept after him. Invited him to several of their meetings. He finally asked if I'd go with him to check them out."

"Why didn't he just call the cops?"

"You know Chester. He said he was going to make up his own mind before calling in the police or anything."

"But if he let them use his land and they were ever engaged in anything illegal, he could've been drawn into it."

"I told him the same thing, but I guess it was more complicated than that."

"How come?"

"He wouldn't say."

"So you went to a couple of meetings with him?"

"Yeah, some farm over near Hurricane. Seemed like just a bunch of bucktoothed crackers running around wearing camo to me, but then I noticed something. A few of 'em had better credentials and were deadly serious."

"What do you mean?"

"I mean most of these folks seemed like they barely knew how to hold a rifle, but a couple of the leaders and a small group of others were experienced people."

"Ex-military?"

"I don't know."

"What did they talk about?"

"The head man gets up and gives some lecture about vague threats from all the Jews and enemies foreign and domestic and how we all need to be prepared. Rahrah-rah."

I shook my head.

"I know. Hard to believe anyone would buy into it, but most of these characters just sat there nodding like bobble-heads."

"What did you say to Chester?"

"To tell you the truth, I found the whole idea of these people out there with their little weapons pretty pathetic, especially since we've got legitimate military ops and people strung out all over the globe. That's what I told him."

"What did he say?"

"He said I was probably right."

"You think one of these militia yahoo types is the shooter who put a bullet in Chester's back?"

"Fifty-fifty between them and some drunk hunter. Like I said, most of 'em didn't look like they could shoot straight if their lives depended on it."

"But you said there were some serious ones too."

"Right."

"What about the guy that gave me this?" I indicated the contusion at the side of my mouth.

He winced. "Now that, I'd say for sure, was one of the yahoos."

"This sounds like something the FBI would be interested in."

"I suppose."

"You and Chester consider calling them?"

"I thought about it, but Chester didn't want me to. He said to just let things ride for a while."

"Maybe he let things ride too long."

"Maybe."

"So what? Now you want *me* to go to the Feds?"

Toronto folded his arms and smiled. "You're at least semirespectable, Frank. You know that."

"I guess I'll take that as a compliment."

"You know what I mean. I start talking to Feds and they get all nervous."

Toronto made a lot of people nervous, me included now and then. I couldn't say for sure, but just looking at him I guessed he was in his best physical condition ever. His eyes blazed with that gaunt, hungry look I'd seen in pictures of marines getting ready to go into battle.

The outside of Chester's house might not have appeared any different from when he'd been alive, but inside the atmosphere was changed. In the main hallway, a small display had been set up with flowers and pictures of Chester and Betty and Jason and pictures of Chester with his birds. One of Chester and Elo stood in a particularly prominent position. A long table had been set up in the dining room to receive bowls of fruit salad, greens, baked goods, and steaming main dishes. A group of mostly elderly people milled about the house, some eating off paper plates, others talking quietly. In the kitchen, four or five women worked at the stove and the counters and the sink.

Toronto and I made our way to a corner where Nicole stood talking with Farraday, who held a plastic glass filled with punch. A stocky man with salt-and-pepper hair and an expensively tailored dark suit with brown pinstripes came toward us, almost as if he'd been looking for us.

"Damon?" he asked. "Are these the gentlemen?"

Farraday nodded. "Frank, Jake, Nicole, this is Chester and Betty's lawyer, Tony Warnock."

"Pleasure to meet you all," Warnock said. He shook everyone's hand in turn. "Sorry for the sadness of the occasion, however."

"Were you expecting us or something?" I asked.

"Oh, yes. I represent Chester's estate and am the executor of his will. Betty is interested in speaking with you about what happened to Chester and so am I."

"Okay."

"Would you like to get something to eat before we talk?"

I looked at Toronto and Nicole but was met by shrugs.

"That's all right. We'll wait."

"Well, *I'm* hungry," Farraday said. "You all go on. I'm going to go get a sandwich."

"Fair enough," Warnock said. "Betty's out back in the barn helping Jason tend to the birds for a few minutes. We thought it might give us a little more privacy."

"Sure. My daughter works part-time for me as an investigator. Any problem if she comes too?"

Warnock cleared his throat. "As long as you're okay with it."

We stepped outside. The big barn in back was a much newer structure than the house and obviously better maintained. Betty had often teased Chester that his birds lived better than they did. Chester had trapped his first raptor, a kestrel, when he was a young man. He'd been flying redtails and Cooper's hawks back in the days before there were any state or federal regs. A heavy work schedule forced him to give up falconry for many years, but when the state of West Virginia finally got around to approving new falconry regulations in 1997, he decided to take it up again. He'd been retired for a while from his job as a chemical engineer and Betty encouraged him — she was worried, she told Toronto and me some time later, that Chester was beginning to lie around the house and be forever underfoot. The irony was he had to find someone to sponsor him and go through the apprentice process just like everybody else.

Toronto and I had been introduced to Chester at a meet in Harrisonburg. There was an instant kinship, and Toronto was honored when Chester asked him to be his sponsor. Since then, the two of us had been hunting many times with Chester in and around the Kanawha Valley. Even though it was a long trek for me to get over to Nitro, I always looked forward to seeing the old man. He liked to tell Jake and me stories about the "old days" of falconry, the wild and unpredictable experience of working with birds of prey before anyone else viewed them as protected species and all the government regulations became involved.

We found Betty and Jason Carew talking next to one of

the weathering cages.

Betty looked up at us, squinting. "Frank, Jake, thank you for coming. Good to see you too again, Miss Nicole."

"Good to see you too, Betty," I said. "How are you holding up?"

"Oh, I'm all right, I guess." She squinted again, this time at my face. "Goodness. I didn't get a look at you at the burial, Frank. You ought to get that looked at. What happened?"

"I'll explain in a minute," I said.

There was an uncomfortable silence while everyone took a moment to digest the situation. Jason hadn't moved from his position by the hawk pen.

"Honey?" Betty said, gesturing in the boy's direction. "You remember Mr. Pavlicek, don't you? And Mr. Toronto? They was good friends of your daddy's."

The boy wiped the back of his hand across his nose and came toward us. He nodded.

"And this here's Mr. Pavlicek's daughter. Her name's Nicole."

The boy nodded again, staring at the four of us with wide eyes.

"Jason's a little shy at first, but don't you worry. He'll warm up to y'all before you know it."

I felt like asking how the boy was handling his father's death, but not with him standing right there.

I crouched in front of him. "Jason, it's good to see you again, buddy."

I held out my hand; he put his small paw in my fingers, and we shook.

"You helping your mom take care of these big birds?"

"Yes, sir." The youngster's voice was halting, still very much the high-pitched tenor of a boy, though now he was being asked to absorb an emotional blow that critically wounded many men.

"Honey," Betty said evenly, "I think we're done out here for the time being. Why don't you go see if they need any help in the kitchen or in the dining room setting up chairs."

"Yes, ma'am." The boy seemed relieved to have something to do so as to not have to engage in further conversation. Without another word, he turned and exited the barn.

"Gotta be hard on him," I said.

Betty nodded. She closed her eyes and shook her head as if she were attempting to will it away.

"I'm sorry."

"Chester loved that boy," she said.

Betty and Chester had adopted Jason when he was an infant. He'd been Betty's niece's son, but when the niece and her husband were killed in a house fire—Jason had miraculously survived—and Betty's sister was too ill to take the boy, she and Chester had volunteered. They had no other children of their own.

One of Chester's birds fluttered from its perch to the ground with a noisy squawk. There were two left: a big female red-tailed hawk named Mariah and a tiercel Harris's hawk named Torch.

Nicole stepped over to the weathering enclosure. "What's going to happen to Chester's birds?"

"Jason's too young to be an apprentice," Betty said. "Damon's been looking after them. I suppose we're going to have to find a good home for them, but I can't even think about that right now."

No one spoke for a moment while the old woman gathered her thoughts.

"But that's not what I asked y'all to come talk about, is it?" She picked up a plastic pail from the floor and placed it back on a post on the wall alongside a couple of others.

"Damon said you wanted to talk with us about how Chester was killed," I said.

"That's right."

"The police are looking for the hunter?"

"Claim to be, anyway."

"I was just up there myself to have a look around. In fact, that's where I got this." I gave her and the lawyer a skeletal version of what had happened to me earlier. "You say you already reported this to the police?" Warnock asked.

"That's right."

"This just confirms what I was afraid of, Tony," Betty said. "Frank, you know about the Stonewall Rangers?"

"I filled him in," Toronto said.

"I told Chester not to have anything to do with those people," she said. "Isn't that what you told him too, Jake, after he took you to those meetings?"

Toronto shrugged and nodded.

"Why doesn't the sheriff just round all those people up, bring them in and line them up for questioning until they find out which one did it?"

"Not so fast, Betty," Warnock said. "We don't know that the person Mr. Pavlicek ran into this morning has anything whatsoever to do with Chester's death, or with any particular group for that matter."

"We don't?" She seemed close to tears.

"Why don't we just let the police handle the matter, the same way they're looking into Chester's accident?"

"I'm telling you I know evil when I see it," she said. "And those Stonewallers are evil people."

"I know. We may not always agree with what other people believe, but they still have rights."

"It still could've been a poacher or someone else," Nicole said. "You can't say for sure yet."

"Hon, I know you're right." Betty wiped a tear from the corner of her eye. "I just get upset is all. I suppose the police are good men, but I can't help wondering if they're barking up the wrong tree."

I gave her a moment to compose herself.

"So what do you want from us?" I asked.

"I want you to, you know, see what you can find out."

I looked over at Warnock, who raised an eyebrow in my direction.

"It's not quite that simple, Betty. Via reciprocal agreement, I am licensed to do investigations in this state, but this is a manslaughter investigation. And possibly, as you say, a homicide. The police—"

"I don't care," she said. "Can't you do *something*?"

Warnock folded his arms across his chest. "Betty, I'm afraid you'd be wasting your money—no offense, Mr. Pavlicek."

"None taken. But I haven't even mentioned money. Chester was a friend and—"

"Dad does pro bono work," Nicole said.

"No," Warnock said. "I mean ... Betty, my counsel is that if you decide you really want to hire this gentleman to look into something for you, you pay him his prevailing rate."

I said nothing. I wondered why Warnock was being such a hard-ass about hiring me and so insistent about the money side of things if I were hired. I'd already decided I was going to work my way into this investigation somehow or another. If those involved insisted I get paid, so much the better. A legitimate paying client gave me a plausible excuse for looking into the matter further.

Provided, of course, there was anything pernicious to be found. Even if Chester really had been shot by an errant hunter and these Stonewall Rangers turned out to be no more dangerous than Rescue Rangers, I could at least bring Betty a little peace of mind. I could always find a way to pay her money back if I felt it was warranted.

"I want to do this, Tony," Betty Carew said. "I want to hire Frank to see what he can find out about Chester's death."

Warnock nodded slowly. "All right," he said. "It's your money."

Betty's eyes met mine. "I've never handled money before. Chester always took care of anything to do with finances. Tony's been helping me. I'd never even written out a check before this week."

Her simple frankness was disarming.

"I tell you what," Warnock offered. "My firm has an account to pay for research and investigations. Why don't I take care of paying Mr. Pavlicek for now. Then we can just add the cost to your bill for handling Chester's estate."

"Would that be wise?" she asked.

"Sounds like commingling to me," I said.

A dark look passed over Warnock's countenance. "Why don't you let me be the judge of that, Pavlicek? I'm not one for always resting on formalities and neither was Chester."

The lawyer and I exchanged hard glances.

"All right then. First things first," I said. "Betty, I'd like to ask you a few more questions—alone this time, if you don't mind. Is there someplace private in the house where we can talk?"

5

Betty Carew sat in the hard-backed chair in a spare third-floor bedroom of the house. 1 stood at the bottom of the bed. Nicole perched on the edge of the mattress across from Betty with her legs crossed and a pen and a pad of paper in her hands while Toronto leaned against a dresser in the comer.

Betty turned to look down through the lace curtains at the cars filling her driveway and lawn.

"Nice of so many people to come. This place may not be much anymore, but right now I'm just glad to be able to hang on to it."

"Money problems?" I asked. I was having second thoughts about Warnock's insistence that she pay me and that the money would come originally from one of his accounts. People who played games with money trails usually played other games as well; sometimes bigger, more dangerous games. Just ask any of the corporate chieftains who'd lately found themselves handcuffed before the cameras. And while there may always be two sides to every story, going on first impressions, I wasn't sure it was Tony Warnock's side I wanted to be on.

She turned back to face me. "Not really. I don't mean to complain. It's just that, like I said, Chester pretty much handled everything financial around here and now I'm left to be dependent on some lawyer."

"You trust Warnock?"

"Oh, I suppose so. We've known Tony for a few years and he's done work for Chester before, back when he inherited that land where he was killed."

"I'm not entirely comfortable being paid for this job, especially with money out of one of his practice's accounts."

"Why not? They're a big law firm, headquartered here in Charleston. If it still makes you uncomfortable, I can tell him I'll write you out a check myself, now that I know how to do it."

"No ... that's all right. I'll just let him play it his way for now. Maybe I'll learn something."

She smoothed out her dark mourning dress, the one she hadn't changed out of, even when she went to help Jason in the barn. "Seems to me you've got to start by trusting somebody, Frank," she said.

"I do. I trust the people in this room. And I trusted Chester. Right now, that's about as far as it goes."

"Okay."

"Putting the money issue aside for a moment, tell me some more about Chester."

"Of course."

"Did he have any enemies that you know of?"

"Enemies? Why, no. Certainly no one that would want to shoot him in the back."

"What about at his work? Anybody hold any old grudges?"

She shook her head. "It's been seven or eight years. The company's been bought out since he left. I can't imagine there'd be anyone."

"Neighbors? Church acquaintances? Anyone with whom he's had a recent dispute?"

Again she shook her head.

I glanced out the window. Some of the visitors were beginning to leave.

"Tell me more about his involvement with the Stonewall Rangers Brigade."

She looked surprised by the question. "I told you what I thought about that. And like I said, I told him too."

"How involved was he with them?"

"I don't really know. Not exactly."

"We know he took Jake to a couple of their meetings."

"Yes."

"Did he ever attend any others, on his own I mean?"

"Not that I was aware of."

"Did you know the group had been asking Chester about using your land?"

"No. Why?"

"We're not sure, exactly. They claimed for some kind of training exercises."

"That's ridiculous. Why those people are just a bunch of ... a bunch of ..."

"Of what, Betty?"

"Of evil charlatans, that's what they are. Of the same ilk as the Klan was in my day."

"What do you think Chester was doing going to their meetings?"

"Well, I don't know really. I remember him coming home and telling me he was concerned some of these people were 'over the top,' as he put it. He was sympathetic whenever anyone started talking about big government eating away at our freedoms and whatnot, but he said they started talking about hating the Jews and that there were a bunch of them who viewed the government in Washington as the enemy. Chester didn't like them saying that. And he said he told them so."

"But he still went back a second time."

"Yes." She looked at Toronto. "What do you think, Jake?"

"Like I told Frank. It wasn't like Chester to let anybody else tell him how to make up his mind," he said.

That brought a small smile to her face, for the first time that day I'd been able to notice. "You're right," she said. "That was Chester."

"Why do you think he wanted to take Jake with him?" I asked.

"I ... I'm not sure," she said. "But I think it was because he was afraid of something."

"You tell the police about any of this?"

"Yes," she said. "But the investigator seemed so certain it was just an accident, a deer hunter or somebody."

"And you didn't know about the Rangers asking Chester to use his land?"

"No. ... But now that I come to think of it, he did get a phone call from a man about ten days ago. He got angry with the caller and they might've been talking about the land. At least I think I remember overhearing something about that."

"Do you remember who the caller was?"

"Chester said his name was Higgins ... something like that."

I looked over at Toronto, who was nodding. "Higgins owns a used-car lot over in South Charleston. He's the guy who gave the talks at the meetings Chester took me to," he said.

"What's the name of the police investigator you talked to?" I asked.

"Nolestar. Deputy Bobby Nolestar."

"Right. The deputies I gave the shotgun to told me he is the investigator working Chester's shooting. Have you talked to him since then? Have they told you whether they've made any progress in finding out who did it?"

"I haven't talked to Nolestar, no. Another fellow called here two days ago and said they had a few leads they were pursuing, but that was all. They put a notice on the TV and radio news too, I guess, asking if anyone has information to come forward."

"Did you get the other man's name?"

"No. I think he said he was a public information officer, something like that."

"I'm sorry to have to ask you all these questions, Betty. Especially today."

"It's okay, Frank. That's what I'm hiring you to do, isn't it? Ask questions."

"Some of your guests are leaving. I better let you go for now."

"All right. Where are you going to be staying?"

"I don't know." I looked at Toronto and Nicole. "I haven't gotten that far yet."

"Well, then, you can stay here. I've some extra bedrooms. You and Jake and Miss Nicole too if she wants to."

"I appreciate it, but —"

"No buts, Frank. Where better to start than right here?"

I couldn't argue with her logic.

She rose from the chair and pushed it back against the wall. "Well, I expect you investigators will want to be talking things over."

"Thanks very much, Betty."

"Thank *you*. I'll be down in the dining room if you need me." She disappeared out the door. The wall vibrated some as her footsteps creaked down the stairs.

"Okay. So what do we do now?" Nicole asked.

"Nicky, listen," I said. "Someone needs to handle things back in the office for a few days."

"What? No way, Dad. It sounds like you may need all the help you can get."

"Now don't get excited. More than likely, it'll still turn out to be a matter of tracking down some panicked hunter or poacher. Besides, we've got a backlog of computer background checks that'll probably take you into this weekend."

"Or I could stay here and help you and work late when I get back to get them done," she suggested.

"Not if you like to eat and stay in school for your last semester. This is part of the business, Nicky, if you really still want to learn what it's all about. We've got obligations to certain people. Plus someone's got to make sure Sprite's taken care of, maybe get her out hunting for a few hours."

My daughter fixed me with her best withering stare, a trait she'd somehow absorbed organically from her mother.

"I guess ..." she finally grumbled.

Sprite was Nicole's own apprentice bird, a kestrel. Since releasing my hawk, Armistead, I'd trapped another first-year redtail and named her Bingo, but despite my best efforts, she'd seemed more interested in sitting on telephone poles all day than going after game, even at a keen hunting weight. I'd had to let her go.

"Only how am I supposed to get home? It's two hundred miles and I can't take your truck."

She was right.

Jake smiled. "There's always the V-Rod."

"Oh no," I said.

"You mean I could take the Harley?" Nicole's enthusiasm for the trip seemed to shoot up considerably. She had, after all, gotten her motorcycle license too, this time without informing me. She didn't own her own bike yet, but Jake had let her borrow his old one for a few weeks.

"Don't see why not," Toronto said. "If I need wheels while I'm here, I'm sure Betty'll let me use Chester's old Suburban. And I can catch a ride either to Charlottesville or back to my place with you, Frank, when we're finished out here."

I stared at both of them. "No way. There's absolutely no way. With all those trucks on the interstate? That long a distance in the freezing cold? What, are you kidding?"

"But you said you needed me back in the office," Nicole said.

Seeing I was outnumbered, I went for the flanking maneuver. "We'll rent you a car."

"A *car*?" she said.

"Wimp," Toronto said.

I shook my head and sighed. "You're going to freeze to death, honey."

"Nah. You just bundle up, right, Nicky?" Toronto flexed his shoulders.

I said nothing, looked out the window again where a white van with brightly colored markings was pulling to the shoulder of the road.

"C'mon, Dad. I've ridden Jake's bike plenty of times before."

"You better take it easy," I reminded her.

"Cool," she said.

"The bike's in the barn, isn't it, Jake?"

"Yeah."

"Head out the back door, Nicky."

"How come?" She stood up from the bed and peered over my shoulder.

"Because the media's just decided to show up," I said.

A minute later, a striking blonde—short in stature but

with long hair, heels, and an ankle-length cashmere coat—
stepped out of the van and approached the house. She didn't
carry a microphone, but a cameraman climbed out right
behind her to shoot some footage. The woman stepped up
onto the porch where I was waiting at the door.

"May I help you with something?" I asked.

"Yes." Her calm blue eyes, trained on mine, narrowed a
bit when she looked at my mouth. She had a feline grace
about her, a short, curvaceous body, and a photoshoot face,
drawn, at the moment, with an appropriate expression of
sadness. There were no wrinkles around her eyes, of course,
and just the right amount of makeup, but what also might
have been the faint beginnings of worry lines. I made her for
early thirties, experienced. A pro. "I'm sorry to disturb you,"
she said. "But I'm looking for a Mr. Frank Pavlicek."

"You're talking to him."

"Oh." She blinked with surprise. "Well, it's very nice to
meet you, Mr. Pavlicek. My name is Kara Grayson. I'm from
KBCX television here in Charleston."

"Pleasure."

"One of our local correspondents picked up your name
and address from the police scanner earlier this afternoon. I
understand you may have run into a little problem today up
in the woods?"

I said nothing.

"They said that someone accosted you with a rifle up
there where that hunter was shot earlier in the week. Is that
correct?"

I still said nothing. The cameraman was taking pictures
of the house and the barn.

"I'm working on a piece regarding local extremist
organizations and I thought you might care to comment."

She really did have pretty eyes. Her gaze finally
dropped from mine. She seemed a little flustered. Maybe she
thought I'd gone brain dead.

"I'm sorry, Ms. Grayson. I don't give interviews."

"Really?" She looked back at me. "Why not?"

"Well ... I just don't."

She looked me over again, especially at my mouth. "You're a private investigator, aren't you?"

I smiled and shook my head, though not in response to her question.

"You look like you've had a run-in with somebody."

I just stared at her. At least it was a pleasant experience.

"Listen, Mr. Pavlicek. I'm only trying to do my job here."

"Listen, Ms. Grayson. These people just buried a husband and a father," I said.

"Okay. Yes, I know. I'm sorry. But I spoke with a Ms. Estavez at your office back in Charlottesville and she told me you were out here for the funeral."

"You're quick on the draw. I'll give you that."

She said nothing—finally seemed embarrassed. A good trait, I thought, for a reporter. Provided it was genuine.

She reached inside her coat pocket, pulled out a card, and held it out to me. "Well, maybe we could talk tomorrow. You can reach me at that number. Anytime, day or night."

I took the card from her. "Don't hold your breath," I said.

She gestured to the cameraman to stop shooting film. "Please pass on my apologies to Mr. Carew's family. I'm very sorry if we've upset you in any way," she said.

She spun around and walked briskly back down the steps and across the lawn to the truck, the cameraman trailing behind her. The door slid open, they disappeared inside, the door closed again, and the van pulled away from the shoulder and drove off.

6

I followed Tony Warnock's blue Lincoln Navigator to his law office in Dunbar, midway between Nitro and downtown Charleston. The office was a nicely converted storefront with a couple of oversized concrete urns supporting impeccably groomed potted evergreens out front. The names of several other attorneys also graced the doorway, along with a different Charleston address. Though it was late in the day, an eager-eyed receptionist dressed in a conservative gray suit greeted us upon entering.

I had wanted to interview Warnock with Jake and Nicole there the same way we'd talked to Betty Carew, but the lawyer had insisted he wanted to talk to me and me alone and that he could take care of paying me my retainer at the same time.

"Any urgent messages while I was out?" he asked the receptionist.

She shook her head. "Just Mrs. Drunger about the divorce settlement again. And don't forget, you're due in court tomorrow morning at nine."

"Got it. Frank, this is Penny Holt, my do-everything person around here. Penny, this is Frank Pavlicek. He's a private investigator who'll be doing some work for us. No calls for the next half hour. I've got some things to discuss with Mr. Pavlicek."

Work for *us*? I was beginning to get the impression Warnock was out to make me a bought man. At least Ms. Holt didn't remark on the bruise splotching my face. Probably too professional for that.

"Will you be needing the special-account checkbook, Mr. Warnock?" she asked.

"Yes, please."

He led me down the carpeted hall and into his office. It was a large room off the back, with the only windows being French doors opening to a small patio. An antique rolltop desk sat squarely against one wall. Next to it was one of those modular workstations with a computer. Several photos of sports teams adorned the walls, some new and some old — Warnock was a Cincinnati Reds and a Bengals fan. In the corner, two chintz chairs framed a small coffee table. Warnock sat in one and I took the other.

"You from Cincinnati?" I asked.

"Originally. Been living and practicing here in the Charleston area though since 'seventy-two."

"You must like it here then."

"It fulfills my needs." He reached for a box on the table.

"Cigar smoker?"

"Never took it up."

"Ah, don't blame you. I like a good Macanudo every now and then myself. Mind if I indulge?"

"Be my guest."

He opened the small wooden box on the table and took his time preparing the cigar and lighting up.

"That's nice," he said at last, once he'd had the first couple of puffs. Smoke drifted toward the curtains covering the French doors. I noticed there was a double set and that one was thick and colored a deep red.

"How long had you known Chester?" he asked.

I thought about it for a minute. "Five or six years, I guess. I met him when he first approached Toronto about falconry sponsorship."

"Sure, right, right. This Toronto fellow, he work for you?"

"Jake works for himself. He and I collaborate from time to time."

He flashed a toothy grin between puffs. "Collaborate ... you make it sound like some sort of academic relationship."

I shrugged.

"You and he were detectives together in New York, weren't you?"

"That's right."

"Got into a little trouble, from what I understand."

I smiled. "Some people thought so."

His turn to say nothing.

"You asked me down here because you said you wanted to see that I was compensated for helping Mrs. Carew."

"That's right. That's right. But there's something more important I want to talk to you about."

"And that would be?"

"To begin with ... West Virginia."

"The state?"

"Our sovereign land." He waved his cigar for a moment as if he were conducting an aria.

"What about it?"

"Ever been over here around Charleston before?"

"A few times to go hunting. Once looking for a skip trace that didn't pan out."

"So you don't know a whole lot about our people or our economy."

"I don't know a whole lot about a lot of things, Mr. Warnock. What's your point?"

"Just that if Betty insists on your looking into Chester's death, well, I hope you'll take your time and familiarize yourself with all the local channels before you go off and—"

"Step on anybody's toes?"

"Exactly. Step on anybody's toes."

There was a soft knocking on the door.

"Come in," the attorney said.

Penny Holt entered carrying a large leather-bound portfolio. "The checkbook you asked for, sir."

"Thank you, Penny." She handed it to him and he took it and placed it on the coffee table before him.

"Anything else you need? Something to drink maybe?"

Warnock looked at me, but I shook my head. "No, that'll be fine for now," he said.

The assistant excused herself and left the room, closing the door with a soft thud behind her.

"Tell me something, since you've lived around here a long time and all. How much do you know about the Stonewall Rangers Brigade?"

"Stonewall Rangers? They're one of these extremist groups you hear about. You know, blame everything on all the blacks and Hispanics and Jews. But like I said, they have rights."

"Free speech and all."

"Yes."

"Did you know Chester Carew had been to a few of their meetings?"

"Betty told me."

"Apparently they were after him to play some kind of war games on his land."

"Huh."

"May I ask what type of law you practice, counselor? Any area of specialty?"

"No particular specialty. I do all kinds of work, from estates, as you see with Chester and Betty, to corporate work, other types of civil litigation, even some criminal work. It all depends."

"Depends on what?"

"On who I think is in the right."

"You aren't going to try to convince me you're the last noble lawyer."

He laughed out loud. "No, no, of course not. A man in your line of work must've figured out a long time ago that nobility is usually in the eye of the beholder."

"Often," I said. "But not always."

He said nothing. He set his cigar down in an ashtray and reached over and pulled the large checkbook toward him on the table, flipping it open.

"I see from the door you've got a few partners."

"Right," he said without looking up. "This is just a satellite office. We do plaintive work, workman's comp, that sort of thing, for a lot of the factory employees in this area. Makes it more convenient for them. All the partners in the firm rotate through here every six months. Doing my tour."

He whisked an expensive-looking pen from his jacket pocket and began writing.

"You don't live in Nitro or Dunbar then?"

"Nope. In the city. South Hills. ... What was the spelling of your last name again?"

I gave it to him.

He began to write out the check. "I was thinking a thousand-dollar retainer to start. That ought to cover your initial time and expenses. Sound good to you?"

I nodded.

"You do much work for attorneys?" he asked.

"Some."

He finished writing and tore the check out and handed it to me. "Good. I know this is a special circumstance, but maybe this will be the start of a mutually beneficial relationship."

He looked at me expectantly as I took the piece of paper from him. It was one of those oversized checks, the kind that stands out in a crowd. In the upper-left-hand corner were the name of his professional corporation, his own followed by the prerequisite initials, and an image of a flying American flag with a Revolutionary War-era musket leaning below it.

"We'll see how it goes," I said. "I do some contract work for another agency but with my own clients I normally earn my keep from case to case."

"Of course. Best way to handle things. No entanglements."

"What's the significance of the flag and the flintlock?" I asked.

"Ah, that. Freedom," he said. "I've always been a big believer in our Constitution. The whole basis of our system of laws."

"I've got no quibble with the Second Amendment crowd."

"That's great."

"As long as it's not being used as a shield for nefarious activity."

He held up his hands and smiled. "Nothing nefarious here, I can assure you. I am worried about something with this whole affair of Chester's shooting, however. I wondered if you were aware of it."

"What's that?"

He picked up his cigar again and took another puff, blowing the smoke upward. "It concerns your friend, Mr. Toronto."

"Jake? There are a lot of people who have to worry about him."

"Yes, but can he be trusted?"

"I don't know what you mean, exactly. Jake knows how to handle himself, he used to be my partner, and I'd trust him with my life. In fact, I have."

"Have you now? You know what kind of business he's in, what kind of things he does, who he works for?"

"Not everything. Jake lives pretty modestly. I'm not worried about him being into anyone for money, if that's what you're driving at."

"No, no." He waved off the thought. "I wasn't talking about money."

"What are you talking about then?"

"You know, it's not that important. If you trust this man, that's good enough for me. I just want you to help bring Betty Carew some peace of mind over this whole business without ..."

"Without what?"

"I don't know ... alienating a lot of people. This is a decent valley, filled with a lot of decent, hardworking people."

"I'm sure it is, but somebody was indecent enough to have shot my client's husband from behind in cold blood. You act like you have your ear to the ground. Any theories on who did it?"

He leaned back in the chair and folded his arms across his chest. A vein grew into prominence in his thick neck. Then he shook his head. "No theories. But I will tell you this. You must've discovered, like me, that there are mysteries about any place, truths and half-truths people don't always speak about.

"Well, around here those truths run deep as a mineshaft, dark as the blackest night. You start stirring around in there, you're liable to be surprised at what might come out."

"Sorry, Warnock. I can't guarantee you anything when it comes to looking into something like this," I said. "If it turns out to be simple, like finding a local poacher or something, then I shouldn't think there'd be any problem. In fact, the police will probably beat us to it, in which case you'll be right and Betty will have wasted her money."

"Exactly. But you should know something, Frank."

"What's that?"

"*I* don't waste money," he said matter-of-factly, reaching across with his free hand and closing the checkbook. "Now, if you'll excuse me, I've got a few letters to finish dictating and some phone calls to make before the end of the day. If you don't mind, please keep me appraised of your progress."

I said I would and shook the man's hand. I took his check and walked down the hall past the pretty receptionist and through the front door. Outside, the temperature had dropped a few degrees. I wasn't sure, but I could've sworn I felt the money burning a hole in my pocket.

7

I drove to a cell phone outlet in South Charleston and picked out a new phone. They were running a special. Thirty-day free trial—only pay the first month's rent and base charge, unlimited minutes and long distance. Perfect, since I'd have to get a new phone when I got back home anyway and I didn't think I'd need this one any longer than thirty days.

After that, I drove to one of those big box stores that sold electronics and showed the salesman the handheld GPS receiver I'd picked up in the woods.

"That's a nice model," he said. "You looking for another one?" He was barely five feet tall, dressed in khaki pants and a clean pressed blue shirt, and had an air of specific, laser-focused knowledge about him.

"No. I was hoping you could show me how to work this one."

"What, you steal it from somebody? Just kidding."

"It belongs to a friend of mine," I lied.

"Sure." He took the unit from my hands. "It's easy."

He showed me how the display and various buttons worked. There were coordinates, called way points, as well as a map on the screen.

"Does it have memory? I mean, does it keep past sets of way points?"

"Of course." He helped me bring up another display that allowed me to scroll through the coordinates. "Looks like your friend already has a few stored in here."

Hot dog. A virtual roadmap to some of the places my attacker in the woods might have been.

"You can use it anywhere on the planet," the salesman was saying. "Except underground or down under the water. It has to be able to get the signals from the satellites."

"Great. Thanks very much for your help."

"Hey. You sure you're not looking for a new one of your own? If you like it after you're through using this one and give it back, you come on by and see me. I'll make you a deal."

"Deal," I said.

Back at the Carews' in Nitro there was a message waiting for me. The driveway had long since cleared out so that only my truck, Chester's Suburban, and Betty's Buick remained.

"Cops called looking for you," Toronto said as I came in through the back door.

"Deputy Nolestar?"

"That's the one. Betty took the message."

"Wonder what took him so long?"

"Maybe they get so many shotgun attacks in the woods around here yours wasn't a priority," he said.

"Right. I'm just glad Betty answered the phone and not you."

"She and Jason are upstairs sleeping. I was just about to take her car and go pick up a pizza."

"With all this food sitting around here?" I indicated the stacked loaves of fresh-baked bread and brownies and pies and the containers of fruit salad and other goodies I was sure were now crowding the refrigerator.

"All this Tupperware makes me nervous," he said. "I need some grease."

I shook my head.

"How was the lawyer?" he asked.

"Very smooth and very professional. Maybe has something to hide. He's also a cigar smoker."

"At least he's got one redeeming characteristic. That didn't stop you from taking his money though, did it?"

"No. And it's Betty's money anyway, at least eventually."

"What's in the bag?" He indicated the plastic shopping bag under my arm.

"New cell phone to replace the one the guy took from me earlier. Plus that GPS unit of his I picked up. I went by a store and they showed me how to pull up coordinates this turkey has stored in the memory. Tomorrow I want to go check them out."

"You bet. I could've showed you how to do that."

"Yeah, but you know me. Mr. Tech-savvy. Sometimes I like to figure these things out for myself."

He shrugged. "I also want to go pay a visit to this used-car dealer you were telling me about."

"No problemo. I'm sure he'll be thrilled to see us. Anything else?"

"All I can think of for now."

He twirled Betty's keys in his meaty hand. "My stomach's growling. Let me know how you make out with the lawman."

I used the wall phone in the kitchen to dial the number Deputy Nolestar had given Betty. It turned out to be a pager so I punched in the Carews' number and hung up. I went to the refrigerator, found a nice piece of untouched pumpkin pie, poured myself a glass of milk and sat down at the kitchen table to wait.

I'd only taken a couple of bites when the phone rang. I went to the wall and snatched the phone off the hook so it wouldn't disturb Betty or Jason any further.

"Frank Pavlicek speaking."

"Pavlicek, I see you got my message."

"You Deputy Nolestar?"

"That's me."

I could hear the hollow sound of the inside of a moving car. He was obviously on a cell phone. His voice was a tenor with a slight wheezing quality that made him sound too young to be an investigator, but who was I to argue.

"I figured you'd call me after what happened," I said.

"Yes, sir. I talked with the other two deputies who took your report. I'd like to sit down and have a talk with you."

"Okay, when and where?"

"How about right now?"

"Right now, tonight?"

"No better time than the present. In fact, I'm headed out your way now. Just across the river in St. Albans."

"All right. But Betty Carew and her son are asleep upstairs. They've had a long day with the funeral and all. Is there someplace else we can meet?"

"How about the McDonald's down on First Avenue? I'll buy you a cup of coffee."

"Give me half an hour," I said.

Deputy Nolestar turned out to be a tall, wholesome-looking (in a Clark Kent sort of way) young man with a dark crew cut and dark hair on his arms. His eyes darted back and forth nervously. They were the color of cobalt; not cobalt blue, which is actually the dark color belonging to a mixture of cobalt and aluminum, but the color of cobalt itself — steel gray. I judged his age at late twenties, give or take.

"You got a good chop on you," Nolestar said, pointing toward my mouth with his thumb after we'd sat down over our coffees in a quiet booth in the back. A huge family of eight or ten — a baby, two toddlers, and multiple other kids running everywhere around a weary-looking mom and dad — sat devouring their Mcfood up at the front, but their three tables were around the corner from ours and mostly out of earshot.

"It'll heal," I said.

He nodded. "So you disarmed this guy, huh? Took his gun and everything? Pretty slick move."

"I thought it was better than trusting to his good graces."

"Heard you were up there looking for information about the Chester Carew shooting."

"I was. Carew was a personal friend. The widow's naturally concerned that whoever shot him is still running around loose."

Nolestar's eyes flicked down toward the table. "Right. I'm aware of Mrs. Carew's concerns, naturally. We're doing all we can to find whoever shot her husband. Other than being a friend, what's your interest level?"

"Well, I'm not really at liberty to say, but I'd sure appreciate any information you can share. Who knows?

Maybe we can help one another."

"Maybe. I'm happy to try to bring you up to speed ... a little. But I hope you don't plan on involving yourself in this investigation, Mr. Pavlicek, without the knowledge or cooperation of the sheriff's department or other authorities."

Nabbed. Time to redirect.

"Other authorities? Now who else might be interested in a supposedly accidental shooting?" I asked.

"Afraid I'm not at liberty to say," he said with a straight face.

I smiled. "Okay. Okay." I blew on my coffee and took a small sip. It hurt my mouth at first, but then felt good as it burned down my throat. "But you said you would bring me up to speed, as you put it?"

"To a point," he said. "I've done some checking into your background, and your friend there ... Toronto, is it? Your record's not exactly clean, but you are ex-homicide and Detective Ferrier in Charlottesville vouches for you. That goes a long way with me, but you got to make sure you understand, Mr. Pavlicek, we're dealing with a different world these days."

"Different world? Sure, I suppose, but you're talking about the accidental killing of a falconer like it's a matter of national security."

There was an uncomfortable silence for a few moments as we both sipped our coffees.

"How about an autopsy. Can we start there? Carew was shot in the back, I know that."

"That's correct," Nolestar said.

"Close range? Long range?"

He looked away. "The M.E. thinks twenty to thirty yards."

"Pretty close range then."

He nodded.

"Still think it was a hunter?"

He said nothing.

"So the shot is what killed him."

"Carew died from massive bleeding and shock related

to the gunshot. Looks like the slug tore into a piece of his heart. No surprise there, I guess."

"What about the gun? What type of load was used?"

"Well, ah, the bullet was recovered, I can tell you that."

"And? What type was it?"

"I'm afraid that's, um, classified information, Mr. Pavlicek."

"Classified? How about shell casings?"

He shook his head. Different world indeed. For the first time I found myself wishing Bill Ferrier's mug were around. At least I could deal with the detective from Charlottesville. Then again, all this guy knew about me was information he'd read from a database and Bill's good word.

"How about the shotgun I turned over to you guys this afternoon? You get any prints off of that?"

He shook his head. "Sorry, sir. Nothing we could use. And without a further description of the guy, he's going to be hard to find."

"Stonewall Rangers," I said.

Nolestar cleared his throat. "What's that?" he asked.

"You know who they are."

"Okay. ... What about 'em?"

"Chester had been to some of their meetings."

"We know that."

"Did you also know they were after him to use his land?"

He said nothing.

"Are they suspects in Chester's killing?" I asked.

"Pavlicek," he said, "look. Don't involve yourself in stuff where you're not needed. I know this guy was a friend of yours and all, but—"

"But what?" I asked.

He didn't answer. We leveled even stares at one another.

"Can you at least tell me what you think happened to Elo?"

"Elo?"

"Carew's falcon. A gyr-peregrine. The one he was

hunting with that day."

"Oh, right. No, sir. I guess the bird is still missing. That's all I know."

"Did anyone talk to Dr. Winston?"

"Dr. Winston? I don't think so, why? Who is he?"

"Veterinarian. He treated that bird for some kind of strange illness — paralysis, that sort of thing — just a couple of weeks ago. But the bird recovered."

"I didn't know that. Maybe the conservation officer — "

"Who's running this investigation, Deputy Nolestar? Are you?"

The deputy shifted in his seat. "I'm afraid I'm not at liberty to tell you that either," the deputy said.

" 'Cause I've got to tell you, this is sounding more and more like a federal operation with you just acting as a gofer."

"Sir, I'm going to have to respectfully request that you and your friend stand down on all this."

"And if I decide not to?" All this sir stuff was starting to make me nervous.

"I'm sorry, but this conversation is over," he said, pushing himself away from the table. "Please tell Mrs. Carew we'll be in touch with her just as soon as we know anything definite about who shot her husband."

"The only thing definite I can see is you stonewalling me about what you're doing to investigate the Stonewallers."

He snickered. "That's good ... I like that."

He left the table and threw the rest of his coffee in the trash. I finished mine as I watched him drive his unmarked cruiser from the lot.

8

"Time to wake up, amigo."

It was Toronto, rapping on the door of the bedroom Betty Carew used to store her sewing machine and dozens of wintering garments. I looked at my watch—5:45 A.M.

"Planning to shake the car dealer out of bed?" I asked.

"Nope. But I hear he's an early riser and I thought you wanted to check out those coordinates first."

"What time does the sun come up?"

"About the time you drag your sorry butt out of the sack, we eat some grub, and get to wherever we're going."

"Right. Bound to endear us to someone." My mouth tasted like dry paste. I stretched and yawned, shaking the cobwebs from my head.

"Your purloined GPS unit has a nifty little mapping feature. I've already localized the three way points this character stored in the memory. And guess what? One of them is up there on Chester's land and another is smack dab in the middle of the used-car lot belonging to our Mr. Higgins."

"Sounds suspiciously like a clue. This Higgins guy going to be armed?"

"That's Lieutenant Colonel Bo Higgins, commander of the Stonewall Rangers Brigade, to you. But I doubt he'll be hefting an M-16 around his lot. Tends to scare off the customers."

"Have you been there before?"

"Not exactly, but Chester drove me by there before we went to the second meeting."

"Be interesting to see what's at the third way point."

"I've got the address."

Two cups of coffee and Betty Carew's sausage, biscuits, and honey had me awake enough to be following Toronto's directions back down I-64 crossing the Kanawha into South Charleston, then along the north side of downtown Charleston to an exit within sight of the gold-domed state capitol. The sky had begun to brighten considerably as the new day dawned.

"Where are we headed exactly?"

"Other side of the interstate. Up the bill."

We climbed a ramp that curved back over the eight-lane highway up toward the steep heights that rose over downtown.

"Turn left here. Then another left."

I gunned the engine and we drove up along a ridge toward an apartment complex of four or five high-rise buildings. What may have once been brick luxury apartments overlooking the city, balconies off the sides, now sported dusty glass windows, decaying trim and railings. A couple pieces of trash from an overflowing Dumpster blew across the parking lot. A sign read Roseberry Circle. We were waved through a guardhouse entrance by a droopy-eyed attendant.

"It's a HUD project."

"Well, what do you know?" Toronto said, surveying the landscape. "I've heard of this place."

"Yeah?"

"Buildings are mostly controlled by rival gang bangers from Detroit and Philadelphia, other cities up north. Lot of dealing going on in here."

Right now the place looked asleep.

"Where is the coordinate exactly?" We were passing over a speed bump, curving uphill between the buildings.

"Hold on a second. Pull over here."

Toronto punched a few buttons on the unit and waited for a response as I pulled to the curb.

"Looks like you're just about right on top of it," he said.

"Okay. So my friend from the woods visited here. A user maybe?"

"Nah. White boy'd be more likely to get his fix over on the West End."

"Maybe Higgins has mounted a new recruiting drive."

"Sure. 'Cept I doubt the brothers who live here would throw him and his bunch much of a grand reception."

"I see your point."

"I think we're going to have to have a talk with Bo Higgins about this one," he said.

"Let's," I said.

We drove back down along the interstate, past the few high-rise hotels and office buildings and state capitol, before crossing the Kanawha again back into the far south side of Charleston, which didn't border South Charleston. Go figure. The way the topography, the interstate, and the river twisted out here, you knew you still had a long way to go before you got to Kansas.

The West Virginia headquarters of the Stonewall Rangers Brigade on MacCorkle Avenue was not as impressive as the name might imply. The building Toronto pointed out as we drove into the lot looked like the sawed-off end of an old tobacco barn attached to the back end of Bo Higgins's used-car dealership—BEST DEALS ON WHEELS—RIDE TODAY FOR LESS! An array of late-model sedans, station wagons, and sport utes with a decidedly made-in-the-USA flavor occupied the lot.

The gray sky had begun to brighten some more, revealing a flurry or two, but despite the cold, a door to the small showroom floor hung partway open. Traffic out front on the street at this hour of the morning was all but nonexistent.

"So let me get this straight," I said, searching for a wide enough parking spot among the mostly occupied spaces. "Chester and you listened to this guy's spiel. What else did Chester have to say about it?"

Toronto shrugged. "He said he thought the speakers raised some interesting questions, even if they were quite a ways off on the answers."

"White supremacists raising interesting questions?"

"Well, just when he was talking to me, Chester liked to call them proletariat whores."

"Proletariat whores?" I was trying to figure what
Chester might've meant by that when a wide spot presented
itself. I twisted the pickup into the slot. "At least maybe
these guys can tell us what happened to Elo."

"Maybe."

"While they're in the midst of divulging all their goals
and schemes to us."

"Absolutely."

"Which we plan to discuss now with this major general
head of the whole operation."

"Not major general. Lieutenant colonel."

"Oh, yeah. I forgot."

The man who poked his head out of the showroom to
see who'd entered his parking lot was a bony figure with a
high-domed head and a coif of white hair neatly combed to
one side. His face had that rugged Western look that said he
mostly didn't give a damn; his uniform, despite his apparent
rank, was a blue-and-white-checked flannel shirt over blue
jeans, black cowboy boots that resembled the pair Toronto
had on, and a white turtle-neck. He squinted suspiciously at
my truck with its Virginia plates until he recognized Toronto
climbing out of the passenger side.

"Jake Toronto, sir. What brings you over here this early
hour of the day? Got someone wanting to buy a new truck?"
Higgins, now grinning, was marching out to greet us. The
air smelled of cold paint and chemicals from an auto body
place next door.

"Not exactly, Bo." Toronto pointed at me as I closed the
door of the truck behind me. "This here is Frank Pavlicek.
He used to be my partner when I was a detective back in
New York."

"Oh. Sure." Bo Higgins stepped forward, extending his
hand. We shook. His grip was firm but not too
overbearing—more like a politician's than a soldier's.

"Frank works now as a private investigator."

"I guess you aren't after a truck then."

"Nope."

"Private investigator." Higgins nodded, Toronto's

words taking a moment to sink in. The car dealer's grin went dead. "Works for whom?"

Hardly the backwoods grammar I'd have expected from a crazed militia leader, but I'd read a couple of articles about these people and knew not to necessarily expect a maniacally raving Hitler type. The question was directed at me.

"That all depends." I smiled.

Higgins said nothing.

"Chester Carew's wife hired Frank to check into the shooting. You know, see if he might be able to give the police a hand and all. Thought we might ask you a few questions, if you don't mind," Toronto said. He was all charm for the moment, I noted, not usually one of my buddy's strong points.

"Chester's shooting?"

"You heard about what happened to him, didn't you?"

The militiaman rubbed at a day's growth of stubble on his chin. "Yeah. Read about it in the paper. That was really a terrible thing, wasn't it?"

"Didn't see you or any of your fellow brigade members at the funeral."

"Oh, well, you know about that, Jake. We mourn along with everybody else, but none of us really knew old Chester all that well."

Toronto nodded.

"By the way, you have any ID on you, Mr. Pavlicek? Maybe a PI license?"

I took out my wallet, pulled out the cards, and handed him both. He looked them over thoroughly, front and back, then handed them back to me.

"Can't be too careful these days, you know," he said. "Cops and federal agents running around checking on everyone like storm troopers. Just because a man may have strong opinions about his country and his liberty don't make him no terrorist."

"You want to talk inside?" Toronto asked.

"Unless you're planning to purchase one of my fine

vehicles, I don't see much good in standing around out here."

We followed him in through the showroom floor where a green-and-white 1958 Bel Air in apparent mint condition stood parked next to a late-model Chrysler minivan. We didn't hit warmer air until we'd reached the back of the room, where a wood-and-glass door led to a small suite of offices.

"It doesn't pay to heat the showroom at night," Higgins explained.

Inside the office door was a small waiting room with a handful of armless polyester-covered chairs.

"Can I get you boys some coffee?"

We each declined.

"All right then." Higgins pulled out one of the chairs, spun it around so the back was facing us, and sat down with his bony legs straddling it like a horse he'd just mounted. "Have a seat and go ahead and ask me your questions. I've got a truckload of used vehicles due in here in about an hour and a truckload of insurance company paperwork to finish before it arrives."

I took a chair on the wall opposite. Toronto, who'd remained standing, looked at me. "Why don't you go first, Frank."

Good cop, bad cop—all right, I'd try to be good. I was still dripping sleep from my eyes, but what the heck.

"Okay," I said. "Mr. Higgins, it's my understanding that you are the leader of a certain local militia group—"

"Hold it right there, my friend," Higgins said. "Commander is the proper term."

"Commander then—"

"And we're not a militia. It's the right of the citizenry within each state to form their own individual militias—check your copy of the Constitution. But since we're comprised of members from more than one state, we don't assume the right to call ourselves one. We're more of a paramilitary club composed of enthusiasts."

"A club of enthusiasts."

"Yes, sir."

"Okay, this *club* of yours then. You're its founder?"

"Not founder. But as I said, I do have the privilege of being the commanding officer at present."

"Sure. You have a military background, Mr. Higgins?"

"No, sir. I was four-F during Vietnam—heart murmur. But some of our members do have direct military experience."

"And what kind of activities exactly does your group engage in?"

"Training exercises, mainly. Weapons instruction and tactical drills and lectures."

"How many members do you have?"

He paused for a moment. "It varies. People come and go. We've had as many as eighty-five at some of our gatherings and as little as twenty or thirty."

"Do you maintain some kind of membership roster?"

"I have a mailing list and we do a roll call, but if you're going where I think you're going, sir, that's private, privileged information."

"Protected under some amendment of the Constitution, no doubt," I said. I had to be a little careful here. Didn't want to antagonize the man too early.

My little dig seemed to wash over him, however. He made no comment.

"Jake tells me that Chester Carew brought him to a couple of your club's gatherings."

"That's right, he did." Something in his eyes told me he'd just as soon that hadn't happened, but since it had, he was trying to make the best of it.

"Had Chester been to many of your meetings before?"

"No, sir. He had some, ah, questions about our organization."

"Questions?"

"Yes. He wasn't familiar with our activities and some of our training, of course, and wanted to know more."

Knowing Chester, I was certain he'd asked a lot more questions than that, but I let it pass.

"How did Chester come to find out about your group?"

"We approached him about permission to use a part of his land. He was the only one who hunted up there and we thought it might be a good place to hold exercises."

"And what was his response?"

"He said no, at first. Didn't want us bringing weapons in there. Afraid for his birds, I guess."

"So why wasn't that the end of it?" I asked.

"Well, we asked him a few more times. Kept after him because his land was really so ideal and convenient for a lot of us. Invited him to a couple of meetings. I guess he must've thought about it and had a change of heart, because he eventually said okay as long as he knew when we were coming so he wouldn't be in the woods hunting with those falcons of his."

"So you've had a few of these exercises, as you call them, on his land?"

He hesitated. "Three so far. And we've got another one planned for next week. Don't know how the widow's going to take to having us back there again though, so we may have to move it to another location."

"How about yesterday morning? Were you having some kind of exercise up there then?"

"No, why?"

"Because I was up there and somebody dressed in camos and a ski mask pointed a shotgun in my face and gave me this." I indicated the bruise and cut on the side of my mouth.

He said nothing.

"Not one of your soldiers, huh?"

"Not to my knowledge."

I looked through the glass down a long hallway and a screen door opening to a room in back. I could see gray feathers flapping and a dark shape darted through the air in front of the screen.

"What've you got in there?" I asked.

"Where?"

I pointed down the hallway. "Down there. In that

room."

He shrugged. "Pigeons," he said. "I race them."

"Homing pigeons, huh?"

"Not exactly. Similar."

"Did you know Hitler was a pigeon fancier? Used them to pass messages back and forth to his spies in England."

"So? The president of the United States is a jogger and a Republican. Does that mean Democrats shouldn't jog? For your information our own country used pigeons to pass messages too."

"Is that right?" Toronto broke in. "Passing some kind of secret codes with your own birds there, Bo?"

Higgins smiled. "If I was, they'd be secret, wouldn't they?"

They glared at one another.

"Okay," I said. "These get-togethers of yours. You just talk about guns, military hardware—things like that?"

"Well, yeah, at least formally, that's all we do. Sometimes a few of the guys'll get together and talk about other stuff ... you know, politics, things like that."

"But you claim you and your people are not part of any extremist militia movement. No budding Timothy McVeighs in your midst."

"Hey, like I tell all those federal agents been sniffing around here since those terrorists attacked our nation last year. One of these days, they might just be glad folks like us are around."

"How's that?" I asked.

"Just saying we're prepared is all."

"How do you feel about the government in Washington?"

"Huh." He snickered. "Now you're sounding like some kind of Red Chinese Commie or something, coming around here and wanting to know all about my politics."

"No," Toronto said. "Excuse me, Frank, but I've had about all of this I'm going to stomach."

"Come again?" Higgins appeared stunned.

"Look, Higgins. Don't try to snooker us with all this talk

about your rights. I've been and I've heard the speeches. You and your little ragtag army spew a lot of venom."

"No crime in speaking our minds. You didn't have to come if you didn't want to. In case you haven't heard, it's still a free country." He folded his arms and thrust out his chin.

"I think you mean pollute people's minds, don't you?"

"I know my people. I know what's in their hearts. It's freedom, gentlemen. Freedom and a pure white race. Not too many citizens left in this nation willing to stand up on their hind legs and fight for that."

"I know some black Americans and a whole lot of others deployed over in Afghanistan and a few other places around the world that would beg to differ with you," Toronto said.

"Oh, spare me the parade, Toronto. Those boys are nothing but tools. You here to accuse me of something? Is that it?"

"I knew Chester Carew," I interrupted. "He was a fine and decent man."

"And he was coming around to where he would eventually join us," Higgins said. "Too bad he didn't quite make it. But I didn't shoot the man and neither did any of my people. And, Mr. Pavlicek, you might be surprised to find out who else is really sympathetic with our views."

Toronto was slowly shaking his head.

"Mr. Higgins, since you don't seem willing to part with your mailing list, I don't suppose you'll be able to tell us the whereabouts of each of your organization's members on the morning Chester Carew was killed?"

"Now how the hell would I know that?"

I'd been saving the best until last. I pulled the GPS unit from my jacket pocket. A glimmer of recognition flashed through Higgins's eyes before they went blank again.

"Took this off of the man who accosted me in the woods yesterday," I said. "Interesting set of coordinates stored in here. Chester's land. Apartment project called Roseberry Circle. And guess what? Your place, right here, Bo."

The car dealer glared at me. "So you say. That doesn't prove a thing."

"Maybe not. But it sure does raise a lot of interesting questions, doesn't it?"

Higgins's eyes narrowed. "Look, gentlemen, I've been polite with you up until now, but I've got a business to run and I'll be damned if I'm going to sit here and be accused of killing some guy just because he came to a few of our meetings. Hell, you guys aren't even cops.... What do you care what goes on up there in Roseberry nigger-land? Probably best you leave."

He stood up to walk back to the showroom, as if to signal an end to our conversation. But he didn't get far. It was not the first time I'd seen Toronto lose it. Maybe one of the most explosive. He burst across the room in little more than a stride and with nothing but a couple of fingers applied to the man's solar plexus had the commander of the local Stonewall Rangers Brigade up against the panel partition leading to the back office.

"Don't screw with us, Higgins. And don't disrespect us. You sent a man up there to Chester's woods yesterday. Why?"

Higgins was suddenly having trouble breathing, but he managed to blurt out, "I don't know what you're talking about."

"Right. We're going to figure out who shot Chester, and if I find out it was you or one of your little cronies, that Constitution you're always waving around ain't gonna help you one bit. You dig?"

He nodded, ever so slightly. His cheeks were turning bright red.

"It's okay, Jake. He's not worth it," I said.

Toronto glared at the man a second longer. Higgins's eyes began to roll back and his lids fluttered. "You're right," Jake said. "And that's too bad." He released his hold.

Higgins crumpled to his knees, coughing and gasping for breath. There was one of those water coolers with a ring dispenser filled with paper cups in the corner. I went over and filled one with the cold liquid, then brought it back and handed it to the car dealer. His hands shaking, he took the cup without looking at me.

"You'll be okay in a minute or two," I said.

Higgins squeezed out a smile. "Just a couple more days," he croaked.

"What's that?" I bent over to hear him more clearly.

"Just a couple more days. Y'all will see."

Toronto grabbed him by the hair. "What the hell's that supposed to mean?"

I held out my hand to stop him. A low vibration rumbled the walls of the building. Outside through the widow, not fifteen feet away, a long tractor-trailer car carrier loaded with used cars and trucks was rolling into the dealer's lot. I guess the driver was early that morning. Higgins's paperwork and the answers to the rest of our questions would have to wait.

9

"What in the world were you thinking? You could've killed that guy."

Toronto didn't answer, simply stared at the multiple lanes of cars ahead of us as we made our way back through Charleston in the direction of Chester's land. We'd left Higgins talking to the car carrier driver, then headed down MacCorkle Avenue and onto the interstate in stony silence.

"Talk to me, man."

More silence. Then finally, "None of this smells right. If Higgins or one of his pals killed Chester, why would he have sent someone back to the scene of the shooting?"

"Maybe they're hiding something. Maybe something about the land."

"And maybe that ties in with whatever happened to Elo," he said.

"We need to find out if Chester's vet has gotten back the results from whatever tests he sent out."

"Seems simple. Chester could've found out about something the Rangers are up to and that's why they killed him. I might buy that. Still ..."

"Still what?"

"Seemed to me Higgins was actually telling the truth, at least about not killing Chester."

"What do you think these GPS way points are all about?"

He shrugged. "Could be just one of their stupid war games."

"Or it could be something serious."

"An actual attack? I suppose Higgins might just have it in him."

"Seemed pretty obvious from talking to Deputy Nolestar that the Feds are watching the Rangers."

"Which means they've probably got them under surveillance and all their phones tapped."

"What do you think Higgins meant when he said just a couple more days?"

"Wish I knew."

"Which raises another question. If they know and have solid evidence that the Rangers murdered Chester, why haven't they moved in to at least arrest those responsible? You pick up on anything specific regarding an attack at those meetings you went to?"

"No. Mostly just a lot of ranting and raving and party line."

"We're going to need to talk to the Feds, either straight up or through Nolestar."

"Unless they decide they want to talk to us first."

"And in the meantime I'll need more names of Rangers to talk to. No doubt Higgins'll be on the phone with some of his buddies just as soon as he gets done unloading those cars."

"I can go to work on that."

"Something else is bothering me though too."

"What's that?"

"Warnock."

"The lawyer? You think he's tied in with these characters?"

"Possibly. But he also seemed to want to make me doubt somebody else."

"Who's that?"

"You."

Toronto smiled. "You ain't taking the guy seriously, I hope."

"No. Should I?"

He shook his head slowly.

"You aren't holding back something on me, are you, Jake?"

"How long have you known me, Frank?"

"I know, I know. But I've never seen you lose it like you just did with Higgins either."

"I'm all right," he said. "I'm all right."

"You sure?"

"I'm sure."

We took the Dunbar exit off the interstate then wound north on back roads that eventually led us to the dirt road turnoff for Carew's land.

There was no gate preventing access from the highway, but an old barbed-wire fence and a string of weathered signs indicated the owner's desire for privacy. The fence ran over a hill and down a ravine as far as you could see. The signs were ubiquitous in either direction. Anyone hunting deer without permission on this property was either blind or malevolently determined. A small piece of leftover crime scene tape dangled from one of the fence posts, the only obvious reminder of the shooting that had occurred here only a few days before.

Before yesterday morning's excitement, the last time I'd been out here with Chester and Toronto had been more than a year before, a few weeks after Chester had acquired Elo from a breeder out West. We'd sent up a pheasant from a radio-controlled launcher to help acquaint the peregrine with that kind of game. Elo missed on the first try. That pheasant gave a nice midair juke as the falcon was about to strike and deserved to go free. But the second bird offered up a paler version of the same move, and this time the peregrine was ready, adjusting his stoop to bag the prey. Elo was a quick learner, a very good sign.

"The spot's about a mile or so in," Toronto said.

"I remember from yesterday."

Toronto consulted the topo of the land he had spread out on the dashboard. A large arrow, drawn by Damon Farraday, pointed to the location. "Don't think I've ever been up the hill that far," he said.

The narrow road, little better than a cow path, climbed steadily, even at a slow five miles an hour, jolting us with a washout every few yards. I had a Billie Holiday CD playing but had to turn it off so it wouldn't skip. We crested a ridge, only to confront a larger one ahead.

Farraday said he had called for help on his cell phone after he found Chester. A couple of sheriff's deputies, probably the same two I talked to yesterday, had arrived about half an hour later.

"Wonder how much they worked the scene." I speculated out loud. "I didn't get to see a whole lot."

"From what Damon says, doesn't sound like much. Unless the Feds were already involved. Damn, Frank. What if it really was an accident, and all this militia business is just so much crap? Cops might even already know who the shooter is, talked with him and decided it was an accident. Just some poor father trying to put venison on the table or something."

"Nolestar didn't seem to think so."

"Sure would make our job a whole lot easier though. We just slip downtown to one of the local honky-tonks and do some asking around. But I guess that's why you're still the professional investigator."

"So what's that make you?"

"A used-to-be investigator. ... Now I is just professional trouble."

I couldn't disagree with that.

We came to a fork in the road and Toronto directed me to pull off to the side in a cleared-out area beneath a large poplar. We climbed out of the truck.

"Guess we need to make sure we're both carrying this morning," he said. "Don't want a repeat performance with the masked marauder."

I nodded.

"Case you get lost way back in here, you can use the tree as a reference," he said, pointing to the poplar.

"Thanks for the vote of confidence. I got out on my own yesterday, didn't I? Even after tracking that guy."

My bush craft had grown considerably since taking up falconry. I'd learned, under Toronto's tutelage, how to build a mews, assorted bow perches, and a weathering pen; how to work with various types of falconry furniture and cordage; how to handle either a bal-chatri or dho-gazza trap; how to take precise bearings; how to gut a rabbit or a squirrel; how to track mammals via signs and gait patterns;

and how to obscure the evidence of my presence in an area if
necessary. Still we both knew I couldn't hold a candle to my
sponsor. On the other hand, I liked to kid Toronto about
growing a little rusty on the street. Problem was, these days
that might have just depended on which side of the street
you were considering. I thought again about what Tony
Warnock had tried to suggest in his office.

"Let's do it," I said.

We went and found the streambed, the exact spot where
Chester had died. The ATV tracks and other evidence of
police presence, not to mention the darkened remnants of
Carew's blood, made the location impossible to miss. It was
surrounded by a stand of oak and maple trees, their bare
branches thick overhead.

For the next hour and a half we canvassed the area
together, marking out a range of fire—just to be sure—of
almost two hundred yards. The woods were overgrown and
gray in the midmorning. All was still except for the
occasional chatter of a squirrel and the wind blowing gently
through the treetops. We took our time, looking for any sign
of the shooter's presence.

"This shooter was very good," Toronto said after a
while. "Seems like it would be tough terrain for just a
hunter."

"What I was thinking too."

"Farraday said Chester was hit almost directly in the
middle of the back. The killer has to be an experienced
outdoorsman to have gotten the jump on Chester."

"Or a lucky shot."

"No luck involved. I've got a feeling what we're dealing
with here may be a pro."

"Meaning?"

"Meaning he or she has gone black, at least as far as this
scene is concerned. The police didn't find any trace and we
won't either."

"You're just full of good news, aren't you?"

I was passing by the tentacles of a red spruce when I
spotted something: a thin black piece of wire buried in the

pine needles.

"Check this out."

Toronto came over. "Looks like a tail transmitter."

"Elo's?" I gently pulled it from beneath the needles. But it was attached to something. A thick bundle of several more transmitters, maybe three or four dozen in all, attached via an elastic band.

"What the —?" Toronto said.

"Somehow I don't think all of these belonged to Elo. Spares?"

"I highly doubt it."

"Why would anybody want so many transmitters?"

"Good question."

"You could track a small army of birds with these."

We searched all around the spruce and the rest of the immediate vicinity but found nothing more.

"What do you make of it?" I asked.

"I don't know. Chester only had three birds. Farraday's been in here hunting and I have too on a couple of occasions, but I don't know of any other falconers who could've left these here."

"I just remembered something ... the pigeons at Higgins's place."

"Right. He said he races them."

"They could be tracked with these too, couldn't they?"

"Yeah, I suppose they could."

"Why would he want to track his pigeons? And more importantly, why would he be tracking them way up here?"

"Let's get back over to the kill site. I want to check out something else," he said.

We threaded our way among the trees to the stream again.

"I picked up on something different when we went through here earlier, but it didn't make any sense to me."

"What's that?"

He knelt down by a section of mud about ten yards from where the body had lain and pointed to the ground.

I followed his finger to a small curved trough in the

mud.

"Looks like part of a heel print," I said.

"I think it is."

"Not in very good shape. Not Chester's boots. It's different from the patterns on his heels I saw in tracks leading up to where the body was found."

"Very good."

"Must be from one of the cops."

"Maybe. But I checked out all the other patterns too. This is the only one that doesn't repeat anywhere else."

"So?"

"Look closer."

I examined the area around the print. Faint brush lines had smoothed what would have been the rest of the print into the surrounding gravel and mud.

"It's been tampered with—someone did their best to erase it, but the ground was too frozen where the heel is."

"You got it."

"Wouldn't be a cop."

"Nope."

"The shooter then."

"Don't think so. From the way Farraday described the wound and the scene, the shooter would have been on the other side of the stream."

"Somebody else was here then when Chester was shot?"

"You betcha."

I thought it over. "I suppose it's possible. You think the cops have considered this?"

"Doubt it."

"Farraday didn't say he saw anybody else though."

"Uh-uh."

"Raises some interesting questions."

"So we've got somebody else at the scene and a pile of bird-tail transmitters in the vicinity," he said. "You see any signs of Elo while we were tramping around?"

I shook my head.

"Me either. Farraday said the cops took Chester's receiver and yagi as evidence, but I took a spare telemetry unit he had from the barn. Left it in my bag in the truck. Not sure if it'll work or not, but it might be worth a try."

As I turned back toward him I saw something unnatural glitter in the distance over his shoulder.

"Jake," I said, keeping my voice even.

"Yeah?"

"You catch that?"

"Catch what?"

"Someone's glassing us."

"Right now?"

"I think so."

The glitter came again, this time even more visible. I nodded.

Toronto kept his voice the same as well and didn't change his posture or make any suspicious gestures.

"Scope?"

"Can't tell. Might be just binoculars."

"Well, given the spot where we happen to be standing, not sure if I'm up to playing Russian roulette over the difference."

"Me either."

"Got a bearing on the location?"

"Dead on. They're right below that water tower we passed on the way in." The tall green structure was visible across the valley from even three-quarters of a mile away.

"How about his line of sight?"

"Approximate. I think if we step on over there around the tree we'll be blocked off. Then we can circle back behind that stone formation and get into the truck without being seen."

"What are we waiting for then?" he asked.

<u>10</u>

I pretended to point to something at the base of the tree. Toronto played along and we both walked — we hoped — out of the line of sight of the potential shooter. Once behind the tree, we circled back to hop into the truck. I started the engine, jammed it into gear, and we spun a three-sixty in the dirt.

"No way to camouflage the dust," I said. "Whoever they are, they're bound to be on the move by now."

"There's an access road up to that tower I remember seeing on the way in."

"One way in or out. Maybe we'll get lucky."

"Unless he goes overland to somewhere else ... the way I'd do it."

"But you're not an optimist."

His smile was the only answer.

The Ford caromed around a curve. I punched the accelerator to climb a steep hill. Just over the rise on the right was the access road Toronto had spoken about, but the way was blocked by a closed gate, chained and padlocked. A sign indicated it was property of the West Virginia Department of Natural Resources.

"So much for optimism," Toronto said.

"Either way we've got to get up there."

Toronto reached down into the knapsack he'd brought and came out with a set of bolt cutters. "Oh, by the way, since I'm about to destroy public property, I forgot to ask, your Eagle Eye Investigations liability insurance current?"

"Well, yeah, but —"

"Good."

Before I could say anything more he'd pushed open the door, jumped over to the chain, looked both ways up and down the highway and snapped the metal links. The chain fell away and the gate, released from the tension, swung partially open. Toronto pulled it wide enough for me to drive through. Then he hopped back into the cab.

"You tried to stop me, but I wouldn't listen," he said.

I floored it and we roared up the dirt road. At the top we came to the water tower, a hundred-foot mushroom with a thick chain-link fence surrounding it, razor wire on the top. But Toronto had been right. There was no other vehicle or even evidence to indicate one had been there recently. Weapons drawn, we took the time to check out the area below the tank where I was sure I'd seen the glass reflection for tracks or any other signs of the watcher's presence, but there wasn't even an unnatural broken twig or leaf out of place.

"Like I said, Hoss. This bird's gone black," Toronto muttered to himself at one point. "And he ain't no rookie.

"You're sure you saw glass?" he asked a few minutes later when we were finished.

"Absolutely. You remember back in the eighties in the Bronx when we had that serial rapist, used to watch all his victims through high-powered binoculars from a nearby rented room for a few days before each rape? Perp kept coming back to the same neighborhood and we set up a stakeout. I still remember spotting the glint off those glasses he was using when we finally nailed the guy. This looked like the same kind of thing."

"All right. What now?"

If we'd both still been in law enforcement, we might've had a chance—assuming we'd called in aerial support from the moment of the spotting, roadblocks to seal all avenues in and out of the area, a massive land search. We might've still been reduced to breaking down state-owned chains on gates in order to try to chase down the suspect, but at least we would've had official sanction. As it was, we had nothing.

"I don't doubt whoever it was got the message that we'd seen them and knew they were watching us."

He scanned the sky and the terrain surrounding the top of the hillside. "If he's that good, might even be keeping an eye on us still. Not from up here, of course, somewhere else."

"He wouldn't be worried we'd find him?"

He shook his head.

"Well, we aren't doing much good standing up here looking like idiots."

We climbed back into the truck and headed down the hill toward the highway. Going down, I noticed, we had a nice view of the interstate and back toward the city in the distance.

After a minute or so, Toronto said, "You let me up here later by myself. Just put me up against your glass guy. Guarantee you I'll track him down."

With Toronto it was not an idle boast.

"You're assuming the person's going to stick around. Maybe they won't."

He shrugged.

My tiny new cell phone bleated like a lamb. I kept one hand on the wheel and dug into my jacket pocket and fished it out.

"Cute," Toronto said. "Does it meow too?"

I ignored him and pushed the answer key and said hello.

"Dad?" I'd called the night before and left the new phone number for Nicole on the voice mail back at the office. She had left a message with Toronto that she'd arrived home safely.

"Hey, precious, what's up? How was the bike ride back to C-ville?"

"Cold."

"Told you."

"But the hog was awesome. Listen, I've got something for you."

"Oh yeah?"

"I hacked into the cell phone company's records" and set up a monitoring program for your stolen phone when I got back last night. It scans the data on any calls made beginning with yesterday morning."

I looked at Toronto. "Bet I know where you learned to do something like that."

"Yeah, well, the guy made a call with your phone. Yesterday, late morning. Must've been right after he got away from you."

"You got a number?"

Toronto was nodding.

"Sure do."

"Wait a minute. Let me get something to write it down." Toronto, anticipating the need, already had a pen and piece of paper he'd taken from one of his pockets. She read the number off to me and I repeated it for him. West Virginia area code. I wasn't sure about the exchange.

"Thanks, Nicky. Great work. We'll get on this right away."

"Don't forget about me back here," she said and hung up.

I flipped the phone shut and tucked it back inside my jacket.

"Guy used your cell phone, right?" Toronto said, looking at the number he'd written down.

I nodded.

"Smart girl. I was going to check the records later myself."

"Recognize the number?"

"Nope."

"But it shouldn't take you all that long to find out who it belongs to."

"Nope."

"Let me ask you something," I said. "A few months back, you called to say you'd be gone for a while. Someone else was taking care of your birds. You'd be out of the country for a few weeks, but you wouldn't tell me where you were going."

"Right." Toronto rolled down the glass and spit out the window.

"Some kind of big job though."

"Yeah."

"And there have been a couple other times like that … you just haven't talked that much about them."

"Uh-huh."

"Listen," I said. "Are you working for somebody else right now, Jake? 1 mean here and now?"

He said nothing.

" 'Cause I thought you were working for me. I mean, we've got federal homeland security, FBI, CIA, special forces, take your pick. ..."

"I'm not working for anybody but you and Chester right now," he said.

"Okay. Then why do I get the feeling you're not telling me something?"

"Chill, Frank. Maybe you're just a little nervous."

"What kind of operation were you involved in that time when you disappeared?"

He drew in a deep breath. "All right," he said. "I'll tell you this much. It was a reunion, of sorts. Guys from my old special forces unit."

"Government backed?"

"Yeah, I'm *almost* certain."

"You're almost certain?"

"Look, we aren't exactly talking on-the-record stuff here. I'm sure nobody in the official chain of command would've even scratched their chin if we'd gotten caught."

"Where'd this take place?"

"Canada. North of Vancouver. Straight of Georgia."

"A dive operation?"

"You said it, I didn't."

When he was in the military Toronto had spent time with the Navy SEALs. When he first joined the NYPD he worked as a police diver before giving it up to go for his detective's shield. He kept diving recreationally, but then gave it up when he started getting into falconry. Or so I'd thought. Where he lived in western Virginia wasn't exactly a hotbed for scuba aficionados.

I, on the other hand, had decided to try my hand at diving in a swimming pool with a bunch of tourist divers while on vacation at a Florida resort when I was still single and working patrol. Not that I was all that into marine science or underwater adventures or anything. I just thought it might be a good way to meet women. And I was right.

Only problem was, take me down below ten feet where I didn't feel like I could just pop right back up to the surface and I started freaking out—some kind of latent claustrophobic thing going on, I guess. I'd never bothered to find out and never went back. I knew enough by then about extreme situations to know that if I panicked, whoever else was diving with me would also be placed at risk. Every now and then, I still woke up in a night sweat thinking about it.

"What did you guys do up there?" I asked.

He didn't answer right away. Then he said, "We took something ... and don't ask me what it was."

Neither of us said anything more for a couple of minutes and I didn't push the matter. If he didn't want to tell me any more details, maybe it was better I didn't know.

When he finally spoke again his voice came out almost like a whisper.

"One thing we both know for sure, Frank, there's people in this world getting burned up by hate."

I nodded. "Like the guys who flew the planes into those buildings."

"And like these Stonewall Rangers. I know, 'cause if my life had been just a little different I could've almost become one of 'em."

An ambulance with its lights flashing passed us as we reached the outskirts of Dunbar and the interchange with the interstate again.

"But not Chester," I said.

"No. Not Chester."

"Let's drop back by the house. Why don't you see if you can find out who that phone number belongs to. And while you're at it, why don't you stop by and see if that veterinarian's got anything."

"All right. What about using the telemetry to look for Elo?"

"I'll get hold of Farraday, see if I can get him out here later to help us. And I'll contact the conservation officer, see if she's interested in coming too."

"What are you gonna do in the meantime?"

"Go stir up some trouble," I said.

11

The town of Nitro, I'd learned from a book Betty Carew had
let me borrow the night before, actually had a pretty
interesting history. The community was formed as a
company town of sorts by the Ordnance Department during
World War I. The federal government needed a centralized
place to manufacture large quantities of gunpowder and
chose the remote yet easily accessible river bottomland not
too far from Charleston. Almost overnight, a boomtown of
about thirty thousand arose from nothing. Looking at the
old pictures reminded you a little of one of those temporary
mining boomtowns out West during the late eighteen
hundreds. The town had been mostly in a state of decay, however,
since the end of the First World War. When the chemical
industry moved into the Kanawha River Valley in a big way
beginning in the fifties and sixties, building a number of
plants in the area, other towns, both upriver and down,
apparently benefited more directly. The population might
have shrunk to just a few thousand, but battered Nitro hung
on, like the steely-eyed war veteran she was.

It took twenty-five minutes to drive from the Carews'
place in Nitro to the Kanawha County sheriff's office at the
courthouse on East Virginia Street in downtown Charleston.
I stayed off the interstate and paralleled the river the whole
way in. The sky was clearing a little and pale sunlight had
begun to warm the cold air.

Downtown, the Kanawha was as pristine as a river
could be, flanked by a few square blocks of high-rise
buildings and the gold-domed state capitol. Now it was just
a moving gray slab of water with the occasional barge or
other commercial boat traffic, but the marina I'd passed and
several private homes with dry-docked cabin cruisers, jet
skis, and other pleasure craft indicated a summertime of
boating pleasure in the shadow of the big buildings.

The county courthouse was a sprawling, fortresslike structure with stone walls and a red tile roof. Scaffolding encircled the back two-thirds of the building and a few workers appeared to be doing something to the stone. Just across Court Street was the headquarters for the Charleston City Police. The cities of South Charleston, Dunbar, St. Albans, and the town of Nitro all had their own police forces too, but since Chester's shooting had taken place on county land, the investigation fell within the sheriff's department's jurisdiction, hence Nolestar's involvement.

A chinless, heavy-jowled female dispatcher with luminous eyes and beautiful hair nodded at me as I entered the department's headquarters. She was on the phone when I walked in. I waited until she'd finished her end of the conversation. Something about a break-in and some petty thievery at an auto salvage yard.

"Can I help you?" she asked. Her hair was blond and so long that, from my vantage point, it appeared as though it might reach all the way to the floor—a size-twelve Rapunzel in a county sheriff's uniform.

"Sure. My name's Pavlicek. I'm a private investigator from Charlottesville, Virginia. I was hoping I might catch Deputy Nolestar in the office."

She gave me a questioning look.

"I'm the guy who got slugged with the barrel of the Mossberg yesterday."

"Up there where that hunter was killed earlier in the week, right?"

"Yeah."

"Let me see if I can find someone to speak with you."

She disappeared through a door at the side for a minute or so then returned.

"Deputy Nolestar's not in," she said. "But if you'd like to have a seat around the corner, Mr. Jackson, our public information officer, said he'll be with you in just a minute."

Great. Now I was getting turfed to the PR person.

"You familiar with the Chester Carew shooting?" I asked.

"Oh, wasn't that awful. Those damn poachers. The county gets a few of 'em every year. First time one's ever shot a human being though that I've ever heard of."

"Is that what the department is still officially saying, the shooting was an accident?" I thought of Kara Grayson's business card tucked in my wallet and wondered what the TV reporter might have to say about that.

"Well, I'm just a dispatcher, Mr. Pavlicek. I'm not sure if I should ..."

She glanced to her left. I looked up to see a tall, athletic-looking man, six feet five or so, with a hooked nose and a pipe clenched between his teeth, come through the door and make a beeline for me. He wore a three-piece suit he could've borrowed from an undertaker and smelled a lot like chestnuts.

"Mr. Pavlicek?"

"I am he." I said.

"Hiram Jackson." He took the pipe from his mouth and shook my hand. "Thanks for seeing me."

"Not at all. That's my job. Why don't you come on back?"

He led me through the door and down a narrow hall to a little alcove with two old vinyl chairs and a rack of magazines and a squeaky-clean ashtray.

He touched the ashtray as he passed. "Not supposed to be smoking in the building but I like to chew on my pipe while I work on the computer."

In the comer of the alcove was a doorway that led us to a small windowless office with a wooden desk mostly taken up by a large computer screen. Jackson pulled a pile of papers off a straight-back chair at the side, gestured for me to sit, and deposited himself behind the desk.

"So you're the man who got surprised by some idiot with a twelve gauge yesterday, huh?"

"That's right."

"And I hear you're a private investigator, from Virginia. Charlottesville. Is that right?"

"You heard right."

He stuck his pipe back in the corner of his mouth. "How did you get into PI work?"

"Used to be a cop."

"In Virginia?"

"No, New York."

He nodded, taking the pipe from his mouth and setting it on the desk. "I take it you were a close friend of Chester Carew," he said.

"Yes, I was."

"Bad business that. We could do with a lot less of that kind of thing around here."

"I'm sure you could."

"So you wanted to talk to Deputy Nolestar again?"

"Yes."

"He's, um, tied up for the rest of the day. Had to go up to Clarksburg for something."

"The dispatcher said you were the county's public information officer."

"Yes, sir."

"Can you tell me any more about the status of the Carew investigation?"

"Well, like I said, that's my job, so to speak, among other things, put a public face on everything. You know how it goes."

"What's the public face on Carew's death? I was just at his funeral yesterday."

He studied his hands, flexing his fingers for a moment, as if there were something about them that might give him special powers of insight or persuasion. "I heard they released some birds at the cemetery, something like that."

"Buteos. Hawks. Released back to the wild."

"Interesting. You're one of these, uh, falconers too?"

"I am."

Now he was examining his fingernails. "So you want to know what the department is doing about Carew's death, is that it?"

"In a nutshell."

He finally turned his gaze back to me. "Well, Kelly probably told you, Bobby Nolestar's the one you really need to speak with, but I can tell you this. Whoever killed Chester Carew didn't stick around to celebrate their feat. I believe the deputies did, however, find evidence of someone else at the scene."

"Evidence? What kind of evidence?" I obviously wasn't about to tell him that Toronto and I had just been out searching the area.

"Sorry, Mr. Pavlicek. They're not giving out those kinds of details. I *can* tell you Deputy Nolestar has been working round the clock on this case."

"What about federal involvement, the FBI?"

There was a barely discernible narrowing of his eyes at the question. "I don't know anything about any federal involvement," he said. "As far as the department is concerned, we're still investigating a hunting accident."

He picked up his pipe again, stuck it in his mouth, and reached to pull open the top drawer of a filing cabinet next to his desk, extracting a piece of paper from a file before handing it to me. "Press release," he said out of the corner of his mouth. "This was just given out to the media this morning."

I read it over. It told me nothing I didn't already know.

"Have you had a lot of press coverage of Carew's shooting?" I said.

"Not much really. I'm afraid hunting accidents aren't all that uncommon in this state. The missing bird made the story a little unusual, mind you. The reporter who wrote up the piece for the *Charleston Daily Mail* did a nice little sidebar about it."

"Anything on radio or television?"

"Just our usual to the news departments, asking for anyone who might have information to come forward. Had a reporter call yesterday from KBCX. She was snooping around about something to do with Carew, but that was all."

"Do you remember her name?"

"Kara something ... why?"

"Just curious."

He leaned back in his chair, took the pipe from his mouth once more. "You said you were a cop in New York. What kind? Patrol officer?"

"At first. Eventually I made detective. Homicide."

"You must've seen some grisly killings in your time then."

"My share, I guess."

"We don't see a lot of homicide around here, thank God. Don't get me wrong, we've got our share of crime."

"How about you?" I asked. "How long have you been working for the county?"

"Less than a year actually. Before that I was in Washington."

"Law enforcement?"

"No, nothing so dramatic, I'm afraid. Department of Labor."

I noticed a pair of hiking boots on a mat in the corner with not quite dry mud on them.

"You an outdoorsman?" I asked, gesturing toward them.

He chuckled. "Not really. But some of my neighbor's cows got out this morning and I had to go help him chase them down."

I nodded.

He sat up straight in his chair and pulled another pile of papers across his desk beside the monitor. "Well, if there's nothing else I can help you with, I need to get back to work. I'll let Deputy Nolestar know you stopped by looking for him."

"Sure."

"Come on. I'll walk you out."

We both stood and I followed him out the door and back down the hallway. This time he left the pipe behind.

At the dispatcher's desk he shook my hand again and turned to go. "Pleasure meeting you. You do want to watch yourself around here, Mr. Pavlicek."

"Yeah? How's that?"

"Wouldn't want you getting hit in the face with any more shotguns," he said.

12

I ate lunch in a yuppified delicatessen a couple of blocks from the state capitol complex. There were trees along the sidewalk, pattern brick in the street, and a prosperous air to the neighborhood.

While I was eating, a young couple at a table across from me couldn't keep their hands off one another, laughing softly and nuzzling and pawing each other between bites of their pastrami sandwiches. They both wore wedding rings and were both dressed in business suits — getting together for lunch obviously.

I got to thinking about Marcia, wondering what she was doing in school at the moment. I still didn't know what had gone wrong between us. I didn't seem to know anything anymore when it came to women. I finished my pity party along with the rest of my roast beef on rye and emptied my tray into the trash by the door before I left.

The studios of KBCX-TV were housed in an old depot that had been converted to office space along the riverfront north of downtown. Plate-glass windows in the lobby offered a panoramic view of the boat traffic and the chemical plant downstream.

"So what's this? A sneak attack?" Kara Grayson was dressed in blue jeans and a sweatshirt this afternoon, definitely *not* her on-camera getup. We were sitting alone in her office with a view of the river.

"Not exactly," I said.

"You're lucky you caught me. This is supposed to be my day off," she said. But there was a hint of mischief in her eyes that told me the intrusion was not at all unwelcome.

"I was hoping you might be able to help me piece some things together."

"Okay. So I take it you must be looking into the circumstances surrounding your friend's death."

"No comment."

"I see."

"I don't want my name spread all over the news and I don't think Betty Carew wants that either."

"Why? What are you afraid of?"

"Misunderstanding, miscommunication, sensationalism, biased reporting, quotes taken out of context ... need I go on?"

She tilted her head slightly, her eyes flashing. "You think that's what I'll do, somehow exploit your story?"

"Not necessarily. That's why I'm here. I'm not willing to go on the record about anything yet. I just want to ask you a few questions."

"Fair enough. As long as you're willing to answer a couple of mine."

"Background only," I said.

She nodded. "Background only."

"All right. You said you're doing a story on extremist groups in West Virginia. Would that happen to include the Stonewall Rangers?"

"Yes. But they're not the largest and most vocal. More of a splinter group actually."

"Not as visible either then, I take it."

"Well, they don't try to march on Washington or anything, if that what's you mean."

"Would you say their more clandestine activities make them more dangerous?"

"Possibly. Then again they may all be dangerous."

"You said you heard my name on the police scanner. Was there some other reason you showed up at the Carews' house yesterday?"

"To maybe get someone from the family's reaction to his shooting. To see if there might be more to it than just the police story about a hunting accident, and if what happened to you up in the woods might be related."

"Makes sense. But how do you tie all that in to your story?"

"Tony Warnock's involvement, for one thing."

"The attorney."

"That's right."

"Why would his representation of the Carew estate be a problem?"

"Because I've spent the last couple of months trying to trace the finances of some of these organizations and where they get their money. Warnock's name has come up a couple of times."

"He a Stonewaller?"

"No. As far as I've been able to determine, he's not a member of any group. He's what I like to call a silent partner."

"A sympathizer."

"More than that. A sympathizer with money."

Alarm bells were going off in my head.

"Okay. So you thought his client, Chester Carew, being shot in the woods might have some bearing on your story."

"Still do."

"You talked to the police or FBI?"

"Yes. They've got their eye on a lot of these people."

"I bet. They give you anything specific?"

"I'm a feature reporter, Frank." She crossed her arms and rolled her eyes. "The words 'the investigation is ongoing' sound familiar to you?"

I had to smile at that. "Always worked for me."

"Now it's my turn," she said. "You're a private investigator. What was your relationship with Chester Carew?"

"Friend. I knew him through falconry."

"You're one of those guys hunts with hawks too, huh?"

"Uh-huh."

"As an investigator though, have you formed any opinions yet about how or possibly why he was killed?"

"No."

"But you're here right now, so you are looking into the matter."

"The 'looking into' is ongoing."

She smiled. "What about what happened up there in the woods yesterday?"

Should I tell her about Higgins and the link to the
Rangers? "Too early to tell if it's related," I said.
    "You know, some of the PIs I've talked to in the past like
to brag about the cases they're working on."
    "Not if they're any good, they don't."
    She nodded. "Anything else you can tell me that might
contribute to my story?"
    I thought about it for a moment. "Not really. No."
    "You married?"
    "Divorced." I'd also noted the absence of a ring on her
finger.
    "Then maybe you'd like to get together for dinner
sometime."
    "Are you asking me for a date?"
    "Does that bother you?"
    "What, being asked or you doing the asking?"
    "Either."
    "Neither bothers me."
    "Good."
    "Let me get back to you on that."
    "Okay."
    On the windowsill sat a large picture frame filled with
several photos of the reporter. In a number of them, she held
a dog or a cat in her arms.
    "You an animal lover?" I asked.
    "Yes."
    "Good thing to be."
    I stood up to leave. "Thanks very much for your time. I
mean, on your day off and everything."
    "You're just lucky I didn't sic a cameraman on you."
    "Camera*person*. It's a PC world."
    "Right," she said softly.
    "It takes guts to be going after the Stonewallers and
some of these other groups."
    She shrugged. "It's my job. People have a right to know
what they're all about."
    "Not to mention giving your station's ratings a boost."
    "Yes," she said. "There's that too."

"Everybody is scared of hatred, but they want to come home at night and watch it on their screens."

"Makes them feel safer, I guess."

"Sure ... to be watching rather than to actually be there falling victim to the hatred themselves."

"But what happens when the tube goes dark?" she asked.

"I don't know. Maybe we all look for someone to cling to."

"Who are *you* looking for, Frank?"

"I don't know yet."

She said nothing.

"So you go ahead and ask your questions and I'll ask mine."

"Maybe they'll lead us to something."

"Just be sure to watch your back," I said.

"Glad to hear you care about it."

"What?"

"My back."

I saw her turn to look out at the river as I went out and closed the door.

13

The GMC crew cab pickup pulled away from the curb in front of the studio as I rounded the corner out of the drive. Traffic was light and the driver hung back a ways. But even after I turned at the next two lights, I noticed he stayed with me.

I was so busy glancing off toward the distance in my rearview mirror I didn't notice the dark unmarked sedan pull in right behind me with its blue light flashing—no siren—until we'd traveled another hundred yards or so. The big pickup was also closing fast. I turned off the street into the parking lot of an abandoned convenience store, its windows boarded over and covered with graffiti, and waited.

A tall black man wearing a green hunting jacket, dark pants, and hiking boots stepped out of the passenger side of the sedan and came around to the driver's window of my Ford. He was built like an all-pro fullback. He had a large, expressionless—at the moment at least—face with brown eyes that looked a couple of sizes too large for his head.

I rolled down my window.

"Frank Pavlicek?" When he squinted, his eyes looked more normal.

"Yeah. That's me."

"Special Agent Jarrod Grooms, ATF." He showed me his Alcohol, Tobacco & Firearms shield. "Wondered if we might have a word with you for a few moments."

"Okay." I cut the engine and pocketed my keys.

"If you'll follow me, please." He gestured with his head toward the other two vehicles.

I climbed out and fell in step alongside him. Our boots crunched across the broken-up asphalt of the lot. He led me through the sickening sweet cloud of exhaust from the sedan, back to the crew cab, the rear windows of which were too dark for me to see the interior.

Grooms opened the door. "After you," he said.

I clambered inside. There was a modified bench seat and space for computers and other equipment, but no one else in back. Two men sat up front. One had his ear to a walkie-talkie. I slid across to the opposite end of the seat.

Grooms hoisted himself in behind me and shut the door. He settled into the seat across from me.

"Been busy lately, haven't you, Frank?"

"That depends," I said.

"C'mon. Neither of us has time for bullshit. You got yourself smacked with a shotgun yesterday morning and you've been kicking around asking questions about the Stonewall Rangers and what they're up to."

"That's right."

"Even though Sheriffs Deputy Nolestar asked you politely to stand down."

"What's being done to find out who killed Chester Carew?"

He paused to look at me for a moment. "That gets complicated. It's being worked on."

"Why are you here, Grooms? You part of a joint terrorism task force?"

He cleared his throat and held up his hand as if to wave away the question. "I don't know yet what happened to your friend the old man. Okay? But we're about to find out, along with a whole lot of other things."

The truck's big diesel engine burbled in front of us. The whole cab vibrated.

"You sound pretty certain."

"I've been on this case for almost a year and you've been here for what... less than forty-eight hours? Yeah, man, I am. I'm pretty certain."

"Toronto and I found a pile of tail transmitters up in the woods a couple of hundred yards from where Chester was killed. Did you know that? They're used to track birds."

He nodded. "Fits in with the information we're working with."

"Which is?"

He smiled and pointed to his forehead. " 'Need to know,' Frank. Everything's on a 'need to know' only basis. You and your buddy Toronto ought to be familiar with that."

I looked up front. The two other agents stared straight ahead as if we weren't just a few feet behind them talking. "How about Tony Warnock? What's his involvement with all this?"

"I can't discuss specific individuals or suspects."

"Have you at least found out what happened to Chester's falcon Elo?"

He hesitated for a moment. "As I said, we're about to find out a whole lot of things."

"Yeah, and how is that? You just going to wave a magic wand and the bad guys will surrender and tell all to you?"

He said nothing.

"You're planning to arrest some people soon then?"

Another smile. Expensive dental work. His teeth were large and white and almost perfectly straight. "We just need you to relax for a couple of days, okay, Frank? Maybe head on back to Charlottesville. You can read about it in the paper. Watch it all on the eleven o'clock news."

"What about Betty and Jason Carew?"

"We'll get around to that eventually. One part of the puzzle."

"So you just want me to trust you," I said.

"You pay your taxes, don't you? 'To protect and to serve.' You know the drill."

"What if you've got some of it wrong though?"

"I don't think we have any of it wrong, Frank. And if we do, well, we'll be the ones to suffer the consequences, won't we?"

You and everybody else associated with this whole mess, I thought.

"I'll think about it," I said.

"Good." He pulled out a business card and passed it across to me. "But don't take too long. My personal cell phone's written on the back. I'd like to hear from you before the day is over."

"I work long days."

He shrugged. "I'm open twenty-four seven myself." He bent down and pulled on the handle, shouldering open the door as he did.

I slid across the seat and followed him back out onto the pavement.

"Oh, and one other thing," he said.

"Yeah?"

"This is very important, Frank."

"What's very important?"

"Be careful who you trust," he said.

14

By midafternoon the sky had cleared to a cold blue. The dry
air smelled of moss and pine. The green Jeep Cherokee with
the brown-and-yellow West Virginia Department of Natural
Resources Conservation Officer emblem on the door came
up the dirt road into the Carews' acreage and pulled in to
park between my truck and Damon Farraday's Scout.

Gwen Hallston opened the door and climbed out.

"So you guys ready to do a little more hunting today?"
She nodded toward the Scout, the backseat of which was
now occupied by the giant hood containing Farraday's red-
tailed hawk, Tawny.

"That's right," I said. "But like I said on the phone, I
thought you might want to help us keep an eye out for Elo
while we're at it, not to mention make another walk-through
of the area around the crime scene, see what we might turn
up."

"The sheriff's people and others have already been
through here looking, haven't they?"

"Yeah, but they're not necessarily outdoorsmen. We
might notice something they missed." I decided not to
mention how Toronto's and my earlier visit had been cut
short.

"Where's your other friend?"

"Toronto? He'll probably join us a little later."

"I assume your paperwork's up-to-date, West Virginia
out-of-state hunting license and all that?"

"Yup. In the truck if you'd like to see it."

"I would, in fact, if you don't mind."

She accompanied me to the other side of the Ford, then
examined the paperwork I produced from my glove
compartment before pronouncing it okay. Farraday was
busy preparing Tawny for hunting. We went over to watch
him make his final preparations with the bird.

"Getting back to Elo, did you know he'd been sick a

couple of weeks ago?" I asked.

"As a matter of fact, I did," she said. "Chester called me when it happened."

"Chester brought him down to see a local veterinarian, Dr. Winston."

"Greg Winston. Yeah, right. He's a good man."

"Apparently Winston told him Elo might've come in contact with some kind of hazardous materials or something."

"I don't know if anything's been determined for sure on that."

"You heard of any other cases of that happening with wildlife here in the area?"

"Nope. Not that I know of. But maybe we should keep an eye out for things with Tawny, just in case."

"Oh, I'll keep a close eye on her, you can bet on that," Farraday said. He'd been listening in on our conversation while he was taking Tawny from her hood. He slammed shut the back door of the Scout with his free hand and walked over with the big bird on his glove. Her eyes were keen and she was already beginning to scan the terrain, looking for quarry.

I turned back to the officer. "Let me ask you something else. What do you know about a group around this area calling themselves the Stonewall Rangers Brigade?"

Her face darkened. "What, those idiots? What've they got to do with any of this?"

I gave her the highlights of my encounter with the masked man in the woods, what Toronto and I had been able to find out so far, and my conversations with the sheriff's department and the ATF agent.

She listened, but said little.

"No one's spoken to you about Chester's death?"

"No. Not directly. I mean, I gave the deputies what I knew about the hunters and wildlife in the area. That was about it."

"Anybody from the ATF or FBI contact you?"

"Look, Pavlicek. You know I'm not supposed to talk

about stuff like that. You used to be a cop too, right? I know Chester was a good friend of yours and all and you had this little run-in with a guy in the woods, but maybe you ought to just back off and let the sheriff's department, the FBI, or whoever else is involved do their job."

"Maybe," I said.

"Don't you think they're as interested as you are in finding out who killed Chester?"

I said nothing.

"Of more immediate interest to me, right now, is what's going to happen to those two remaining birds of his. Do you know if Chester ever stipulated in writing where he wanted his birds to go if something happened to him?"

"I don't know. You'd have to ask Betty, although I'm not sure now would be a good time. The hawks are kind of an important link to Chester, I think, especially for the boy."

"I understand that, but if anything happens to them while I'm — "

"Listen, Jake Toronto and I are staying there for now and the birds are being well cared for. Maybe you could just cut them some slack for a while? No one's taking them out to hunt or anything where they might get injured."

She looked at me for a moment. "All right," she said. "I'll give it a few more days."

"Thanks. I'm sure they'll appreciate it."

"But you should let Mrs. Carew know she's going to have to come to a decision on the birds, barring anything found in writing from the permitee, Mr. Carew. Since her son is still a minor, and unless Mrs. Carew is interested in acquiring her falconry licensure. I'm afraid we may have to intervene and take temporary possession of the birds in order to seek a permanent home for them."

"Sure."

We still had about three more hours of daylight, but the bright afternoon sun was already beginning to angle down toward the horizon.

"Well, aren't we going hunting?" she asked.

For the next two and a half hours the conservation

officer trooped along with us while Tawny swooped from tree to tree and we circled deep into Carew's woods. I carried Chester's spare telemetry unit, holding the yagi high in the hope I might get lucky and catch some sort of signal from Elo. But after five days I knew it was a real long shot.

After an hour or so, Farraday said he'd run out of tidbits for his bird so the agent and I surveyed a part of the acreage I hadn't been on before while he and the hawk went back to his truck to retrieve his spare bag. Upon his return, we went back to the hunt.

Farraday's big redtail caught nothing, but it wasn't for lack of trying. A squirrel tumbled from the treetops, barely escaping her talons before scrambling to safety inside a hollow tree. She also put a rabbit to cover in a dugout den beneath a stand of fallen logs and made point to it. Try as we might, however, neither Farraday nor I was able to flush the bunny to her again.

Along the way, we all kept a lookout for any signs of hazardous materials or any agitation or other problem among the wildlife in the area, or in Tawny for that matter. There was no evidence of nasty stuff, Tawny looked healthy and keen, and as for the wildlife we saw, including a few deer, all appeared to be normal. There didn't seem to be a large number of small game present, but that was typical with a hawk in the woods — most potential prey would've bugged for cover at the first sensing of the raptor.

We were unable to serve anything else to Tawny until, finally, as we were heading back toward the trucks, she swooped after a field mouse only to check to a flight of doves taking the air from the branches of a jack pine about a hundred yards in front of us. I was about twenty yards ahead of the others with my beating stick and had the best view.

The chase didn't last long though. Killing smaller, quicker birds was not totally impossible, but rare for the big buteo, and they soon outflew her. All, that is, except for one that seemed to sky up irregularly, twirling and zigzagging as if it were injured. Tawny had a bead on the dawdler, but the bird seemed to right itself and was soon making steam after the others. The redtail, sensing this, broke off to alight in the branches of the pine from which her erstwhile quarry had just departed, maybe in hopes of pouncing on any other hidden stragglers.

"You see that?" I asked.

"What, she try to hit on those doves?" Farraday was making his way toward me. Hallston hung back checking out a dried-up streambed for any evidence of chemicals.

"Yeah."

"Should've stayed on the mouse, she might've at least caught her dinner."

"Can't blame her, can you, when there's bigger meat in the air?"

"Nah, I guess not."

"But one of that flight was flying funny, kind of dopey-like, until it righted itself and finally got under wing."

"Huh. Maybe it was injured."

"Maybe. Funny thing was, it looked a little different from the others too. I couldn't make out the markings but the straggler didn't have quite the same shape as the others."

He shrugged.

"What happened?" Officer Hallston caught up with us.

"Just thought I saw a strange bird — part of a flight of doves she flushed out of that pine where she's perched now. Tawny took off after it, but she broke off."

"Really. Probably nothing, but let's have a look."

When we made it to the tree and took a look around, it did seem like nothing. There were no other birds in evidence, living or otherwise.

"What did you say you saw again?" the conservation agent asked.

I described it again, this time in more detail.

"Probably just a bird with an injured wing," offered Farraday.

"Probably," she said. "But I'll tell you what — since we've got precious little else to show for our little outing so far, I think I'll bag a few samples of droppings from down here in these pine needles." She produced a few clear plastic bags and some latex gloves from inside her coat pocket and proceeded to scoop several handfuls.

"Great hunt," Farraday said. "Now we're out here skimming up bird shit."

"Could be worse," I said. "Nobody's pointing a gun at me this time, or shooting at us the way they did Chester."

"Not exactly a clean crime scene, eh, Detective?" Farraday said.

"You know I've thought of something else," Hallston said. "What if someone were illegally storing chemicals or other materials out here without Chester's knowledge?"

"Possible, I suppose," I said. "You have anybody in mind?"

"No, but I could contact the EPA and see if they had any ideas."

"Not a bad thought. Might as well cover all the bases. Jake's supposed to be talking to the vet too. Let's see if anything comes of that."

The sun had dropped below the trees and was dropping fast toward the horizon. We had a half hour, maybe less, before dusk.

Approaching the trucks in the gathering shadows, we saw that Toronto had finally decided to join us. Chester's old Suburban was parked behind the conservation officer's Jeep and my pickup. He had to have been there awhile since I hadn't heard the sound of his engine.

Farraday and the conservation agent went to settle the redtail in the back of the Scout.

"What happened to you?" I asked Toronto.

"Got a little waylaid," was all he said.

"You talk to the vet?"

He shook his head. "Sat in his waiting room for two hours. Emergency surgery — somebody's dog got run over by a truck. Nurse said to try back later."

"You ask if they'd gotten in any test results for Elo?"

"She said she didn't think so. In any event, she said we had to talk to the vet about it."

"Anything else?"

"I got a line on that phone number your masked bandit called yesterday."

"Yeah?"

"Had a memorable conversation with another Stonewaller."

"Who is it?"

He glanced at Farraday and Hallston. "I'll tell you about it when we're alone."

We went over to the Scout. Hallston said she had to get going so she and I broke away and I walked her over to her Jeep.

"Thanks for coming," I told her. "I thought we might stumble onto something more, but not for the moment, I guess."

"It was worth a shot," she said. "If there's some foreign substance up here making birds sick, I'm as interested as you are in finding out what's causing it. I'll let you know if anything turns up on these samples." She opened her rear hatch and stuffed her pack in next to the rest of her equipment, then slammed the door shut.

"I appreciate it. And thanks for holding off a bit on Chester's other two birds."

"You're welcome." As she came around the side of her vehicle, her gaze drifted back toward Toronto, who was holding something for Farraday.

"Chester's told me a few stories about your friend over there."

"There are a few to tell."

"I guess he's a bit more of a ... colorful personality."

"Right. I'm the one who specializes in drab."

"Then again, he was Chester's sponsor and all."

"That must be it," I said.

She laughed and climbed into the Jeep. She started the engine, turned the vehicle around in the grass, and waved as she headed off down the dirt road.

She'd only traveled about fifty yards when I heard it. A hissing noise, like the air being let out of a tire, escaped from the bottom of the Jeep. A ball of fire enveloped the cab and at the same instant the roof appeared to implode briefly; then the entire vehicle exploded with a deafening roar.

I dove for the shelter of a nearby ditch.

"What the heck was that?" Damon Farraday screamed.

Flaming bits of foam and other pieces of what was left of Gwen Hallston's Jeep rained down across the woods. Farraday and Toronto had been standing another fifty yards farther away, shielded from the blast by the front of his Scout. Tawny was screeching inside her giant hood.

I jumped up and ran to my pickup, opened the door, and grabbed the fire extinguisher I kept behind the seat. Hallston was assuredly beyond help, but with the dryness of the brush and timber we could also have a major forest fire on our hands.

Toronto had grabbed a blanket from somewhere and he and I ran together to the remains of the Jeep. There was not much left of it or Gwen.

"Take the other side!" I yelled. I began shooting down the flames with the foam from the extinguisher while Toronto beat at several smaller flares that had already sparked in the grass. We spent four or five minutes knocking down what we hoped were all traces of the fire, but with the smoldering wreckage of the Jeep, now nothing but a charred piece of chassis filled with body parts, the danger remained high.

I called 911 on the cell and the dispatcher said people were on their way. She wanted me to stay on the line, but I was too busy watching flares. I walked back up the hill and gave the phone to Farraday, who appeared to be in a mild form of shock. He took the phone and started babbling. At least he would keep the line open.

"Hey, Frank," Jake said, coming up behind me. "This may not be over."

"What do you mean?"

"Whoever planted that device on her Jeep might've armed the Ford and the Scout too."

I looked at him for a moment.

"Get away from the vehicles!" I said to Farraday.

"Wha—?"

I grabbed him and helped him to his feet, walking him to a safe distance. Toronto lifted the entire giant hood from the back of the Scout and carried it over to us out of potential danger.

"Wha—what's going on?" Farraday asked.

"I'm going to go check it out," Toronto said.

"I'll help," I said.

"No. No sense *both* of us getting killed."

He approached my pickup first, dropped to the ground, and rolled under the bumper.

A couple of seconds later he called out calmly. "There's another bomb here."

"Oh, Jesus, mother of God!" Farraday was blubbering into the phone. I took it from him and explained to the operator what was happening.

"I've seen this type of unit before," Toronto said. "It's on a timer. Set to go off a short while after the drivetrain starts rolling. You got any wire cutters?"

"In the tool chest in the bed," I yelled.

"How about a flashlight?"

"There's one in there too. You need my help?"

"I need your prayers," he said.

He got the tools and the light and rolled back under the truck. He was under there for maybe a minute and a half.

"How's it going?" I asked.

"Done. I've disarmed it and I'm removing it from the frame."

"Good idea."

He finished with what he was doing and crawled carefully out from beneath the Ford with the device in his hand. It looked like a large pale brick with wires sticking out of it.

"C-four," he said, setting it down in the grass. "Pretty harmless by itself now. Needs an igniter to start the detonation chain."

"Stonewall Rangers?"

"Maybe, although this work's pretty clean. Has to be someone with experience."

Next he moved to Farraday's Scout.

"Same thing here," he said from under the vehicle. "Not as well done though. Sloppy ... they crossed a couple of wires. This one would've been a dud. Must've been in a hurry."

He slid back out from beneath the Scout with the second device.

"You see anybody when you were driving in here?" I asked.

Toronto shook his head.

"How long had you been waiting for us?"

"I don't know. Fifteen, twenty minutes maybe."

Sirens could be heard in the distance. Darkness was gathering and the glow from flashing lights appeared over the nearby hills.

"Look, man," he said. "This dirt road continues all the way through to another highway on the other side of the ridge. I can make it in the Suburban so I'm out of here."

"You're what? Jake, we just had a bombing and a murder here. The sheriff, the FBI ... they're going to be all over this."

"I know. That's why I can't stick around."

"What are you talking about?"

"I'll explain later," he said, trotting to the Suburban.

"You'll what?"

Farraday was still talking to someone on the phone. The skeleton of the Jeep was still burning and the sirens were getting louder. Toronto hopped into the vehicle, fired up the engine, and kicked up a cloud of dust and stone as he disappeared over a rise up the road.

15

"Pavlicek, I want to talk to you. Inside. Now."

Two hours later, our macabre gathering in the woods still included a fire captain, two big red pumpers, several firemen, about a half dozen Kanawha County sheriff's deputies and their cruisers, not to mention the state police bomb squad, a gaggle of swarming FBI agents, and my newfound friend, ATF Agent Grooms. Darkness had fallen. Flood lamps and headlights lit up the cold. Some kind soul had stuck a cup of hot black coffee in my hands.

Grooms pointed toward the back of a large black panel van parked in the line of rescue vehicles. I took another sip of coffee and followed him. The van's doors opened as if by magic to reveal a mobile command post of sorts. Radios and terminals and sensitive monitoring equipment, most of the uses for which I could imagine but not precisely identify.

"This some kind of game to you, Pavlicek?" The doors closed behind us. With a gesture he bid me sit down in a rolling desk chair by one of the consoles while he took another opposite.

I kept my mouth shut. Shook my head.

"Now we've got a West Virginia Department of Natural Resources conservation officer murdered."

"You finally ready to start arresting anybody?"

"Shit. You don't even know what you've stuck your foot into and you want me to start arresting people."

"*Somebody* put those bombs under our vehicles."

"You're right. Somebody did. And we're going to find out who it was." He looked at a screen on the console for a moment. "What the hell were y'all doing up here in these woods this afternoon?" he asked.

"Hunting."

"Hunting."

"Yeah. You saw Farraday and the redtail."

An ambulance had whisked the apprentice falconer off

to the hospital for a checkup. The bird was calm and quiet now, sitting inside its giant hood in the back of Farraday's Scout.

Grooms rubbed his hands together. "What was Hallston doing up here with you then?"

"Helping us look for Elo."

"Elo?"

"The missing falcon that had been ill. Remember, I asked you about him?"

"Right. So what's the big deal about a missing bird?"

"Well, I'm still curious about what caused Elo to get sick in the first place. So was Hallston."

He thought about that for a moment. Then he appeared to dismiss it. "Mighty impressive the way you defused those other two bombs," he said.

I shrugged, wondering if Farraday would back my story the way I'd asked him to, that he and I and Hallston had been the only ones present at the bombing.

"Something seems to be missing here."

"You can say that again," I said.

"Where's your buddy Toronto?"

"I haven't seen him this afternoon. He's supposed to be following up with Chester's veterinarian."

"Back to the bird thing again."

"Right."

He propped his big foot on the counter and retied his shoe, then let it slide back down to the floor again. "So you think by us moving on the Stonewall Rangers now we can end all this, huh?"

"I don't know. You still know a lot more than I do and I'm beginning to wonder. ... But it sure seems like it would make a great start."

He leaned forward in his chair with his elbows resting on top of his knees. He put his head down for a moment and massaged his forehead. He looked tired.

"All right, Pavlicek. Look, what I'm going to tell you right now is a matter of homeland security. You understand?"

I nodded.

"If it leaves this trailer, in any way whatsoever, both your ass and my ass will be so hard fried the charcoal will look worse than what's left of that Jeep out there."

"I get it."

He let out a long sigh. "I can tell you we're on the inside of this one and we think we're ahead of the curve."

"That's it?"

"That's it."

"The Rangers are definitely up to something then."

"Yes."

"And you've infiltrated their organization."

"Not exactly. Better than that."

I wondered what he meant, but knew better than to probe further about it. "So you think they're feeling the heat and have started killing people?" I asked.

"I don't know."

"What do you mean, you don't know?"

"I honestly don't know." He stared at me, looking a little uncertain.

"But it sure is making the waters muddy for you at the moment, isn't it?"

"It damn sure is."

"So you're saying, don't let finding out who killed an old man flying his bird in the woods get in the way of catching some terrorists."

"In the short run, maybe I am. Yes. If there were anything illicit about Chester Carew's shooting, I can almost guarantee you it will come out in the wash."

"But now they're killing people with bombs."

"You must've really pissed them off then. You're just lucky it wasn't you and your friend Farraday too."

"The bombs were all on timers."

"Appears that way ... random ... hoped to kill as many of you as they can."

"When are you going to make your move?"

"Soon," he said. "Very soon."

"Seems to me we're right back to where we were a

couple of hours ago. You want me to trust that you guys have got it all correct."

"That's right," he said.

"But what if the devil's in the details?"

"What if the bigger question is: can we trust you?"

"You want to arrest me? Is that it?"

"No. I don't want to arrest you. That might tip our hand to the Stonewallers. I just want you to be a team player."

There was a knock at the back of the van. Grooms wheeled his chair over and pushed one of the rear doors open.

A woman in a dark jacket with the large letters ATF stenciled on the front stood there holding a printout in her hand.

"What's up?" Grooms asked.

"We've got something we thought you'd want to see, boss."

"What is it?"

The woman made a point of glancing over the top of her paper at me.

"It's all right, Sally. Just give me what you got."

She coughed. "The two remaining car bombs, you know, are C-four. And we're pretty sure the one that boomed was of the same type. But in spraying the area with detection agents we've come up with a trace of Group One Inorganic Nitrate along the road."

Grooms's brow furrowed for a moment. "Ammonium nitrate? How much?"

"Like I said, just a trace. Minute amount. Could've even come in on any of these vehicles' tires."

"Probably just some spilled fertilizer."

"That's what we were thinking too."

"Do a broader analysis though, as much as feasible. Check up and down the road for any more of the stuff."

"You got it."

"I'll be right with you guys," he said.

"Something unexpected?" I asked.

"*You're* what's unexpected, Pavlicek. But I've got to go."

He pushed himself out of the chair and I followed.

Halfway through the door of the van he turned to me. "So is this the end of it for you then? Or do I still have to wait for your call?"

"I'll let you know," I said.

He tapped his watch. "The clock is ticking. Remember what I said earlier. ..."

Be careful who you trust.

"What about my truck?" I asked.

"We're done with it for now," he said.

"And Farraday's hawk?"

"Farraday wasn't injured, was he?"

"No, just a little shell-shocked, I think."

"I'll get somebody to drive the bird down to him at the hospital in just a little bit," he said.

The inside of my truck was still warming up as I threaded my way among the various law enforcement vehicles parked along the dirt road and rolled down the hill toward the highway, following a state police van that was also leaving. At the intersection with the main road a police barricade blocked the exit. Two sheriff's deputies nodded at me gravely as they let me pass.

There was another large assembly of klieg lights and vehicles parked along the shoulder here. A half dozen media vans, huge video cameras, and a satellite truck. I heard the guttural chop of air and saw the blinking red lights from a helicopter circling in the dark sky over-head.

The county sheriff, Hiram Jackson, and another man stood before a group of fifteen or twenty reporters. Squinting into the bright lights, the sheriff was speaking into a bank of microphones.

Toward the back of the gathering, I noticed Kara Grayson. She was hard to miss, what with her bright blond hair and long dark coat, the same one she had worn at the house the day before; but she appeared content to remain in the background while the other reporters fired their questions at the officials. She turned from watching the sheriff to look at my truck as I passed.

We locked eyes for a moment before I'd driven completely by.

16

I wouldn't see Jake Toronto again for almost twenty-four hours. He didn't answer his cell phone, and when I called Betty Carew she said she hadn't seen him or heard from him either. I picked up a sub and a couple of sodas in Dunbar and drove into downtown Charleston again, circling along the river and up around the surrounding hills through various neighborhoods, thinking about all that had happened. At night, the city was a bright beacon of civilization built up around a cold river running out of dark mountains.

Not a huge metropolis, but big enough to spawn the likes of Roseberry Circle and pique the business interest of the gangs from up North, where a five-dollar vial of crack up there might go for as much as twenty dollars down here. Simple economics. Supply and demand. But what were the economics of hatred that spawned the likes of Bo Higgins and the Stonewall Rangers?

All I had were more questions. Had Chester Carew, being sucked into the Rangers' orbit, gotten too close to something volatile and been sacrificed simply to silence him as Grooms seemed to suggest? Or was something else going on? Why come after me and Farraday and Conservation Agent Hallston all at once?

Where was Toronto and what was he up to? I'd never known him to leave the scene of a crime like that before. Was Grooms right? Was it really time for me to stand down? I had no direct counterterrorism experience, domestic or otherwise. And that's what we were talking about, weren't we? That's what Grooms and Nolestar, and now even potentially Toronto, were embroiled in: some act or potential act of terrorism. No matter what kind of spin the sheriff and the media put on it for public consumption. And it might just well have been my own boneheaded inexperience that contributed to Gwen Hallston's being blown to bits instead of her being back home with her friends or family tonight, wherever and whoever they might be. It suddenly occurred to me I hadn't even thought to ask her about a husband or kids.

I didn't call Grooms. I shut off my cell phone and returned to the house in Nitro, where Betty and Jason Carew had gone to bed early once again. I let myself in through the back door into the dimly lit kitchen. There was a note from Betty and two pieces of pie left in the refrigerator, only one of which would be consumed that night, I now felt certain.

Later that night, I fell into a dream. It was one of the most vivid I can ever recall having and brought me back in time to a place and realm of experience I thought I'd long since left behind.

One fall morning, near the end of a shift twenty-five years before, my first partner and I had a floater down by an old set of docks that were later demolished, just below Battery Park.

"Friggin' A. Just what we friggin' need," Zak Dolinski said.

"Right," I said.

The Manhattan skyline had begun to brighten only a half hour before. The call had come over the radio as we were finishing a roust on a couple of copulating junkies who'd temporarily taken over the heated doorway of an otherwise deserted Laundromat only a block or two from Wall Street. Wouldn't do for any early arriving investment banker types in their pressed woolen suits to be exposed to such an apparently dark underside of humanity.

"Ever see a floatie before?" He switched on the beacons and burped the siren, gunning the engine around a corner, turning south toward the river.

"Nope." I was just emerging from the Cro-Magnon phase of my early twenties and didn't have any more to say about it.

"Oh, they're loads of fun. Depends how long he-she-whatever's been in the brine."

"Peachy," I said.

I was still fresh meat, a little too cocky. Less than ten months out of the academy. Assigned to work the dog shift between Canal Street and the Battery with Zak, who was a twenty-year veteran and had a wife and three teenage children, though for reasons known only to the brass and bureaucracy of NYPD, two months later I'd be transferred north to the war zone of the Bronx. Dolinski, although he couldn't have known it at the time, was less than twelve months from the five-car pileup on the BQE, on his way to work one evening, that would mangle the cab of his brand-new Chevy, crushing his pelvis so severely he would bleed to death internally before the paramedics could get him stabilized and into the ER at Forest Hills.

But all either of us knew then, on our way down to the Battery at six thirty in the morning, was that the hungry chill of the Hudson awaited.

We found the spot a couple of minutes later. The vie in the water turned out to be a Puerto Rican male, naked to the waist, with four medium-size gunshot wounds, three to the torso and one larger one to the back of the head. The witness who had called it in looked to be one of those Wall Street types, obviously a local, who still held his dog, a Great Dane named Harriet, on a short leash.

I took down the man's statement before letting him go, then turned back toward the water's edge where Dolinski knelt on the pavement above the body.

He shook his head. "Jesus ... these spies just keep doing each other in."

For the most part, it was what he had tried to prepare me for. Bloated arms and fingers, bits of brain salad still leeching into the slick surface eddies of the Hudson. The body had somehow gotten tangled in an old fishing net, making the portion that remained below the water, even at low tide, a good target for crabs. My gaze swept involuntarily past the body toward New Jersey.

"You know," he said, "we ain't supposed to touch anything before the dicks and the divers get here."

I nodded.

"Thing I'm worried about is this current." He pointed at the oily sluice of water rushing against the dilapidated pilings. And indeed the body, temporarily snagged against the giant-sized broken-toothpick remains of the dock, seemed in peril of breaking free at any moment.

"Must be the tide starting to pull."

He got on the radio asking how much longer until the divers got there, and was told five, maybe ten minutes.

"Yeah? Well, we may not have five more minutes," he told the dispatcher. " 'Less those frogmen want to go searching for this corpse downriver."

There was a delay then the crackled, dispassionate response from dispatch. "Don't let it go."

Dolinksi shook his head. "Don't let it go. Christ ..." He looked at me. "You believe this shit? Roger," he said into the radio, then keyed off the mike. "You up for this, Pavlicek? Maybe we should just let José here float on down to Davy Jones."

"And let the crabs have the rest of him?" I said. We locked eyes for a moment.

He grunted. "Goddamn crabs. ..."

But as he was speaking the top half of the body in the water suddenly began to rotate out from the pilings. Without thinking, I leapt down into the river, which came up to my waist. The cold slammed into me like a shock wave and the current almost forced me to lose my balance.

"Grab the netting!" Dolinski was yelling behind me. I reached out toward the slimy lattice already thinking the same thing. A moment later, he was splashing into the water beside me.

The netting was slick with the accumulated muck of the river, not to mention whatever unspeakable fluids had oozed from the corpse. The body was much heavier than I'd expected — it took all of my strength, leaning against the current to hold it in place. Dolinski grabbed hold as well, and between the two of us we managed to shoulder the net and the attached weight of the dead man back toward the pilings where we might gain some relief from the relentless pull of the tide.

"Whoa!" he said. "We gotcha, chico. We gotcha." My hands and lower body had already gone completely numb. The chuck-chuck of another siren could be heard in the distance.

"What a bunch of crap!" Dolinski was laughing maniacally now, shaking his head. "Both of us gonna have to burn these sets of blues."

I almost gagged. Mist rose like cannon smoke from the flat dark green of the river.

"Don't worry, kiddo. You done good ... you done good. ..."

I must have turned to look away from him then, away from the pockmarked body and the stinking crap of the water, my gaze somehow instinctively drawn toward the sky. High above the rising clouds of fog, the early-morning sun struck the tops of the twin towers of the Trade Center, turning them a fiery red.

If you worked in lower Manhattan then, you knew those steel monoliths, finished just a couple of years earlier, were always there, but you didn't stop and gawk at them. As cops, most of our action was down at street level anyway. Concrete and stone. Bankers floated up there in those towers. Bankers and traders and their lawyers. People mostly immune from the types of things we had to deal with.

But then Dolinski was suddenly screaming in my ear, the way he must have screamed at the rescue workers trying to free him on the BQE that morning later on. Only it wasn't Dolinski. In my dream it had become Toronto. I couldn't understand a word he was saying and I began to lose my grip on the net.

The buildings high above were mainly empty at that hour. The last thing I remember was that their orange glow gave me something to look at so I wouldn't freeze.

The next morning, after waking to a cold clear sunrise, I sat out in the barn with the Harris's hawk and the big redtail for a while. The birds were in fine shape. Jason and Betty had been doing a good job feeding and looking after them. Still, Torch had a gleam in his eye I could've sworn hadn't been there two days before. These two wanted to be hunting — it was what they'd been created to do and what Chester would have wanted.

Maybe Gwen Hallston had been right. The state could take possession of them and arrange for transfer to another West Virginia falconer, or, in the case of the red-tail, a captive release. But I couldn't help thinking that for Jason, taking the remaining birds away at this point would be like ripping away an integral part of his father to which the boy could still cling. The decision would have to be made soon, however, one way or another.

Betty Carew was still in her housecoat and slippers, standing at the stove with her back to me, her white hair stringing down above her shoulders, when I appeared in the kitchen an hour later. Several strips of bacon sizzled in the pan.

"Mornin', Frank. You fellas were out late last night. You use the key under the mat?"

"I let myself in and put it back where I'd found it before I locked up." I said.

"Where's Jake? Sleeping in this morning?"

I didn't say anything. She'd poured two glasses of orange juice and set the table for both of us. I sat down at one of the places and took a sip.

She turned the heat down on the burner and turned to look at me. "Something's wrong, isn't it?"

"I'm afraid so. Is Jason up yet?"

"No, he's still sleeping. Now what's wrong? Has Jake been hurt?"

"No, although I'm not quite sure where he is at the moment."

"What happened?"

I explained about the bombing but left out a lot of my conversation with Grooms and some of the more gory details.

"So you don't know where Jake went afterward?" she

asked when I finished.

"Nope. And let's keep that to ourselves for the moment. My guess is he's found something he doesn't want me knowing about just yet. In the meantime, I was thinking maybe I could get your help with something."

"Of course. Anything."

"Have you had a chance to look through any of Chester's papers or files since he died?"

"No, I haven't. I tried for the first time yesterday after y'all left, but it was hard for me being in there with his desk and all his things. I stopped after just a couple of minutes."

"I understand. Would you have any objection if I took a look myself? It's a long shot, but I might find something that will help Jake and lead me toward Chester's killer. Now that they've got a bombing on their hands, I suspect the police or the FBI may want to have a look at those papers pretty soon too. I wouldn't mind getting there first."

She nodded. "I suppose it will be all right. But I'd rather not have to go back in there again myself right now."

"I promise I'll be careful not to disturb things too much," I said.

"Thank you, but you're going to have some eggs and bacon first, no argument."

No argument from me. She transferred the bacon onto a plate, placing it in the warm oven to keep the pieces from getting cold, then cooked the eggs. I was struck by how these little acts of domesticity seemed to help create a home for her, one that would insulate her not just from the pain of her husband's passing, but also from the terrible possibility of his having been coldly murdered by someone or some group with even larger malevolent intentions.

Now that someone was my cold quarry. And Toronto's. And that of Nolestar and Grooms and the ATF and the FBI and whoever else might be in on this investigation. I'd decided the night before I was going to try to focus on Chester and find out who shot him, Grooms be damned, and not get too distracted by terrorist bombings or whatever else might happen.

Yeah, right. Like trying to ignore the blaring big-screen TV inside a house trailer. It might take all I had in this game just to keep from being shown the inside of a jail cell.

Eating, I wondered idly why I hadn't heard any more from Grooms. He knew where I was staying. He might even have somebody watching me right now. I looked out the kitchen windows but saw no sign of surveillance or anything else to mar the early-morning light. Which didn't mean those eyes weren't there.

Chester's office was small. It was not much more than a large closet really, just beyond the door off the kitchen Betty had pointed out to us the afternoon before. A half window looked out on the driveway behind a plain, student-style desk. The hard-backed cane chair sported a worn corduroy pad tied to the back to cushion the seat. Above the desk sat an old postal-style credenza with various envelopes and pieces of paper stuffed into several of the slots. The only other object in the room was a single two-drawer filing cabinet wedged between the desk and wall.

I sat down in the chair and could immediately sense why Betty would have had a hard time doing this right now. The entire nook of a work space spoke of Chester, reeked of Chester. From his bills and correspondence, to the leftover smell of his pipe smoke in the draperies, to a King James Bible on the blotter opened to the book of Proverbs, its well-worn cover frayed at the edges and several small pieces of paper stuck in to the pages as bookmarks. These items were among the last things in this house Chester Carew ever touched.

I started with the filing cabinet. As far as I knew Chester had always been reasonably fastidious when it came to the care of his birds, and his files were no different. Each drawer held an orderly row of hanging files, neatly arranged and labeled. Nothing out of the ordinary. Bills, bank account records, insurance information, a file containing documents related to the house, and a file concerning Chester's pension and a couple of brokerage accounts.

I spent about half an hour looking through all of the

documents as well as all the scraps of paper stuffed in the credenza, but came up with nothing. I also found nothing that might incriminate Bo Higgins and his cronies, or Chester or anyone else, for that matter. No hidden diaries with Nazi ramblings. No reading material from white supremacists or anything of that ilk. I felt a little like a peeping Tom after a while, which was saying a lot for a gumshoe. From everything I could tell of his life in this little cubicle, Chester Carew had been a decent man who somehow may have gotten mixed up with the wrong people; and for that he'd paid with his life. It was not a new story. It was one of the saddest ones I knew.

I was just about to pack it in when I noticed a sticky note stuck to one of the envelopes in the credenza. The envelope itself was empty, but on the attached note the following was written in large letters and circled with a red felt-tip pen:

NH_4NO_3 — *Benzene, toluene, and xylene!!!*

I knew Chester had been a chemical engineer, of course, but I had no idea what the bright yellow note might have been referring to. Some project he'd been working on? Most likely it was irrelevant, but I copied down the information anyway and put the envelope back in its place.

17

Back in the kitchen, Betty and Jason both sat at the table, where the boy was pushing corn flakes and milk around in his bowl.

"Find anything?" Betty asked.

I shrugged. "Not really. I put everything back the way I found it."

She nodded as if she'd been expecting this.

"Good morning, buddy," I said to Jason. "How're you feeling today?"

"All right," the boy said. He had a dog-eared copy of a book sitting next to his place at the table, *The Cat in the Hat.*

"You're a reader, I see. That's a pretty good book for someone your age. Glad to see you reading it."

"Mamma says I have to. But it's funny ... I kind of like it," he admitted.

"I tell you what. When you finish with your breakfast, how about heading out to the barn with me to check on Mariah and Torch?"

His eyes grew wide with anticipation. "Sure."

Ten minutes later, I entered the barn for the second time that morning. Jason was quick on my heels. The boy wore a heavy winter jacket, a ski hat with a long tail that flopped halfway down his back, and rubber boots that were a couple of sizes too big for him.

The birds sat on their respective perches in their separate enclosures. Torch stretched his wings and squawked at our presence, but the big redtail merely stared silently at us.

"Now, Jason. If you want to be a falconer someday, like your daddy probably told you, you understand it takes a certain amount of work."

"Yes, sir."

"These creatures aren't like dogs or cats. You can't just feed them, give them love and a warm place to sleep and that's about it. You've got to weigh them every day using the scales. You've got to keep track of their diet and monitor their health closely."

"Uh-huh."

"And you've got to make sure they get regular exercise and are hunting often during hunting season."

"Like now," he said.

"That's right."

"How come you and Mr. Jake don't take Mariah and Torch out hunting then?"

I smiled, thinking again about what the conservation agent had said and wondering what would happen now that she was gone. I expected it would be a little while before her eventual replacement got around to dealing with Chester's birds. "That gets complicated," I said. "You see the government has special laws to protect all birds of prey like this."

"Right. That's what my daddy told me. That's why I can't have one right now."

"That's right. And those laws also are pretty strict about who can handle a bird. It wouldn't be right for Jake or me to come in and start handling your daddy's birds. The state and your mom have to decide what's going to become of them first. They might decide to release them back to the wild, which would be okay. A game officer would come and take them away to release them then."

"Could I go watch?"

"I'm sure you could."

"What if they didn't want to release them yet?"

"Then whoever's going to take care of the birds would get them and begin to handle them and work with them."

Jason thought about all this for a few moments. Then he asked, "Mr. Frank?"

"Yes?"

"Do hawks go to heaven?"

"When they die you mean?"

"Yeah."

"Yes, I suppose they do."

"Is that where Elo is right now?"

"I don't know, Jason. No one's been able to find him. Why?"

"Because that's where my daddy went when he died," he said. "And I'm gonna tell Momma, that's where I want Mariah and Torch to go too."

The chemical symbol NH_4NO_3, I discovered via a quick stop at the Nitro Public Library, stood for ammonium nitrate. Maybe Chester's little sticky note was not so insignificant after all. The ATF technician working with Grooms had mentioned picking up a minute trace of ammonium nitrate on the road near where the bomb blast had occurred.

Ammonium nitrate, I knew, could be used to build bombs, but that wasn't what it was made for. NH_4NO_3 was commonly used as simple fertilizer. Millions of pounds of the chemical were sold legally every year. As such, traces might be found in many different places in our environment, particularly near farms, so Grooms was right not to jump to any conclusions regarding the minute quantity his tech had come up with. If more massive traces had shown up, for example, in some more atypical places such as on someone's clothing or in a nonfarm vehicle, then that might raise suspicions.

I really hit the jackpot though with the second part of Chester's sticky note. A simple online search pointed me to the fact that benzene, toluene, and xylene were "aromatic compounds" and that they typically made up about 35 percent of another very common commercial product: fuel oil. The potent mixture of fuel oil and ammonium nitrate, commonly known as ANFO, was used for controlled blasting in mining but it could also be used to make gigantic bombs, like the one that had destroyed the federal building in Oklahoma City.

Could this have been what caused someone to murder Chester Carew? Had he discovered that someone, most likely the Stonewall Rangers, was building an ANFO bomb? Had he somehow detected traces of these chemicals on his

land?
      It all fit with what I'd learned so far and the
information, scanty as it was, that Grooms had given me.
But if the Rangers were building a big bomb, surely the ATF
knew about it from what Grooms had indicated about the
Feds being on the inside of their operation. Had Grooms
simply discounted the technician's finding in front of me to
try to keep me in the dark? Or was there more to the story?
      Dr. Gregory Winston's office in Dunbar was a long gray
rectangular building with rectangular windows at the
roofline and a glass entrance. In back, a blacktopped
driveway led to a modest two-story colonial home of recent
construction. A large sign in front read K-VALLEY ANIMAL
CLINIC AND HOSPITAL – DR. GREGORY WINSTON,
MRCVS, and in smaller letters *Member of the Royal College of
Veterinary Surgeons.*
      Inside, the rectangular waiting room, empty of any
patients at the moment, was filled with dog and cat toys,
chewy rawhide bones and fuzzy scratch poles. In one corner
was a large electronic scale for weighing the animals before
they were taken back to the examining rooms. Peering into a
computer screen behind the counter sat a plump, middle-
aged woman wearing teardrop-shaped eyeglasses from
which dangled lengths of chain on either side of her neck.
      "Yes, sir," she said, looking up at me. "May I help you?"
      I handed her one of my business cards. "I was hoping to
speak with Dr. Winston if I could."
      She took off her glasses, letting them hang across her
ample bosom, and read the card. "A private investigator?"
The term seemed to leave a bad taste in her mouth.
      "Yes. I was a friend of Chester Carew. My associate
stopped by yesterday."
      "Oh, yes … that poor man. Hold on a second. The
doctor's just finished with a procedure. Let me see if he can
speak with you."
      She pushed back her chair, rose on seemingly unsteady
legs, and left the room. Less than a minute later, a door at
the side opened and a casually dressed woman came out

walking a bright-eyed golden retriever on a leash who seemed none the worse for wear. She was accompanied by a younger woman wearing surgical scrubs under a short lab coat and they were both followed by the woman with whom I'd spoken behind the counter.

"He said to go ahead and bring you back," she said.

I followed her as she ambled down a narrow hall to an office in the corner of the building. The door stood open and the vet was seated behind his desk.

"Thank you very much," I said to the woman.

"You're welcome."

The vet rose to his feet and stuck out his hand. "Mr. Pavlicek? I'm Greg Winston."

"Pleasure to meet you," I said as we shook.

"The pleasure's all mine."

His voice carried a strong hint of a British accent. I made him for early thirties. Athletic, good-looking. Dark hair beginning to go prematurely gray around the temples. The office was tastefully decorated, but nothing overly ornate.

'Would you like to sit down?" he asked.

"No. That's okay. I'll stand."

"So I understand you knew Chester Carew?" He still held my card in his hand.

"That's right."

"And you're a private investigator."

"Yes."

"A falconer too?"

I nodded. "You're originally from Great Britain?"

"That's right. I did a lot of work for a falconry school over there when I was in training."

"How did you end up here in West Virginia?"

"Actually, my mother was born here. I love it. I guess you could say I've become addicted to the outdoors."

"Sure."

"I'm sorry, but how can I help you this morning, Mr. Pavlicek?"

"You performed some tests on Chester's falcon when he brought the bird in recently."

"That's right. Elo was experiencing respiratory distress and I was afraid he might've ingested some kind of toxin, so I drew some blood."

"What exactly do you think could have caused Elo to take ill as he did?"

"Any of a number of chemicals or liquid agents, if present in sufficient quantities. My guess is something caustic that would have irritated the respiratory tract."

"Do you have the test results yet?"

"No. Not yet," he said. "We don't perform that kind of analysis here. I sent them off to a lab, but I'm expecting them back. Maybe even later today or tomorrow."

"I'd appreciate it if you would share those results with me when they come in."

"Why? Do you think they might have something to do with Chester's death?"

"I don't know. Just want to make sure I'm covering all my bases."

"Not a problem. You can call or stop by later if you'd like."

"Have you heard anything from the police?" I asked.

"No."

"All right. Well, thanks for your time." I turned to go. "I hope Elo is all right and that somebody finds him," he said.

"Me too," I said.

Later that morning I drove back to Tony Warnock's office. Ever industrious for a Saturday morning, Warnock was in his office just as he said he would be when I'd met with him the first time. A woman in a brown pantsuit, not the same receptionist as two days before, said Mr. Warnock was just sitting down with the parties for a real estate closing. I told her who I was and that it was very important I talk with him. She smiled and said she thought he might be willing to break away to talk with me for a moment.

Stopping to refuel the truck, I'd had a chance to peruse the Charleston paper. There was a piece on the car bombing that had killed Conservation Officer Gwen Hallston. Thankfully, there was no mention of me or Farraday by name. Good thing Kara Grayson wasn't a print journalist.

I'd taken a circuitous route to Warnock's office, pulling in a couple of driveways and doubling back to make sure I wasn't being followed. I saw nothing, but that didn't have me convinced the Feds were no longer interested in my comings and goings.

Warnock was tight-lipped and serious when he appeared in the hallway and ushered me into an adjoining empty office and closed the door. He had a sheaf of papers in hand, some kind of legal document, and wore reading glasses that rode down the front of his nose.

"Something to report?"

"Yeah. You're not friendly with local reporters, are you?"

"No. Why?"

"You heard about the bombing yesterday?"

"Yes. It's disturbing."

"I was there."

"Oh."

"But that's not half as disturbing as learning you're hooked up with the Stonewall Rangers."

He stared at me over the top of his glasses. "What are you talking about?"

"You know what I'm talking about."

"I really have no idea."

I said nothing.

He sat down in an office chair next to the empty desk. "So as far as Chester's death, you think there's more to this, do you, than some drunk hunter blasting away?"

"More to this? Are you kidding?"

He raised his eyebrows. I decided not to tip my hand.

"Where's your friend Toronto?" he asked.

"I want to know what your skin in the game is on all this, Warnock," I said. "You were casting around doubts about Jake a couple of days ago."

"What do you mean?"

"For all I know, you've been playing everybody. What's your relationship with Bo Higgins, and who else, besides the

Stonewall Rangers, are you involved with?"

Warnock made a bridge with his fingers, folded them across his lap, and stared into them. "You're not making any sense. Higgins? And why would I possibly want to cast aspersions on your friend Toronto? My doubts about him are based solely on some questions I asked about him of the local sheriff's office. They did some kind of background check and came up with various nefarious dealings he was suspected of being associated with."

"Is that right? Listen, Warnock, I've seen the police sheet on Jake Toronto. It doesn't look much different from my own or that of any other ex-cop who happens to be in our line of work."

"Well, maybe I'm just not used to dealing with that many people in your line of work."

"Or maybe you're a liar. Maybe someone else dropped some icy piece of propaganda on you and you've been spreading it around to the cops, the Feds, and anybody else who'll listen."

"Frank, look. I understand how you might be upset if you were present at this bombing like you say. But I can assure you —"

"You're not assuring me of anything, Warnock. You're making me more nervous." I stood up to leave.

"Where are you going?" he asked.

"Oh, I'll be back," I said. "Count on it."

Back in the truck, I used the cell phone to call Nicole on hers. She answered on the third ring.

"Hey, Dad. I've been dying to hear from you. What's going on?"

"Any more progress on those background checks I asked you to do, honey?"

"Some. Nothing unusual to report though."

"Well, keep at it. Don't stop with the surface stuff. I want to know everything I can about anybody who is involved with this thing out here."

"Okay. I heard something about a bombing on the news," she said.

"Yeah, there was a bombing."

"Were you anywhere near where it happened?"

I snickered. "You might say that."

"Dad, what's going on? Was Chester murdered?"

"Yes. At this point, I really think he was."

"What do the police say about it?"

"They say a lot of things, but it doesn't seem to be their primary concern right now."

"So you and Jake are going to find out who did it, right?"

"I sure hope so."

"Where's Jake? Is he with you?"

"I'll have to get back to you later, Nicky. Call me later if you come up with anything, all right? Anything at all."

"I love you, Dad."

"Love you too," I said.

I had just stuck the nifty little phone back in my pocket when it chirped at me. Great. I plucked it back out and pushed the TALK button.

"Listen, Nicky," I said. "I can understand you're curious and all —"

But the voice was low and agitated on the other end. "Hold on, Frank. It's not Nicky," Toronto said. "It's me."

18

Finding Felipe Baldovino's cabin wasn't as easy as, say, just calling the old man up and asking for directions. Toronto's father didn't have a phone at his ramshackle hunting lodge, which was a forty-minute drive from Charleston, a two-mile climb up a peak out toward the headwaters of the Kanawha, Fayette County, and the New River Gorge. For Felipe, cell phones, e-mail, or other modern forms of communication might as well have been alien devices from another planet.

Locating the right road was my primary problem, since it wasn't on any of the maps I had in the truck, and it had been three or four years since I'd been to the cabin for the one and only time. Toronto had taken Chester and me up there on that particular November morning with Chester's first bird, a gargantuan female redtail who was a fierce hunter. Her name was Maltese and Chester would forever after talk about her as his standard for a falconry bird. She'd been killed eighteen months later by a stupid encounter with a high-power-line transformer — stupid because the local power cooperative in the county where it happened had refused to spend the relatively small amount of additional money needed to build the simple protective perches on their high-voltage lines.

Fortunately, the day we took Maltese up to Felipe's empty cabin was etched pretty firmly into my memory. I only drove up one wrong back road before being forced to turn around and backtrack. I located the correct turnoff about a mile farther on down the highway.

As soon as I began the climb, I remembered certain landmarks: the rusted-out hulk of an old Volkswagen Beetle inexplicably stuffed into a narrow ravine alongside a small pile of equally rusted-out hulks of ancient refrigerators; a massive eastern hemlock, part of its root structure exposed by the washout of the road, sprouting from a steep moist slope where water normally cascaded across the road —

except that now with the drought the rivulet was reduced to a thin muddy bog.

The end of the road leveled out some at the summit and the cabin, a one-story frame structure with weathered wood and rotting shingles, came into view. The house itself hadn't changed much since my prior visit. But instead of Felipe's old Pontiac station wagon he used to drive all the way down from Queens there was a mud-splattered Chevy Tahoe parked alongside the Carews' Suburban in the driveway next to the front porch.

Toronto was waiting for me on the brown grass beside the two SUVs. There was a little more snow here at this elevation, but still not much. The pale earth broke through in mud-packed sections everywhere. The lack of moisture had bleached the tree trunks and stones, even the old wood siding of the cabin.

"Thanks for meeting me way up here," he said as I climbed out.

"What'd you expect? You got my curiosity up, wigging out of there yesterday like that."

"Mmm. ... Dad's inside, but I'd just as soon he not hear most of what we have to talk about."

"Sure," I said.

He blew on his hands to warm them. Toronto hardly ever wore gloves, except when stealth or the bitterest of cold required it. My hands were bare too," but still warm from the truck.

"So you said you think you've got a lot of this whole mess figured out."

"Yeah," he said. "Like I told you on the phone, I talked to someone who gave me most of it."

"And that someone would be?"

"Sorry, Frank. No names. I know this guy from some ops a few years back. He's a heavy hitter. Ex-CIA. Not someone to screw around with."

"I wasn't exactly planning to screw around with him."

"I know, but that's how it's got to be."

"All right. How did you know this guy had info on

Chester?"

He shrugged. "You might say I happened to bump into him. He surprised me. I didn't realize he was involved with this whole affair."

I hadn't told him much about my conversation with Grooms, figuring it was best to find out what he had to say first. "So this guy's take is?"

"Here's the deal: he's taking down the Stonewallers for the Feds."

"Okay. And how is he doing that?"

"It's a sting operation. They've been setting up for months. You know that GPS you picked up, those pigeons we saw, and all those tail transmitters we found?"

"Yeah?"

"Apparently the Stonewallers have got great plans for them. They think they're about to acquire some actual weapons-grade chemical materials. Something real nasty. My guess would be Sarin, maybe even VX gas."

"Lovely. And just what are they planning to do with this crap?"

"For starters, use the little coop flyers to spread some of it all around Roseberry Circle."

"The population of which they no doubt feel is polluting their Aryan blood."

"Exactly."

"Okay. And let me guess. They're going to track all these little buggers using the transmitters and GPS technology."

"You got it. Courtesy of our own defense department, who so kindly descrambled the signal a couple of years back so that now any Tom, Dick, or Harry can find his way to anywhere within a couple feet of where he wants to go."

"Wouldn't want the high-end Beemer with the two-thousand-dollar computer to get lost trying to evade traffic somewhere."

"You betcha."

"How're they planning to physically deliver the chemicals from the birds?"

"That's where it gets a little dicey. But my source claims they think they've got it worked out. Ever see pictures of those old-time homing pigeons you were talking about, like the ones Hitler used?"

"Yeah. I guess so."

"Turns out they've got a long tradition of being used in warfare. You can strap little capsules right onto their backs. They used the capsules to hold messages, but now you just launch the birds from up there where Chester's land is, they boogie straight toward the coop back at Higgins's place, and with a little radio-controlled signal when they're over the target ..."

"Bombs away."

"You got it."

"No one will even be able to figure out where the stuff is coming from."

"Not quite as birdbrained as it first sounds."

I looked down the mountain, where a small cloud was passing just in front of an adjacent peak. "But back up—you said the Stonewall Rangers *think* they're getting these chemical weapons."

"That's the whole point," he said.

"The Feds have helped your pal set the whole thing up?"

"Right. They take out the Rangers, track down their source of funding, maybe even lobby Congress to reform the GPS protocols while they're at it. The whole shooting match."

"How much money's involved?"

"I didn't ask, but my guess would be in the millions."

"You think Warnock's the player making all that happen?"

"Looks like it."

I thought about everything Grooms had told me. "This contact of yours is working with the ATF then?"

"ATF, FBI, locals, you name it."

"So they think Chester just stumbled onto something— maybe with the birds or whatever—and the Rangers killed him to keep him quiet."

"Something like that."

"What about the bombs?"

"That's why I took off yesterday. I'd seen this guy earlier, but that's when I knew I needed to talk with him. They're thinking the Rangers are getting real nervous and wanted to try to take out you and me and anybody else snooping around up there on Chester's land."

"Well, I've already gotten the message loud and clear the Feds want us out of their hair."

He folded his arms across his chest and drew in a deep breath. "I'm wondering if for once maybe we ought to listen to them."

The wind kicked up and blew a swirl of white powder snow at our feet. My hands were beginning to feel the cold now.

"Something just doesn't add up," I said.

"What do you mean?"

"What about the ANFO bomb?"

"ANFO bomb? Ammonium nitrate and shit? Who said anything about that?"

"I found evidence in Chester's desk at home. It looks like *that* could be what he found that got him killed. Not something to do with tracking birds to drop chemical weapons."

"Maybe the Rangers have some kind of an alternative plan using a bomb."

"Maybe. Or maybe the story's not quite so simple as your friend indicated."

"Hey, don't get me wrong. This guy's no friend. I know who my friends are. I'd call him more of a professional contact."

"Not sure you trust him then?"

Be careful who you trust. Grooms's words still echoed through my mind.

Toronto thought about it. "I think he was giving me some straight dope. It jives with all the evidence we've seen. It explains what happened to Chester. But if you're asking me would I trust this guy with my life, the answer is no."

"How come?"

"I've seen too much of the way guys like him operate. Working both sides of the fence. In it for themselves mostly in the end."

"Everybody seems to be going on the big assumptions here. But what if the Rangers *didn't* kill Chester."

"How do you come up with that idea?"

"The guy who hit me across the mouth with the Mossberg. If you're the Rangers and you're planning this big attack, and you've just killed a potential witness, why would you send somebody right back up there a couple of days later to the scene of the crime?"

"Maybe they're just making preparations for their operation."

"No. I sensed this guy was looking for something. He freaked out when I showed up."

"So what are you saying?"

"I'm wondering if the guy wasn't sent there to look over the scene because the Rangers are trying to find out who killed Chester too."

"Which would mean there are other players here we don't know about."

"And the scary thing is, maybe the Feds don't know about them either."

"Only one way to find out for sure and that's talking to the guy who socked you."

"Uh-huh. You come up with anything on that phone number he called?"

"As a matter of fact I did. But I wasn't going to go anywhere with it."

"How come?"

"It's not good news. Turns out he's one of Higgins's lieutenants and he's a state trooper," he said.

"You talk with him in person?"

He beamed. "Yeah. We ... uh ... played some chin music together yesterday. That's right."

"Chin music." Where did he come up with this stuff?

"Yeah."

"And?"

"He wouldn't give me the name of the caller, he said. He gave up our buddy Tony Warnock instead."

"Back to Warnock again."

"Call it corroboration," he said. "Rats from a ship."

"You think your trooper's state police superiors know he's been involved with the Rangers?"

"Nope. And now he swears he's got religion. Won't ever talk to Higgins again and won't go to another meeting either."

"All from talking with you."

"Yup."

"You can be very persuasive."

He nodded, beaming again.

I stamped my feet, thinking the whole thing over. It wasn't getting any warmer up there on the top of that mountain.

"So what do you want to do, boss? Punt and just let the Feds handle it? We're talking about some pretty big kahunas involved here."

"I want to find out who killed Chester Carew," I said.

He smiled. "Like a mad dog on a bone. I was afraid you were going to say that, Frank. But you know what? Me too."

19

The Bitter Angler sounded more like a watering hole for frustrated bass fishermen than a redneck haven. I bit anyway. The establishment occupied the end cap of an otherwise crumbling strip mall on the river between Dunbar and the north side of Charleston. Out the back, the Kanawha flowed wide and strong, and in the evening light even the visible fire stacks from the first of the chemical plants upriver glowed with an almost pastoral aura.

"This is the place I was telling you about," Toronto said, sitting across from me in my truck again. He was eating peanuts from a small plastic cup. He popped one into his mouth.

"Warnock will be showing up here around nine?"

"Uh-huh. If not a little bit before. Thinks he's coming to meet the trooper," he said, chewing.

"Nice work." I looked out the window at the building.

"But explain something to me, will you, Frank?"

"You bet."

"You already said you think the Stonewallers may not have killed Chester."

"Right."

"So why are we still wasting our time chasing after Warnock?"

"Two reasons. First, we can lean on him to tell us the name of the guy who made the phone call. You said the state trooper claimed Warnock knew who it was."

"Right."

"And second, Warnock looks like the money man for the Rangers. And money men are usually middlemen."

"Which means he gets to see whoever's on the other side of the fence."

"Exactly."

"I love this game," he said.

We stepped out of the truck. The assortment of vehicles

in the parking lot ranged from a muddy Toyota pickup with a missing side mirror and a broken taillight to a sparkling new Corvette sporting temporary dealer plates. The swinging glass doors to the bar were reinforced with steel bars and duct tape.

"Guess we get to hang out with the local talent for a while," I said.

"Staggers the mind, doesn't it? But they've got a decent jukebox."

"Fifties music?"

"A song or two. Mostly country though, I'd say."

"Any Elvis?"

"Oh, yeah, there's Elvis. Always Elvis."

"We just might survive," I said.

Trace Adkins was crooning "Help Me Understand" through the speakers as we entered. I judged from the number of chairs, almost all of which were occupied, that there were about twenty-five people altogether in the place, a fair crowd for a Saturday night. There were about a half dozen seats at the bar and the rest of the tables were arranged in diagonal patterns. Smoke drifted toward the ceiling and the room was dim, tailor made for intimate conversation; that is, unless you decided to raise your voice. Pictures on the walls generally seemed to follow a sports or hunting or fishing motif, with the exception of a couple of dramatic nighttime shots of what looked like flying saucers.

"There are a couple of stools open over by the window," Toronto said, nudging me in that direction.

A few eyes had turned our way as we entered, but most went back to their conversations, laughter, or beer. We found the two empties—high chairs actually, next to one of those tall round bar tables—and sat down.

"Figured I might see you back in here tonight."

The voice belonged to a large auburn-haired woman wearing rectangular tortoiseshell eyeglasses facing Toronto. She was hoisting a tray filled with used beer glasses.

Toronto nodded in return.

She eyed me cautiously. "Don't know what you two are

looking for exactly, but you both look like the type that'll get it."

"Frank, this is Roswell Parker. She owns The Bitter Angler."

"Roswell. Like the town in New Mexico with the UFO spacemen?" I asked, glancing at one of the photos on the wall.

"You betcha." The proprietor beamed. "My original name was Shirley. Had it legally changed."

Oh, boy.

"Roswell, this is Frank Pavlicek. He and I used to be partners. Frank's a private investigator."

"Is that so? We had one of those in here not long ago—start of the month. Greasy-looking fella said he was looking for a lady used to work over to the plant in Dunbar. Showed me a picture, but I'd never seen her before."

"Did he say why he was looking for her?" I asked.

"Not really, as I recall." She shrugged. "I guess I must've just figured he was working for some husband whose wife had been whorin' around on him. Ain't that mostly what you fellas do?"

"On our good days." I tried to smile.

"I heard Tony Warnock comes in here every now and then," Toronto said.

"Tony? I suppose so, but I don't keep a surveillance on my customers, as a rule. What you want with him?"

"Just to ask him a couple of questions," I said.

"Lawyers don't usually like you asking *them* questions, you know."

"Let me ask *you* something," I said. "Did you know Chester Carew?"

She put the tray down and folded the dishcloth she was carrying over her arm. "I knew who he was, had seen him in the grocery store a couple of times. Fine old man. Damn shame, what happened."

"The party line seems to be a hunting accident, poachers."

"What I heard too, but don't you believe it."

"Why not?"

She looked at one of the UFO pictures then said in a softer voice, " 'Cause if you ask me, a man gets shot to death right square in the back like he did in the middle of the woods for no reason, it ain't no accident. It's 'cause he knows something."

I was almost afraid to ask but I did. "Like what?"

Her tone became conspiratorial. "The next time they come, they ain't gonna leave no spaceship for the air force to steal."

I nodded and looked across at Toronto, who had somehow managed to keep a serious expression on his face. After she'd gotten this off her chest, however, the owner's expression brightened considerably.

"So what'll you two boys be drinking? Something light or something dark?"

"How about a couple of bottles of Rolling Rock?" Eagle Eye Investigations' standard sipping beer for alcohol-related stakeouts.

"Coming right up." She bustled off and disappeared through a door in back that appeared to lead to some kind of kitchen.

I let out a low whistle. "This is better than watching sitcoms," I said.

"How would you know? When was the last time you watched anything but the news?"

"Does nineteen ninety-seven count?"

We hadn't waited long, in fact were only about a quarter of the way through our beers, when Tony Warnock came swinging through the glass doors into the room. He moved purposefully and with almost catlike efficiency toward the bar. The top half of him was wrapped in one of those red-and-black checked three-quarter-length hunting coats.

"Here's our target," Toronto said under his breath.

I glanced over his shoulder. "Looks like him."

"Let's wait and see if Roswell lets him know we're looking for him."

Sure enough, as soon as Warnock had picked up his

drink—it looked like Scotch and water—from the bartender, who said something in his ear, he turned and made a beeline in our direction.

"I understand you folks were ask—" He stopped in midstride when he recognized Toronto and me. "Hey, fellas. What're you guys doing here?"

"Waiting for you, counselor," I said.

"Oh, really? Well, er … I'm supposed to be meeting somebody else."

"Yeah, we know," Toronto said. "He ain't coming."

Warnock looked as though he already needed a second drink. He acted like he didn't know whether to stay or run.

I pushed a free stool from an adjacent table toward him. "Why don't you sit down and join us, Tony?"

He looked at his drink for a moment.

"Go ahead. We don't bite. Pull up a chair."

He dragged the stool over to our table, plunked his weight down on it with a loud crackle of scratching leather, and looked at us warily.

"Guess you must be wondering how we knew you'd be here."

"What?" He was busy staring at Toronto, who was grinning crazily. Warnock's face registered a trace of cold fear for a moment, like he was seeing his own death.

"I said you must be wondering how we knew you'd be here."

"Sure. Yeah."

I fished in my pocket for a small notepad I kept there, pulled it out and flipped it open to an empty page. Then I uncapped the felt-tipped pen I kept attached to the binding and handed it to Warnock. "I'd like you to please write down the names of all of the Stonewall Rangers with whom you've had contact, as well as whoever else you might be funneling money from or to," I said.

"What?" He seemed to snap back to reality. "Are you crazy? I can't do that."

"Oh, I think you can," Toronto said. His voice carried a casual undertone of malice, but the words had their intended impact.

"Look, Pavlicek, you people have no idea what you're messing with here."

"Really?" I said. "Why don't you tell us then?"

He searched my eyes. "This is bullshit," he said. "Complete and utter bullshit."

I said nothing.

"You can't touch me."

"Oh, no?"

"We *all* have civil rights. Not just some of us."

I didn't need to look at Toronto to sense that his jaw was clenching and the little vein on the side of his neck was throbbing.

"What was that guy doing in Chester's woods?" 1 asked. "The one who socked me with the shotgun?"

Warnock snickered. "You really want to know who killed Chester, huh? Well, how do you know it wasn't someone from your own government? You think the FBI and the ATF and all those faceless bureaucrats and phonies in Congress are immune to corruption?"

I smiled. "We're not here to argue politics with you, pardn'r."

Another snicker. He pursed his lips and shook his head. Then he took another sip of his Scotch.

"Well," I said, "do you know who killed Chester or not?"

He lowered his voice and looked around. "No, goddamn it. Why do you think Higgins sent the kid back up there in the first place? And I don't want my name dragged into any of this, do you hear?"

Chalk one up for hunches paying off.

"Of course not, Tony," I said. "You're a fine upstanding member of the bar. You happen to know this kid's name and where I can find him so I can thank him for the bruise on my face?"

"Y'all are going to get me killed too," he said. "You know that, don't you?"

"You could end up that way anyway," Toronto said. He

had whisked out a very serious looking stiletto and was now cleaning his thumbnail with it. His eyes never left either of us.

Warnock took one look at the nail cleaner and swallowed hard. He glanced over his shoulder at the rest of the room to make sure no one was watching us too closely. Then he flexed his jaw and stuck out his chin. "All right." He picked up the pen and wrote down the name.

I read it and showed it to Toronto.

"Is this guy another Higgins lieutenant or just a lackey?" I asked.

"I don't know what he is."

I tore the piece of paper from the notepad and glanced at the name once more, committing it to memory. "Jake, you got a match?"

Toronto produced a book of matches from one of his pockets. I ripped one from the cardboard, struck it, and touched the flame to the piece of paper with the name on it.

Warnock looked at me with wonder. "What are you doing? Are you mentally disturbed?"

"You might say that. What else do you know. Tony? You're good with money, aren't you? Who are you moving money from and who are you moving it to?"

"Just accounts. I only know account numbers. I swear."

The paper was completely engulfed in flames now. 1 transferred it to the ashtray on the table so it could finish burning out. One thing was for certain: we now had the attention of almost everyone else in the bar.

"Hope you didn't have any further plans for the evening, Tony. You looked like you planned to spend a long time here drinking when you came in."

"What are you talking about?"

"The guy whose name is on this paper," I said. "He in the bar right now?"

"No. Of course not."

"Good." I pushed my chair back from the table. "Then you're going to get up from this table and go out that door with us and help us find him."

"What? You guys are too much. Look, you're being paid, Pavlicek, and I gave you the name, didn't I?"

"Oh, I'm being paid now, am I?" I looked across at Toronto. "Did you know that, Jake? Did you know I was being paid?"

Toronto shrugged.

I fished out my wallet and took out Warnock's nice legal check. I stuffed it into the ashtray, where it caught the last few sparks from the ashes of the other piece of paper and made its own new flame.

"Hey!" Roswell Parker yelled out from across the room. "What're you fellas doing over there? Fixin' to burn the place down?"

Toronto smiled in her direction and held up his hand. "Got it under control," he said. We watched it burn for a couple of moments until the flames died down.

I clapped Warnock on the shoulder and shook his hand so that everyone in the bar could see us. "Time we took a walk outside, don't you think?"

Meanwhile Toronto placed a hand on Warnock's other arm. To anyone across the room, it would've looked like a friendly gesture. To Warnock, who was feeling Toronto's grip, it was obviously something else. "Yeah, Tony. Mr. Pavlicek here and I would be delighted to have your further company."

Warnock's eyes darted back and forth between Toronto and me. "What time is it right now?" he asked.

I checked my watch. "A couple minutes past nine."

"I can tell you exactly where you can find him," he said.

I examined his eyes for any signs of deception. "All right," I said to Jake. "Let him go."

Toronto released his grip. Warnock was hunched over, wincing and rubbing his elbow.

"Tony, now don't do anything crazy on us. We might be back to talk to you some more later," I said.

He looked out at us again with fear-filled eyes. But this time I don't believe it was Toronto or anyone else he was afraid of. He seemed to be staring beyond us into the darkest abyss of his own clouded soul.

20

There was no crowd at the Burger King in South Charleston. Dinner hour had long since come and gone, and the only patrons at present were an elderly couple lingering over their burgers and milk shakes and two little children, one in diapers and the other a wild man of a toddler who seemed to be fascinated with making the swinging trap doors on all the garbage bins rock back and forth while his young mother, barely out of her adolescent years herself, kept her nose buried in what must have been a fairly current issue of *Seventeen* magazine.

I asked for the manager. The order taker behind the counter, a fiftyish woman with leathery skin and hair dyed brunette, took one look at Toronto's motorcycle jacket and the almost fiendish gleam in his eyes and retreated to the back as if she were about to become the victim of a stickup. A half minute later, she was back with the person in charge, a short, owlish man whose bushy mustache and eyebrows made him look like a fast-food Albert Einstein. The name badge attached to the pocket of his shirt said he was the assistant manager.

He too cast a wary eye toward Toronto's olive complexion and muscle-bound physique. "May I help you gentlemen?"

"Yes, sir. My name is Frank Pavlicek and this is my associate Jake Toronto." He shook my hand and I showed him my PI registration and gave him one of my cards. "I'm looking for one of your employees. Caleb Connors? I was told he'd be working here tonight."

He twisted my card between his fingers, reading. "Private investigators." He snickered, looking around the wall at the customers seated in the restaurant and lowering his voice. "Figures. What kind of trouble have they gotten into now?"

"They?"

"Yeah. They're brothers. Matt and Caleb. They both
work here."

"I don't know if they've gotten into any trouble, sir. We
were just hoping to have a few words with Caleb."

"About what? Something to do with the restaurant?"

"No," I said. "Nothing to do with his work here."

"That right? Well, maybe I can help you find him then.
And maybe you can help me. I've just been on the phone.
They're my weekend closers, but neither of 'em showed up
for their shift tonight. Leaves me real short-handed with the
cleanup and everything, you know?"

"Sure. You have home addresses for them?"

"Yeah, yeah, in the files in back. They were both still
living at home with their mother, but they moved into a
place of their own not too long back. Rented a house over on
Chandler Road. I can get you the number."

"I would really appreciate that. Is it like the two of them
to miss work?"

He shrugged. "It's happened once or twice before, but
they've both been with me here steady for a couple of years
now and Christ, you know how hard it is to find kids who'll
stick around through the training and then show up for
work even halfway regular these days?"

"Either of the Connorses work anywhere else?"

"Not that I know of. I try to make sure they each get
thirty or forty hours a week here. They're usually pretty
good workers. Which is why I'm so screwed without them
tonight. Hey, you find 'em, you tell 'em Mr. Quinones is not
happy."

I nodded my sympathy, wondering what the two
brothers — both in their twenties — could've earned at jobs
like this and if they might've been in the market for some
kind of income supplementation, maybe the off-the-books
kind. "We'll be sure and do that," I said.

The assistant manager disappeared in back, leaving us
to stand uncomfortably with the woman for a few moments.
There was another younger woman in back working the
grill. She was flipping burgers and not looking too happy

about it.

Quinones came back with the address written on a blank time card. "Hey, you know, I hope these kids aren't in some kind of real trouble or something, 'cause I'd hate to see that happen. Some of these kids, I try to give 'em a break and everything, you know? These two, from what I know, they don't got much of a family backing 'em up or anything." He handed me the card and I took it and shoved it into my coat pocket.

"You mentioned the mother," I said.

He turned his back to his other employees and lowered his voice again—the woman at the counter, while she was pretending to wipe down some counters, had obviously been eavesdropping.

"She's a drinker," he whispered. "Been in and out of work. In and out of rehab a few times too now, I guess. Last I heard, she was even turning a few tricks now and then on the street."

"No father?"

"Not that I've ever heard much of anything about. The older one, Caleb, I remember him saying something once about how his old man had been in the army, but that's the only time either of them ever mentioned him."

I tapped the card in my pocket. "This address you're sending us to, how's the neighborhood?"

He made a show of looking Toronto and me up and down again. "This time of night? You two fellas look like you can handle yourselves, but I wouldn't be going over there by myself, if you know what I mean. That's one thing about those Connors boys—they always seem to stick together."

"Thank you very much, Mr. Quinones. You've been a great help."

"Don't mention it. Listen, you find those two, you tell 'em I said to get straight on back to work here and keep their noses clean. I really need them."

I shook his hand and thanked him again—he even shook Toronto's hand this time after a slight hesitation. We

left there with me wondering if this little man in his empty
fast-food place on a Saturday night could even begin to hold
back all the forces arrayed against him.

Charleston's west end is a residential district of steep
hills and small houses running down to and beyond the
main drag, which is Washington Street. Along Washington
are several commercial establishments, everything from a
Laundromat to biker bars, redneck bars, and just about
everything in between. There are also a couple of projects;
not as bad as Roseberry Circle, but the clash of cultures in
the west end, mixed with greed, crack, crystal meth, and
booze, makes for a potent mix.

Toronto told me all this as we drove down there to look
for Caleb Connors. He said the cops referred to the area as
the Wild West.

"Sounds just like your kind of place, Jake."

We found the house, a dark blue bungalow with a
sagging porch on Chandler Road, just as Quinones had
described. There was nobody home, but a sallow-eyed next-
door neighbor shoveling a pile of sawdust beneath a
floodlight beside his garage told us he thought the Connors
boys had gone out for the evening, probably to one of the
bars down on Washington.

"Usually do," he said. "About the only time I get any
real peace and quiet around here."

We spent the next hour hitting bars up and down
Washington Street, coming up empty. All we left with was a
better description of the brothers and the car they drove, a
bright orange classic GTO.

"I feel like we need a gear change," I said as we climbed
back into my pickup for the tenth or twelfth time.

"Yeah? How's that?"

"We can waste all night trying to chase down these two
French fries. We might be better off hitting them bright and
early tomorrow when they're sleeping it off back there at
that little shack of theirs."

"Maybe we should go back, find Warnock, and lean on
him some more."

"Or we could go see if we can follow up with that vet, Dr. Winston."

"The place won't be open though."

"Right. But it looked to me like Winston owns an entire property with a house out back where he lives. Must make for a short commute to the office."

"Ties up a loose end, either way."

"You said you didn't get to see him earlier like I did, but you met him once before with Chester. You think he'll remember you too if we show up at the house?"

Toronto smiled but said nothing.

"All right, I know ... people have a way of remembering you," I said.

The parking lot at the veterinary clinic in Dunbar was empty and the office building dark. Away from the traffic off the road to one side stood a row of exercise runs surrounded by chain-link fence. The vet probably boarded pets overnight or kept some for observation when needed after surgery. Lights blazed from the house out back, and there was a fairly new Range Rover parked in the driveway.

As we climbed out of the truck, the echo of barking from inside the animal hospital hit our ears, mixed with the faint sounds of traffic in the background. There were several dogs and they sounded agitated. Lucky thing for the vet, his neighbors on either side and in back were all commercial establishments — an outdoor tree nursery, a small office building, and an auto body shop — all of which appeared to close up at night so there was no one around to complain about the racket.

The house was built of wood but had a brick foundation and a set of brick stairs leading up to a small open front porch with wrought-iron railings and twin lantern porch lights glowing brightly on either side. I followed Toronto over the short walk and up the stairs and waited as he pushed the lighted button to ring the bell. The cold air smelted faintly of an odd mixture of auto exhaust, earth, and animal waste.

Several seconds passed, but there was no answer.

Toronto tried the bell again.

Still no answer.

There was a heavy black door knocker that matched the railings so Toronto grabbed it and knocked three or four times.

Nothing, not even a hint of activity or movement from inside.

"Maybe he's gone out," Toronto offered. "Young guy. Saturday night. Probably decided to leave some lights on for security."

"But the Range Rover's still in the driveway."

"Maybe he's got a second car."

"Maybe," I said.

Instinctively perhaps, Toronto had already begun to scan the security on the front door, gently attempting to turn the knob just in case. It was locked tight, with a mortise lock and decent cylinder dead bolt, not to mention an alarm system, judging from the sensor foil taped just inside the window frame; none of which would have been insurmountable obstacles for my companion had we not been standing in a brightly lit area with our backs to a distant line of moving cars.

"Why don't we take a look out back?" I suggested.

We looped around the sparse foundation planting to check out the rear of the house, which was also well illuminated by a couple of floodlights attached to the top corners of the house just below the roofline. There was a wooden table and chairs alongside a gas grill, both draped in vinyl weather coverings for the winter. A set of sliding glass doors led into what looked like a neatly furnished and undisturbed family room. The doors were also locked, and apparently armed by the alarm. Otherwise, we found no sign of anything out of order.

"Okay, what do you think?" Toronto asked. "Just leave the guy your card for now and I write him a note?"

I nodded. "Don't see any cause for breaking and entering. What about the office?"

"Let's check it on the way out."

Toronto ripped a page from my notepad and wrote a brief message, signing his name. Back in front, we wedged the note along with my card in the tight space between the front door and frame.

The dogs were still barking from the clinic. We piled back into the truck, reversed into the turnaround beside the Range Rover, and drove toward the highway again before turning into the office parking lot.

Though the building was dark, light from bright halogen lamps along the road gave enough illumination to the area for us to have a good look around. I also brought my penlight just in case — didn't want to shine too much light or arouse suspicion from drivers on the road.

The front entrance, a glass enclosure around a small portico, was closed and locked, as you might expect. We found no access to the building at all in back, but there was a side entrance and here we encountered a problem: the door had been left open an inch or two and, judging from the splinters of wood on the floor just inside, had clearly been jimmied.

"This doesn't look right," Toronto said. The dogs inside, sensing our presence, boomed out an even louder chorus.

"Monster dog?" I said.

"Uh-huh."

"Your weapon in your bag in the truck?" I asked. Toronto nodded. He'd been carrying a small satchel when I'd picked him up earlier back at the Carew house and had stowed it in front of him on the floor. I kept my own .357 beneath the seat in the truck.

"You know where mine is. You better go get them, plus another flashlight."

I stayed by the door while he went to the truck. Warm air flowed out from the narrow opening. I could hear the building's two heat pumps whirling behind the building, a pulsing background beat for the noisy canines. I shone my small beam of light around the frame looking for any obvious trace evidence, signs of tool marks, or prints, not really expecting to find anything. The metal ridge was bent where the door had been forced, but beyond that no other marks or signs were visible.

A few seconds later, Toronto reappeared and handed me my weapon and a larger flashlight.

"Just a precaution," I said, slipping on my shooter's gloves.

He nodded.

I pulled open the door.

If the dogs had been loud outside, once inside the cacophony was almost deafening. There must've been eight or ten, from large deep-throated voices to smaller tinny ones—their pens lined the back of a large room visible just beyond the short entranceway.

I clicked on the bright beam Toronto had just brought me. Nothing appeared amiss in the hall. There was a push broom and a snow shovel, a mop, and a large yellow pail on wheels. The walls were made of cinder block and were empty, except for a cork bulletin board that had been taken over by the usual state and federal bureaucratic mumbo jumbo you see posted on bulletin boards in any business. This was obviously the employees' entrance.

The air reeked of animal, a musty aroma made worse by the transition from the fresh air outdoors. The cold from the door left ajar had lowered the temperature inside some, despite the heat pumps, so that the dogs and perhaps other animals inside must've felt the chill. I motioned Toronto to my left. We moved farther into the building, each hugging a wall.

At the opening into the larger room, you could see the silhouettes of the dogs, tensing and straining as they barked. A few were howling or growling. I trained my beam on a few of their faces: black and brown fur, gleaming yellow eyes, red gums, and white teeth.

All at once, the room was flooded with a blinding light.

21

"Just what in the world is going on in here?" a woman's voice said.

It was Kara Grayson, wearing the same elegant long coat I'd seen her in the night before. She stood by the opposite door where she'd switched on a panel of overhead lights. Her eyes went wide with fear when she saw the guns.

"I-I," she stammered, taking a short step back to the safety of the doorway and perhaps meaning to throw the room into darkness again. At least the dogs had calmed down a tad at the warm glow of the lights and the sight of the woman. They still barked, but the change in scenery seemed to have broken their panic and reduced the volume.

"It's okay, Ms. Grayson." I lowered my handgun to my side. "It's Frank Pavlicek."

"Yes, I-I saw you again yesterday ... at the bombing."

"We came by hoping to talk to Dr. Winston about a recent patient, but no one answered the door at the house. We heard the dogs making a racket here in the clinic and thought we'd check out the building—found a door broken into on the side of the building."

"I see," she said, although her look said she wasn't quite sure whether to believe me. She was looking at me, but she kept glancing at Toronto. She moved to the pens and began reaching out a hand to stroke the head of a German sheperd. "It's okay, babies. Nothing to worry about." Tails began to wag and the occasional bark turned into drooling pants with smiles.

"You here after another story?" I asked.

"No, I'm not, actually." After calming the animals, she turned back toward us. "I volunteer here a couple of times a week. One of the nurses is a friend of mine. She had to go out of town for the weekend so I guess she gave my phone number as backup for the alarm company to call in case they couldn't reach Dr. Winston. I saw your truck and heard the barking."

"Brave girl. Why not just call the cops?"

"Kids are always breaking in here because it's on a major road. Maybe it gives them some kind of a thrill, I don't know. I just figured it was another false alarm."

"Did you try calling Dr. Winston?"

"Sure. I tried both the office and the bouse. I got the office voice mail and there was no answer at the house. So I decided I better drive on over here to make sure everything was all right."

"I take it you have a key to the front door?" I asked.

"Of course." She seemed to have relaxed a little.

I stepped over to her and she showed it to me. She still had the key ring in her hand. The shepherd and another dog, a black-and-white husky, let out fearful barks.

"Shhh, babies, that's okay, now, shhhh," she said, reaching in again to pat the shepherd.

"That Winston's Range Rover out back in the driveway?"

"Yes."

"He own any other vehicles?"

"No, not that I know of. You don't—you don't think there's something wrong, do you?"

I glanced over at Toronto, who returned my look.

Her eyes narrowed. "Just what is it you and your friend wanted to talk to Dr. Winston about?"

I was about to answer when a loud bang like a falling pan reverberated from the darkness of the hallway that led toward the set of examining rooms and offices where we'd seen the dim light.

"Get down," Toronto shouted.

The first shots struck the back wall. Then bullets hit the floor and began to scatter through the cages. One of the dogs yelped, throwing the others into a renewed panic. They were large-caliber rounds; the *tat-tat-tat* bursts of fire from the front of the clinic suggested an AK-47.

I reached out and grabbed Kara Grayson by the sleeve of her coat, pulling her down hard and toward me as we lunged behind a barrel of what looked like kitty litter on the floor. A bullet slammed into the side of the barrel next to my head. Using the container and my body to shield Grayson as best I could, I twisted the muzzle of my weapon around and fired toward the sound. Toronto had long since dropped into a prone position and returned a flurry of fire at our assailant.

But just as quickly as it had begun the hail of shooting stopped. A couple of seconds later, we heard the glass of the front door of the clinic shattering.

"Runner," I said.

"I'm on him. Sweep the rest of the building." Toronto was already up and moving across the room. The sound of his running footsteps faded as he disappeared down the darkened hall.

"You okay?" I asked the reporter.

She nodded slowly, her eyes blank with terror. I helped her into a sitting position and looked her over. No wounds, as far as I could see. I reached for the cell phone in my jacket pocket and could've kicked myself—I'd left it on the seat in the truck.

"Do you have a cell phone?"

"What?" She was still trying to process what had happened.

"A cell phone. Do you have a cell phone with you?"

"Yes." Her voice was flat. "In my purse."

For the first time I noticed the small black night purse clutched between her fingers. She fumbled with the clasp, managed to undo it, and pulled out one of those folding cell phones and handed it over. I flipped it open, punched in 911, and spoke with the dispatcher, giving her my name and our location.

The dogs were still barking. A painful whimper sounded from one of the cages. It was the German shepherd. Kara Grayson rushed to its pen, undid the latch, and went to the animal's side. The big dog lay on its side in a growing puddle of blood, its breathing labored, its huge chocolate eyes searching ours for answers.

Grayson applied pressure to the creature's wound to stop the bleeding.

"Can you look in that gray utility closet over there?" she asked, pointing toward the corner with her free hand. "I think that's where the bandages are kept and I could use some gauze."

It was good she could concentrate on helping the wounded animal. Her momentary disorientation after all the shooting had passed and focusing on the dog would help dull the sting of the news I was afraid she was about to hear.

I stepped over to the cabinet, pulled open the door, and found what she wanted.

Toronto reappeared in the doorway. "Lost him. He went into the woods in back. Might've been able to start tracking, but I heard sirens and figured I better give it up for now."

"So you decided to stick around this time?"

"Figured it'd be hard to explain the slugs from my gun being in the wall and all my fingerprints if I don't."

"Just one shooter?"

"Far as I could tell."

"You get much of a look at him?"

"Fast. Looked like he was wearing some sort of dark outfit."

"All right," I said, handing him the cell phone. This was shaping up to be a repeat of the day before with Farraday. "You stay here with the woman and keep the line open with the dispatcher." I pushed the phone into his hand. "I'm going to have a look around."

"But what about Dr. Winston?" Grayson asked. Her face was scratched from where I'd pulled her down so roughly on the concrete floor.

"I'm hoping he's okay." But even as I mouthed the words I felt an icy knot twist in the pit of my stomach. I knew I was lying. I knew what I or the police would probably find, either here in the vet's office or somewhere back in the house.

The German shepherd would live, but Dr. Gregory Winston, MRCVS, hadn't been so lucky. I discovered the young veterinarian slumped over the desk in his office at the end of the hall, a large ragged bullet hole through the right posterior quadrant of his head, suggestive of a weapon fired at close range. There were contusions and cuts on one of his arms as well as marks on his wrists from having been bound, and his bloodstained mock turtleneck was torn at the sleeve. The man had not gone down without a fight.

What's more, the room was torn apart. A large tiling cabinet drawer had been overturned on the bloodstained carpet in front of the doctor's desk. Charts and notes and other miscellaneous pieces of paper littered the carpet, a small table and lamp were overturned, and most of the desk drawers had been opened, their contents thrown to the floor as well. The perp had been looking for something and apparently had found it. A priority mail bag, its contents gone and the shipping label missing, lay cut open next to the vet's outstretched hand.

Those test results from Elo? Did they confirm what I'd learned from Chester's note, possibly corroborate the massive presence of ammonium nitrate and fuel oil ingredients? As Winston had said, it wouldn't take much for a falcon's sensitive olfactory system to react to the strong chemicals, if they were present somewhere in sufficient quantities.

I wasn't going to get the chance to speculate any further, however, or try to search for more evidence in the room, because you could feel the shattered glass on the floor of the office vibrate a little as the whoop-whoop of the police sirens closed in on the parking lot outside.

Back in the dog's pen, I was just bringing some more gauze over to Kara Grayson when two county sheriff's deputies, their weapons drawn, stepped into the room.

"Freeze! Drop the weapon!"

I realized I was still carrying my gun in my other hand. I raised the hand with the gauze in the air and slowly bent down and placed my revolver on the concrete. "It's all right,

Officers. I'm a PI. Frank Pavlicek — the one who called."

"He's okay," Kara Grayson said. "These two gentlemen saved my life. But I've got a seriously wounded animal here."

"Yeah?" The deputy who spoke was the older of the two and clearly in command. He had red hair and a bushy brown mustache. He looked at my face. "Jesus. You're the same guy who was up there with that truck bombing yesterday, the same one who claims he got slugged with the shotgun the other day." He shook his head. "Must be trying to set some kind of world record."

Toronto turned slowly to face the deputies, which only caused their stances to stiffen. His big Beretta was now tucked into his waistband.

"Please take the weapon out and place it on the ground, sir, just like your friend."

"Not a problem," Toronto said. He did as they'd instructed.

More sirens arrived outside.

"You'll find that both weapons have been discharged," I said. "We were defending ourselves. May I take this gauze to Ms. Grayson here for the dog?"

"Go ahead," the redheaded cop said. He nodded to his partner and they both lowered their weapons. He turned and spoke into the microphone strapped to his shoulder. "Dispatch, this is eight. We've got an animal down here at the clinic. Looks like there's been some shooting but the situation is now stable."

"Roger, eight. All units stand down, except four and eleven. Eight, be advised I also have Nitro rolling."

"Copy that."

I ripped open the package of gauze, stepped into the pen and gave her the bandage.

"Thank you," Kara Grayson said.

Her coat and hands were covered with blood, but she didn't seem to care. She quickly switched hands and used the new compress to apply pressure.

More deputies were entering the building — you could

hear the sound of them moving toward us with their gear.

"Anyone else in the building?" the deputy asked.

I exchanged looks with Toronto. Kara, still bent over the dog, looked up at me as well. She seemed to hold her breath.

"The doc's in the other room." I squatted down to make eye contact with Kara. "I'm sorry," I said. Her hand went to her mouth in horror.

I stood and faced the two cops. "He's in the office," I said. "You'll want to make sure you secure the scene. No need to rush."

22

Deputy Bobby Nolestar leaned against the clinic waiting-room door and exhaled a line of smoke through his nostrils. He went to an empty Coke can someone had deposited in the corner and snuffed out his cigarette.

"I don't quite get all this," he said. "You guys in the habit of entering someone else's private property with your guns drawn? You've got yourselves an assault, a car bombing, and now a firefight."

"Don't forget two more murders," I said.

He shook his head in disgust.

"You got people checking the woods for the shooter?" Toronto asked.

"We're searching ... nothing so far."

"Not even any footprints?"

"Look, I've had it with being polite. We're talking about obstruction or something here. I ought to cuff you both right now."

"Where's Grooms?" I asked.

He stared at me. "Oh, don't worry, I'm sure he'll be here directly. Had to go back up to the regional office in Pittsburgh this morning for some kind of meeting with the FBI."

That explained why he hadn't been hounding me.

"Something's about to go down."

"No shit, Sherlock. What you think we've all been doing around here, picking our noses?"

"What I mean is, something's about to happen, and it may not be what you all are thinking it's going to be."

"What's that supposed to mean?"

"It means Chester Carew wasn't killed because he knew about the Rangers' plans."

"What?" Nolestar looked at Toronto then at the floor, thinking it over. He had already taken statements from Toronto and me and confiscated our weapons. A shift commander had also shown up and helped take charge of the crime scene. A couple of technicians had arrived shortly thereafter, and by now had been in and out of the doctor's office a few times. A female sergeant had also arrived and seen to it that Kara Grayson and the German shepherd were taken care of. The sergeant had been on the phone with an emergency animal hospital elsewhere in the city and two officers had taken both Kara Grayson and the dog off in their squad car.

It was late and I was suddenly bone tired — the adrenaline had long since ceased to flow. "I'm telling you, deputy. ..." I tried to keep my tone neutral.

"You let me worry about what's going to happen or not happen, Pavlicek. Tell me again what the two of you were doing here."

"As I told you before, we were looking for Dr. Winston. We heard the dogs barking and after we'd left the note at the house we went to check it out. Found the door and it had obviously been jimmied. That's when I sent Jake for the guns."

Nolestar shook his head and rubbed his eyes. He subconsciously patted his jacket pocket. He looked like he wanted another cigarette. "You guys are just wonderful," he said to himself. "Just what I need here. Cool Hand Luke and his sidekick Arnold Schwarzenegger.

"Okay," he continued. "Let's say everything you've been telling me today is the truth. You and your pal here still haven't explained to me why the weapon he just so happened to be carrying wasn't registered. We could get you both on a weapons charge right there."

That nasty little detail had emerged about twenty minutes into our conversation when one of the officers, after talking outside on his radio, had come into the room and whispered something into the deputy's ear. I'd hardly been shocked, since we were talking about Toronto and all, but it didn't exactly bolster our reputation with the local constabulary.

The detective turned to Toronto again, who by now

looked as if he were about to nod off into dreamland. "What was it you told me you did for a living, Mr. Toronto? Corporate security? Funny, I don't find you registered in any database of licensed private security agencies."

Toronto barely opened his eyes, shrugged a little, and said nothing.

"Maybe a night in a jail cell would help improve both y'all's ability to impart information," Nolestar said.

While he spoke, I noticed two large vans pull into the clinic parking lot. The deputy, whose back was to the waiting-room window, turned and followed my gaze.

"Something interest you out there, Pavlicek?" We watched as a man in a dark suit climbed from the first van and showed something to one of the officers outside. Then a woman in blue jeans and a plaid shirt and hunting vest, accompanied by two more men in suits, stepped from the back of the van. The woman was talking on a cell phone.

"Now who the hell is this?" Nolestar said.

The entourage swooped in past the propped-open front door, its frame still dangling broken glass. The woman was in the lead. She was about five feet nine, solidly built, with short-cropped brunette hair topping a pair of darting green eyes and a handsome Scandinavian/Midwestern jaw.

She lowered the cell phone to her side. "Deputy Nolestar?" Her voice was mezzosoprano.

Our inquisitor eyed her suspiciously. "That's me. And who might you be?"

"Agent Colleen Briggs, FBI." She held up her shield.

The two men next to her held up both their shields and ID.

Nolestar looked at them all and asked the same question I had. "Where's Grooms and his people from ATF?"

"On his way from Pittsburgh," she said. "Be here in about an hour. But as head of the task force, he just gave us directions on the phone."

Nolestar twisted his mouth a little as if he wanted to say something smart but kept it quiet. "Oh, yeah? Well, ah, what can I do for you, Agent?"

"You've been questioning these men about a shooting and a murder that took place here tonight. Is that correct?"

"Yes, ma'am. "

"And these were the same two men present at the car bombing yesterday afternoon that killed a state conservation officer."

"Just Pavlicek."

I didn't like the way this was sounding.

"Thank you very much for your help, Deputy," she said. "We'll take over from here."

"Wha —? What do you mean?"

"I mean, please stand down. I've got one of our analysts on the phone who's attached to the CTC at Langley. He'll give you a short debriefing." She handed him her cell.

"Great." Nolestar snickered under his breath and gave her a look, then stepped outside with the phone.

Agent Briggs turned her attention to me. "Let's see, now. You must be Frank Pavlicek." She didn't raise her voice or show any sign of threat.

"I am," I said.

"You're a private investigator and you've been asked by Betty Carew to look into her husband's shooting. You also met with the family's lawyer."

"That's correct."

Her cheeks creased around a flat smile. "I know Chester Carew was a friend of yours, and, given your background and, ah … line of work, I can appreciate your desire to want to run around asking questions of people, but I'm afraid it's becoming counterproductive for our investigation."

"I've already been given that message."

"But you didn't do anything about it, did you? Didn't know when it was time to step away. Seems like everywhere you turn up, people are getting killed."

"Well, as far as I can see, nobody else around here seems too interested in trying to find out who killed Chester, other than officially trying to pass it off on some poacher or something while dropping vague hints about Stonewall Ranger involvement. And I'm beginning to believe you may just be wrong about even that," I said.

"What you believe, Mr. Pavlicek, and what the facts are may be two different things. Case in point. ..."

She turned and looked dispassionately at Toronto. "This, of course, is our famous Mr. Jake Toronto."

Toronto, still slumped back in his chair but fully awake now, stared defiantly at her.

"I've been looking forward to this one, Jake."

"Been looking forward to what?" I asked.

She motioned to the agents on either side of her, who moved into position beside Toronto and firmly pulled him up from his seat. He didn't resist.

I rose to my feet. "What the ... ? What are you doing?"

"Serving a warrant," she said. "Cuff him, please," she said to the other two agents.

They did as she ordered. I looked at Toronto, whose face had gone as blank as the concrete walls.

"This must be some kind of mistake," I said.

"Not this time," she said. "Jake Toronto, you're under arrest for the murder of Chester Carew. And for conspiracy to commit acts of terrorism against the United States."

23

On Presidents' Day two winters before, I'd brought my first redtail over to Chester Carew's to hunt. Toronto was busy doing something else that weekend. Jason was still too young to be of much help, so it was just the old man and myself that afternoon. Carew had enticed me with the promise of watching his new gyr-peregrine, Elo, train to the lure, as well as what he claimed was some of the best rabbit hunting around.

It snowed off and on during my drive through the mountains over to Charleston. By the time I'd reached Nitro and we'd driven up to Chester's private hunting grounds with Armistead in the back of my truck, the flakes were coming down fat and heavy and a couple of inches had already accumulated. Wind gusts cut visibility to just a few feet.

Needless to say, we didn't get a whole lot of hunting in that day, but I did enjoy the privilege of a snowed-in overnight at the Carews'. Betty cooked up a wonderful dinner and we played a card game with Jason before his mother went off to read to him and put him to bed. Chester and I stayed up late by the crackling fire, talking of hunting, of the old days when as a teen growing up just a couple of valleys away he'd fallen in love with and flown his first raptors.

There was no such thing as licensure and the formal sponsorship program back then. Chester said a lot of folks, especially around his neck of the woods, would just as soon shoot any hawk or falcon that came near as try to trap and take to manning one. Chester had an old library copy of Frank and John Craighead's *Hawks in the Hand* as his only guide. The rest he pretty much had to figure out on his own, with predictable mixed results.

A gleam came into his eye that night by the fire, making him seem younger. He reached behind him and brought out

a dog-eared Bible and pulled out a slip of paper on which
he'd written a prayer.

It was for falconry birds that died, for any who died, he
said. He still remembered how he'd lost a couple to
automobiles, one to a bad bite from a squirrel he hadn't
known how to help heal, another to a shotgun-toting farmer
who'd been so aggrieved when he'd found out the bird
belonged to Chester he'd offered to give the young man an
entire wagonload full of sweet corn in return.

*I am crossing into a high country where the winters are
always green and the air as sweet as ivory, where your grace
abounds forever. Come, Lord Jesus, come.*

"You a believer?" he asked me matter-of-factly. He took
a long draw on his pipe.

"I guess that depends," I said.

He nodded. "I know. Up North, where you come from,
folks see things differently, don't they? You got your
Catholics and your big white churches with all them steeples
and all, but have any of them got the fire in them?"

"I'm not sure what you mean, Chester."

"You think the world's getting any darker, Frank?"

"Darker?"

"Yeah. Lots of people I talk to think the world's getting
darker. You know, all that stuff you see on TV these days.
Killings and kidnappings and rapes and such."

"Maybe," I said.

He flipped through the pages of his Bible, took out a
handkerchief and wiped his nose. "You read some of the
stuff in here, you want to know what?"

"What?"

"It was worse."

"Yeah?"

He put his finger on a passage. "It says right here in the
Book where Jesus is talking and he says, 'I am the way, the
truth, and the light. No man cometh to the father, but
through me.' "

"No man, huh?"

"No man, that's right."

"That's a hard thing Jesus said. It's hard for some people to accept."

"Lots of things is hard to accept," he said. "Like cancer. Like that snowstorm we ran into today. Doesn't make 'em not so."

Deputy Nolestar came back in through the front door, passing the two agents with Toronto on their way out.

"All right, lady. You win. I just talked to the sheriff too, but we've now got three fresh killings in our jurisdiction in less than a week, and I want to question Mr. Pavlicek here about them myself."

"No way," Briggs said.

"You got a problem with that, you or your people in Washington can talk to the sheriff about it."

Way to go, Bobby, I thought.

The FBI agent glared at the deputy for a moment.

"Fine," she said. "But you know, we've got a major op going on."

"I know about your damn major op, Special Agent. I'm not going to get in the way. But the sheriff says if you want the department's continued cooperation, y'all need to give us a little more latitude around here with all these folks suddenly getting killed."

No one said anything for a moment. Briggs took a quick look outside at the van.

Then she said, "I apologize, Deputy. As you know, the timing of all this can't be helped. By all means, feel free to go ahead and question this man. But I insist on remaining present during your questioning."

Nolestar shrugged. "No skin off my back. You've placed Toronto under arrest, right?"

"That's correct."

He turned to me. "Please sit down again, Mr. Pavlicek."

The thought occurred to me that the deputy was already on the way to becoming a good detective. Mistrust too much authority. Always treat your suspects with respect.

I sat down.

"You saw what just happened," he said.

"Yeah," I said. "All of you are wrong. Toronto didn't kill Chester and he certainly is no terrorist."

"You don't think so, huh?"

"Tell me what you've got on him."

"We don't have to tell you anything," Briggs interrupted.

Nolestar just looked at her, then back at me. "They've got ballistics, Pavlicek. Turns out the rifle that killed Carew belongs to your buddy."

"Plus, he's had sniper training," Briggs interrupted again. "Plus he's been to Stonewall Ranger meetings, not to mention some of his not-so-stellar associations with various and sundry characters."

Nolestar said, "The thinking is, Toronto's been helping the Stonewallers. They're planning some kind of terrorist attack. Carew found out about it. Toronto murders him to keep him quiet."

"Nice and neat and simple," I said.

He shrugged. "Does it need to be complicated?"

"No. Just needs to be the truth. Where did you come up with the murder weapon?" I asked.

"This afternoon we took a couple of unmarked Chevy Blazers and served a search warrant on Felipe Baldovino, Toronto's father, up at his mountain cabin," Briggs said. "The rifle is a legal one—surprisingly enough, from what we've been able to ascertain about Mr. Toronto's activities—and registered to him. And don't even try to suggest his father could've shot Carew. The old guy couldn't even make it ten feet in the woods anymore."

After talking with Toronto earlier, we'd gone inside to see Felipe before leaving. I remembered seeing the gun case filled with several hunting rifles.

"Have you checked to see if Toronto has an alibi for the morning of the shooting?" I asked.

"I questioned him three days ago before you came out for the funeral," Nolestar said. "He was already out here when it happened. Claims he was visiting his father, but won't detail his whereabouts that morning. Neither can the

old man."
"He has the right to an attorney," I said.
"He'll get one," Briggs said.

I leaned back in the waiting-room chair, thought for a moment about dialing a lawyer I knew from Charlottesville with a lot of experience in dealing with the Feds, but decided that might only aggravate the situation further.

"Frank, from what I know of things, I'm not sure you've appreciated, up until now, the seriousness of this whole situation, and your own precarious position," Briggs said. "Mr. Toronto is now under arrest for murder and is also under suspicion of having conspired with potential terrorists. Convince me you're not a coconspirator."

What followed was more than an hour-long string of questions by the two of them. Back and forth, first one and then the other. About my relationship with Toronto, where I was on Monday morning. (I had a solid alibi. I had been in a meeting with a judge in Charlottesville about another matter.) No bright light blinded me. No one threatened to harm me or tried to coerce me in any way. But after a while, Agent Colleen Briggs's voice really began to annoy me. It was as flat and monotonous as a long stretch of Iowa blacktop and seemed almost forced.

I guessed that, in addition to somehow infiltrating the Stonewallers, the Feds had been employing surveillance, court-ordered wiretaps, and possibly bugs as well for some time. That would be the SOP anyway. I was operating at a serious information deficit, compared to them.

"Pavlicek, I'm going to assume, for the time being, that what you're telling us is accurate," Nolestar said finally. "That you haven't had much contact with Mr. Toronto in the past year and that he never discussed in too much detail his relationship with Chester Carew or his attendance at some of these militia get-togethers."

"I'm not so sure about that," Briggs said.

Nolestar ignored her. "Don't you think it's time you separated yourself from this whole business, Frank? Head on back to Charlottesville to your normal work. You know as well as I do this is big-league stuff."

"You expect me to just walk out on my friend?"

"That's exactly what we expect, Mr. Pavlicek. In fact, we require it, unless you want to end up in a cell next to him," Briggs said.

"But Jake didn't do this," I said. "Can't you see that? He's a former homicide detective. If he were even remotely involved with such a killing, you think he'd be so stupid as to leave the murder weapon lying around like that for someone to find it? It's too staged. Somebody's trying to set him up for this."

Nolestar seemed to consider the possibility, but Briggs dismissed it.

"We'll be the judge of that," she said. "I think we have just a wee bit more information than you. And we're far better equipped to handle this sort of thing, at this point, than you are."

"What about the rest of the killings? The reporter is another witness right here, besides myself, who'll tell you it wasn't Jake who was spraying bullets at us just now."

"Maybe not. But how do you know for certain he didn't set those bombs yesterday? Don't try to pretend he doesn't have the skills to have done it. And how do you know he didn't come in here sometime earlier today and kill the veterinarian? This whole shoot-out at the OK Corral you just had could've been some kind of crude attempt at a cover-up. Other than the dog, no one was hit by any of the bullets, were they?"

She was right. The M.E. might establish a different time of death on the vet, but we'd have to wait to know for sure.

"I'm sorry this is happening to a friend of yours," she said. "But we're at war, mister."

That did it. I held out my hands. "Hey, don't let me get in the army's way. But this war is about justice and defending the innocent, isn't it? Don't sit here and try to tell me it's right to be arresting an innocent man. ..."

I stopped, realizing I was making a fool of myself. I don't know why I suddenly decided to start sparring with this robotic clone of a federal agent. It was like arguing with somebody's lawyer or press release. I couldn't really talk to her now, any more than I'd been able to talk to certain members of the review board at the hearing on the shooting Toronto and I had been involved in all those years ago in New Rochelle. You could rant and rave all you wanted about what was really going on between the lines and behind the scenes, but unless you were really willing to do the legwork to find out some of those nettlesome details you weren't about to come any closer to the truth.

For years, Toronto had operated in a sort of shadowy nether world of security and intelligence "consulting" and "operations" for various unnamed clients and entities, much of which, I imagined, was never recorded in anybody's official budget or records. As far as I could tell, his services were always high in demand, and since his material needs were few, he seemed beyond compromise.

It didn't take a huge leap of logic, however, to imagine someone with clandestine and sinister motives putting Toronto's talents to use for their own purposes. They would have to be good. Very good, in order to pull the wool over Toronto's eyes about their intentions. Or they would've had to somehow tap into Toronto's loyalty or something that was important to him.

And that left only one option: the contact he'd said was on the inside of their sting operation and had given him all the details about the Rangers' plans. Problem was, that wasn't something I could talk to these two about.

Not yet, anyway.

Nolestar rubbed the growing stubble on his youngish face. "Your choice now, Pavlicek. Either agree to our request to stay out of this business from now on, or join your friend outside in handcuffs in the van."

"I'm not so sure I feel comfortable giving this man any kind of choice," Briggs said.

The other agent in the room, who'd been standing against the far wall like a mannequin during our conversation, seemed to twitch involuntarily, as if anticipating the opportunity to throw me in with their other catch.

"You haven't got any real evidence to hold him, do you?" Nolestar asked. I didn't know why he was suddenly sticking up for me, but I was thankful for it.

Briggs said nothing.

"I'm telling you right now Jake Toronto is no terrorist," I said. "Sure, he may have been involved with the wrong people from time to time, but you both know as well as I do, that's sometimes the nature of getting things done. If all of you only dealt with upstanding citizens, you wouldn't have a clue what was going on in some of these groups, would you? So who's to say Jake Toronto hasn't been trying to accomplish the same sort of thing? I go back more than twenty years with this guy."

"Oh, yes." Briggs snickered. "We know all about that. You two shot to death an unarmed African-American teenager years ago in New York, isn't that correct? It just could be that the seeds of that anger were—"

"You're kidding, right? What, you just get that off one of your daily intelligence faxes? I suppose you've never had to make a decision like that. You probably would've already labeled that kid a terrorist and had him in custody as a threat to national security. We did not have that luxury. We did what had to be done. And in case you haven't read the complete record, that was over fifteen years ago and we were both exonerated. Completely."

Exonerated, at least, in the courts. My heart and my sleep at night were another matter, but I wasn't about to give her any quarter on this one, not when it came to my partner. I'd been the senior detective on the scene that night. If there were any seeds of subversion growing in Toronto since then, I and I alone would be responsible.

Except that there weren't. She couldn't have been more wrong.

"Most of us can't work outside the system, Mr. Pavlicek," she said. "We have to work from inside, utilizing all the resources at our disposal, as imperfect as they may be."

"Spare me, will you? I know all about the system. Just look what it did for Toronto and me. You don't see me sitting here and complaining. You're the one who brought it up, in fact."

She said nothing.

"Okay, let's say I agree to what you want. When do I get to talk to Jake?"

"You don't," Briggs said. "Not until this operation is over."

Again I thought of the lawyer in Charlottesville, but I realized even he wouldn't do much good. At this point, she had all the cards in her favor. And if it helped her stop a bunch of white supremacists from dropping nerve gas on a bunch of people, or whatever they were planning to do, who was I to say she wasn't right?

In the end, just so I could walk out of there, I ranted and raved a little more for show before agreeing to their demand. Thankfully, they didn't make me put anything in writing.

I'd agreed to a lot worse in my time, compromises good and bad. Some, maybe half, were the source of a lot of pain and frustration in my life, decisions I'd regretted at the time and some of which I was regretting still.

I tried to think about the other half as I walked back outside toward my truck, past the van with the blacked-out windows where they were holding my best friend.

24

"I'm coming back out there, Dad."

I could visualize my daughter's pout through the phone and her blowing an errant strand of hair from in front of her face. After giving her a few more details about the night before, I was just coming fully awake, torn between memory and reality. I'd called and left word on her personal voice mail from the truck on my way back to the Carew place in the wee hours of the morning. When I got back to the house, I'd plugged in the cell phone for charging overnight, but had left it on. Sleep had been slow in coming, and even when it finally did come, had lasted only a couple of hours.

Out the window though I could see that it had snowed a little while I'd slept. An inch or so of the white stuff coated the lawn, the driveway, and the branches of the trees.

"Look, Nicky. I still need you back in the office."

"While Jake is in jail? No, you don't, Dad. You just want me to be back here where you think I'll be safe or something. Besides, it's Sunday. Nobody's in their office today and my classes don't start up again for another week."

"What do you have for me on those backgrounds I asked you to check?"

"I've been working on them. The cops you gave me all check out."

"Yeah, well, I have another one to add to the list, but go on."

"Tony Warnock looks like your run-of-the-mill attorney, as far as I can tell. I did find something from about twenty years ago when he was just out of law school. He represented a member of the Ku Klux Klan regarding a cross burning. But he's done nothing that looks that controversial since that I can find."

"How about Higgins?"

"Well, you already know about him and the Stone-wallers, right? I also found a property tax lien that had been placed on his property."

"Conscientious objector?"

"Not sure. Looks more like it might be simple financial problems to me."

"Figures." No way a guy like that came up with a few million to finance a bunch of chemical weapons without Warnock. The question was, where was the money's ultimate source, and who did that give the leverage to?

"Let's see," she said. "Damon Farraday is just a plumber, but you know that too. Nothing unusual on his record, financial or otherwise. I did talk to his boss on the phone—told him I was from a credit reporting company verifying information. He said Farraday's a good worker. Always shows up on time and does his work, even if he does wear an earring, the guy said."

"Earring? I've never seen him wear an earring."

"Maybe he took it out for the funeral. I think he's kind of cute. And I hate to tell you this, Dad, but you and Jake are kind of like, thirty-years-ago sometimes. You know?"

It was way too early and I was too tired to deal with being thirty years ago.

"Okay," she said. "Moving on to the conservation agent, Gwen Hallston—"

"She's dead, Nicky."

"Oh." There was a new edginess to her voice.

"She's the woman who was killed in the bombing on Friday."

"Right. I don't know why, I didn't make the connection."

"It's okay. You have anything on her?"

"Nothing unusual. She had four kids. ..." Her voice caught in her throat.

"You all right, Nicky?"

"Yeah. Sorry."

"Don't worry about it. The best way we can help her now is to find out who did this."

"Sure. I know."

"You come up with anything on anybody else?"

"Nope. Nothing so far."

"How about Felipe, Toronto's father?"

"Just that he's retired and receives a pension — dull — but that's about it."

"I hate to ask, but how about Chester? Skeletons in the closet?"

"Nope. No marks or dings or anything. And his credit report's practically perfect."

"All right," I said. "Good job. Keep at it."

"What about me coming out there?"

I ignored her question. "How's your boyfriend?" I asked.

"What?"

"How's Mark?" Mark Burke was a solid electrical engineering major, an amiable, square-jawed young fellow with a four-point-oh GPA whom Nicole had been dating since the end of her junior year.

"He's gone skiing up at Snowshoe with a bunch of our friends. What difference does that make?"

"Just guys, or guys and girls both?"

"Guys and girls both."

"Why didn't you go with them?"

"We've had this discussion before, Dad. You said yourself I shouldn't be sleeping with him if we're not married."

"Going skiing with a bunch of friends doesn't mean sleeping together, does it? Or is Mark starting to put pressure on you?"

"He's *not* putting any pressure on me, Dad. How'd we get into this anyway? Besides, I promised I'd help you in the office while I'm on break and it cost almost five hundred dollars for the long weekend with lift tickets and all. I don't have it myself and I didn't want to have to ask you for the money. And you know Mark's family is not rich."

"Where'd he get the extra money then?"

"He's working extra shifts in the computer lab this month." She sounded exasperated. "Could we get back to my coming out there?"

"Am I paying you enough for helping me out in the office?" I asked. "I know you're only still a student and all, but — "

"The pay is just fine, Dad!"

I said nothing.

"You need me out there," she said.

"We've got other clients to take care of," I countered.

"Most of them can be put on hold, can't they?"

"They're not paying us to put them on hold, honey."

"But Da-ad! Jake's in trouble!"

Why do kids, especially grown kids, have this way of getting under our skin with the truth sometimes?

"All right. Listen, this is not some form of entertainment."

"I know it's not."

"At least three people now may have already died over this situation out here."

"But why would they arrest Jake? No way would he have shot Chester, not in a million years."

I hoped she was right. Then again there was the not trivial matter of his rifle being used to commit the crime.

"You understand that, and I understand that. But the police don't. They're just following the evidence the way any investigator would. And right now the trail happens to be leading to Jake. The real question is why does someone want the police and the Feds to think Jake did it?"

"Maybe it's these Ranger militia people."

"Maybe. But I've got an idea it may be somebody else."

"Who?"

"Can't get into it over the phone."

"Then when do you want me out there?"

"I'll tell you what," I said. "First thing I'm going to do is have another talk with Betty again after it gets light and she's awake. I need to know more about what Chester might or might not have been doing with the Stonewall Rangers."

"How about the vet who was killed?" she asked.

"I think he may have been murdered over some pending lab results. I'll call a reporter I've met out here who

does volunteer work for his clinic. She was actually there
last night too. She may know the name of the lab where they
send their tests."

"If you get a name and address I can run it down when
they open up first thing tomorrow morning."

"Good. After that, I'm going to drive back over to
Felipe's cabin. The Feds claim that's where they found the
gun that killed Chester. Haven't heard anything about it
from the old man and I don't think Jake had either, and that
concerns me. And after that, I'm going to head on over to
Leonardston — it's only a couple of hours from here. You can
meet me there."

"Leonardston? How come?"

"I'm sure the Feds either have already or are about to
search Jake's place. If somebody's trying to frame him, I
want to have a look around the place myself. If we're lucky,
maybe we'll even beat them there. I also want to make sure
whoever is taking care of his birds for him doesn't freak out
about everything."

"Couldn't that get you into trouble, Dad? I mean, didn't
you say in your message that you told that FBI agent you
would stay out of things now?"

"You let me worry about that, honey."

"I know! You could just send me in. / didn't make any
promises to the FBI."

I found myself shaking my head. "We'll discuss it in
Leonardston," I said.

"What about Mom? She's right down the road and it's
been a couple of months, you know. I got a letter from her a
few days ago she dictated to her nurse."

"Sure, we can stop by to see her too for a few minutes, if
you'd like."

"I'll meet you at Jake's place in Leonardston then. What
time?"

I checked my watch. "How about three o'clock? I should
be able to get over to Leonardston by then."

"All right."

"After we go over the situation at Jake's and visit your

mom, we can head back out here together. We'll have to be careful knowing the Feds are all over the place now, but I want to start visiting a few of these Rangers, one in particular Jake and I didn't get to last night. I've got a strong suspicion he's the one who stuck that Mossberg up my nose the other day."

"Sounds good."

"And remember what I said. These people are playing for keeps. You have your weapon with you?" I'd spent a lot of time with Nicole on the range over the previous year, getting her certified and bringing her up to speed on a slick little Glock 27. Not that I relished the idea of my daughter playing with guns, but she seemed determined to be in this business when she finished school, and if that were going to be the case, I was going to make sure she was prepared. Let alone the fact she'd also begun studying tae kwan do on her own.

"All set," she said.

"Good. I'll see you at Jake's place at three then. If you get there before I do, do not attempt to enter on your own. If the Feds haven't served their warrant there yet — and even if they have — we're going to have to be cautious."

"Okay."

"And leave Jake's bike at home. Bring your car instead. You may need it. Plus, you've got that painting you want to bring for your Mom too, right?"

"Right ... and Dad?"

"Yeah?"

"I love you."

"I love you too, sweetheart. Call me if anything comes up in the meantime."

We said our good-byes and broke the connection.

I rolled over in bed and peeked out the bedroom window through the curtains to what was becoming another wintry steel dawn. I'd just given Nicole a somewhat precise account of how I saw things progressing over the next twenty-four hours if we were to attempt to help Toronto. A plan, neat and orderly — I thought it might give her some confidence that things could work out as intended in this business, at least on occasion, that you could always try to anticipate your obstacles and out-think the objects of your investigation.

I should've known better than to try to give her an idea like that.

25

His mother stroked the boy's long dark hair. "Jason has something he wants to talk to you about, Frank."

"He does?" I said. "Okay."

The boy said nothing.

We were standing by the windows in the dining room, Jason holding his mother's hand. A mantel clock ticked in the other room.

"Go ahead, honey," Betty Carew said. "Remember you said you could only tell Mr. Toronto or Mr. Pavlicek and nobody else?"

The boy let go of her hand but still said nothing.

"He won't even talk to me about whatever it is, Frank."

I squatted down in front of the boy and searched his eyes. "Something about your daddy's birds, pal?"

He shook his head.

"Is it about what happened to your father?"

He pushed his lips into a pout and nodded.

"Betty, maybe I, uh ... ought to take him in the other room, see if he'll talk to me in there alone."

She smoothed out the apron she had tied around her waist. "It's all right," she said. "I'll just be in the kitchen." She turned and left the room.

"Okay now?" I asked when she was gone.

"Yes, sir," he said. "I don't wanna tell nothing in front of my momma. They might hurt her."

"Who might hurt her, Jason?"

The boy finally looked up at me with a pleading expression. "I know who killed my daddy," he said.

Half an hour later our breaths pushed rolling clouds of smoke up the hill below the stream where Jason's father had died. The sun angled a bit higher in a sky changing from pale to cerulean blue.

"All right," I said. "We're almost there. Can you tell me now?"

Jason stopped and listened. The woods were quiet,
except for the faint sound some crows were making over the
nearby field.
"The men in the masks. That's who killed my daddy,"
he said.
Hairs rose to attention on the back of my neck. "Men in
masks?"
"The men who come up here."
"How many men?"
"Two men."
"What kind of masks?"
"The kind you wear when you ride a sled. You know, it
covers up your head."
"How do you know they killed your daddy?"
"I know 'cause I saw them. I saw them and they said if I
ever told anybody, they'd kill me and my daddy and my
momma too."
"But you didn't tell anybody, did you?"
He shook his head.
"Then why do you think they killed your daddy?"
" 'Cause he must've found their hideout."
"Their hideout?"
"Yeah," he said. "C'mon. I'll show you."
He turned sharply and led me on a path perpendicular
to the one we'd been on. We forded the stream and passed
through a washout area of loose earth and large rocks. The
night's snow had turned the surface of the stones slick and I
had to watch my footing, but the boy moved like a gazelle
over the ice and the moss. After a few hundred yards, he
turned off the faint path and we climbed uphill again,
grabbing on to branches and rocks where we could gain a
handhold to pull ourselves up, scrambling for several
minutes until we reached the very top of the ridge.
"How far're we going, Jason?" I finally asked.
"Just down there," he said, pointing down the opposite
side of the slope.
We now began to descend, which was even slower
going than the climb, given the steepness of the hill and the

lack of footing. About halfway down the boy stopped and looked up and across the slope to a spot about fifty yards distant where the ridge turned into an almost vertical cliff.

"Are we going to have to climb that?" I asked, thinking we would've been better off to approach from above.

"Ain't that far."

He scampered across the incline and I followed until we reached the bottom of the cliff. At the base of the rock wall where it turned straight upward was a stand of long tree trunks that had fallen together into a gigantic tangle perhaps a few years before. Jason waded into them.

"You got to bend down to get in here," he said.

I wedged myself under a huge fallen pine trunk. On the other side, hidden from everything else around it, was a narrow opening in the rock wall. The boy went over and stood beside it.

"What is it?" I asked. "A cave?"

"Yes, sir. My daddy said they was going to cut a quarry or maybe mine something in this hill a long time ago, but they stopped. It don't go in very far. I found it last year."

"This is where you saw the masked men?"

He nodded.

"When did you see them?"

"Before daddy died."

"How long before your daddy died?"

He thought about it for a moment. "I'm not sure," he said.

"Was it a long time, like before your last birthday?"

He seemed confused for a moment. Then he said, "No, it wasn't that long. You want to see inside?" He started to move into the opening.

"Wait," I said. I stepped along the wall in front of the opening. "Better let me go first. I wish you'd told me earlier. I could've brought a flashlight."

The boy said nothing.

The opening was quite narrow, barely large enough for a full-grown man to squeeze through. Just enough light filtered down from a crack in the ceiling overhead to see all the way to the back wall, maybe ten yards deep inside the fissure. I'd only taken a half step through the opening when it hit me: the pungent odor of ammonia, a telltale indication of a high concentration of ammonium nitrate. I stopped and held out my hand.

"What?" he asked.

I didn't answer but squinted as my eyes adjusted to the dim light. Was there a bomb here? Not anymore. None that I could see, at least. No large containers of chemicals or wire or fuses or large man-made devices of any kind. Then I spotted something on the floor of the cave. A dead bird lay only a few feet to my right, its half-mangled carcass entwined in a patch of wet leaves. A mourning dove from the looks of it, or maybe a pigeon.

But there was more. A little farther along the floor of the cave I saw another dead bird. And another. And, if I wasn't mistaken, among the leaves there was also the whip end of another tail transmitter. Was Elo, or what might be left of him, somewhere in here too? I took a half step forward then remembered what Toronto had told me about the plan to set up the Stonewallers by luring them into a deal to purchase bogus chemical agents. His contact had told him the Feds had a handle on all that. But the way things were going, what if it turned out some of those agents weren't exactly counterfeit either?

"Jason, let's go. We're out of here." I turned, grabbing him by the shoulder, and pushed him away from the cave, following closely behind.

"Why?"

"There's something inside that might be dangerous."

"What do you mean dangerous?"

"Well, it might not be all that dangerous to us." Not unless someone knew how to rig a bomb together with it, I thought. "But it could be," I said.

"I saw a dead bird," he said.

"Come on. We need to call for some help." I took him by the arm and led him back through the tangle of trees and down the slope a few yards. Then I took out the handheld

GPS unit I'd acquired courtesy of the yet-to-be-met Mr.
Connors, pushed the buttons and waited for the unit to
triangulate its position with the nearest satellites to plot the
coordinates on the screen. Once the device had displayed its
results, I used my cell phone to dial Agent Grooms's cell.

"Good morning," I said when he answered.

"Who's this?" he barked.

"Frank Pavlicek. You arrested my friend last night."

"Damn right we did. And you're lucky I didn't have
them take you into custody too. I hope you're headed back
to Charlottesville."

"Not exactly," I said.

I explained in very vague terms where I was and what
I'd found. The string of profanity that spewed forth from
him arose, I guessed, as much from his frustration over my
failure to go away as the possibility that I just might've
discovered something significant of which they hadn't been
aware.

"If this is all on the level, how'd you know about this
place, Pavlicek?" he demanded. "What kind of game are you
and your buddy Toronto playing now?"

"No game, Grooms."

"We've got your pal for Chester Carew's murder. We've
got him cold. We know he and Carew had been to Ranger
meetings. Our guess is your pals joined Higgins's army as a
Grade A recruit and that Carew got cold feet and maybe
knew too much about their plans, so Toronto simply
eliminated him. Don't try to tell me he couldn't have done
it."

"You've got the wrong man."

"I wouldn't be so sure if I were you."

I debated how much to tell him of what I knew.

"I'm putting out an APB on you, Pavlicek. This has gone
far enough."

"Not if you want me to keep feeding you this
information, you won't."

"Is that a threat or something?"

"Do you know everything that's happening with your

situation, Agent? Do you believe that everything is for certain, that all the people you've staked this sting operation on are legit?"

"How the hell'd you know it was a sting?"

"You need a wild card in your hole," I said. "Maybe I'm it."

He said nothing at first, then muttered "Shit" under his breath.

I told him I'd call back again in a few minutes and give him the exact GPS coordinates of our location so he could send a team up to thoroughly check the place out. Which of course would give Jason and me a chance to clear out of the area first. Given enough time and the right resources, Grooms might have even been able to trace the approximate location of the source of my call, but he must have known I'd be long gone by then. I hung up and turned the cell off.

Jason stared at me as I stuffed the phone back in my jacket pocket.

"This is all my fault, ain't it, Mr. Frank?" he said.

I put my hands on top of his small shoulders and made sure I had his complete attention. "No, buddy. It's not your fault. Don't ever think that. You understand?"

He nodded.

"Come on. Let's get out of here," I said.

As we turned to head back down the hill, I pushed another button on the GPS unit, scrolling through the list of the stored way points.

"Hang on a second." I held out my hand for him to stop. I scrolled through the list again.

"Isn't that interesting?" I mumbled to myself.

None of the saved coordinates matched our current location. The closest, while also on Chester's land, was more than a quarter of a mile away.

26

Bo Higgins was in the process of closing a deal on a nice late-model Dodge pickup when I showed up at his car lot. Through the glass I could see him sitting with a young Hispanic man and woman in one of the offices in back. The fire-engine-red truck had been shined and detailed and was parked by the door to catch every possible gleaming ray of the sun.

The car-lot owner shot me a cold stare, which might have had something to do with my attire: a black ski mask I'd slipped over my head as I'd driven onto his lot. I'd also driven Betty's Buick instead of my truck and swapped out her plates with a set of expired North Carolina ones I kept bolted to the inside of my truck's bumper for such occasions, just in case Grooms had decided to put out that APB after all. The ATF agent's mood hadn't improved much when I'd called back to give him the coordinates of the small cave.

Another foray to the Connors bungalow on Chandler Road had yielded no sign of either brother. For all I knew, maybe they'd ended up like Chester, and Gwen Hallston, and Dr. Winston. I had considered slipping the back door lock and letting myself in the house, but since it was broad daylight the last thing I needed right now was a neighbor calling in to report me for a B&E.

Higgins was still staring at me. He didn't move, maybe hoping his customers wouldn't notice. I stepped across the showroom and climbed inside the unlocked Bel Air. Higgins stood up for a moment, but apparently changed his mind. He sat down again and went back to the business of obtaining the necessary signatures from his customers.

The car was a two-tone two-door hardtop. Tropical turquoise under arctic white. Original everything too, from what I could tell. Dual exhausts. Four barrel three forty-eight V-8. You could bury the speedometer at 120 and still have some jambalayas left. I could almost hear Chubby Checker shouting through the silent radio.

I wondered how Higgins's clients might feel if they knew about his little sideline as commander of the Stonewall Rangers Brigade, if they might check out the odometer on that new vehicle of theirs a little more closely. Even white supremacist leaders have to make a living, I suppose.

"Help you?"

I turned to see a bald, muscle-bound man of about my age with gold-capped teeth, narrow deep-set eyes, and a small swastika tattooed on the side of his neck. He was packed into a dark tank top and blue jeans that looked like they were about a size and a half too small. No bone lay clenched between his teeth or anything, but give it time.

The window was half open. I rolled it the rest of the way down. "I'm here to see Higgins," I said.

"You're dressed like an asshole." He folded his arms across his chest.

I shrugged. "I just figured this was the right uniform for all good Stonewall Rangers."

"You're full of shit is what you are," he said under his breath, shaking his head. "What do you want to see Higgins about?"

"Looking for a new sports car. Lamborghini," I said.

"Listen up, smart mouth, Mr. Higgins is in the middle of something right now. So maybe you ought to pack your tail on down the street to somewhere else."

"Did you just grow on a tree around here or are you the product of some sort of chemical experimentation gone awry?"

"Say what?"

"It's okay, Wayne." Higgins was emerging from the office, the man and woman trailing behind him. "I'll deal with him."

Baldy worked his jaw around in a circle as if he'd lost his chewing tobacco in there somewhere then disappeared out the side door without a word.

Higgins turned to the couple. "Keys are in the ignition, folks. You need me to answer any more questions or go over anything on the truck, just give me a call."

The man and the woman stared at me for a moment, then thanked him and shook his hand. They went out and climbed into the Dodge's cab. They started the engine, took a few seconds to get charged up on a few more whiffs of that new-car-smelling aerosol Higgins had probably sprayed throughout the cabin, then drove the truck off the lot.

"Nothing like free enterprise," I said.

Higgins turned and glared at me. His face twisted a little in recognition. "Aren't you ... ?"

I held up my finger to my mouth to shush him. "Come on, Bo. Climb in here on the other side where we can talk."

He went around to the other side, opened the door and climbed in, closing it behind him with a hollow thud. Nothing like the sound of that big fifties chrome and steel. I rolled up my window.

"Where's your friend Toronto this morning?" he asked.

"Off on other business," I lied.

"Uh-huh. So what, you just decided you'd come harass me by yourself?"

"Close. I've just come from Chester Carew's land, not too far from where he was shot to death. Found some interesting evidence in a cave up there. Called the authorities and sent them up there to check it out."

"Cave? I don't know anything about any cave," he said.

"I know you don't. You don't know who shot Chester either, do you?"

He leaned back in the seat, blew out a breath, and examined me with reptilian eyes. "What are you hustling, friend?"

"The cops are looking for me," I said. "They think I might've done it."

"Yeah?"

I couldn't quite tell whether he bought it or not, but his posture seemed to slacken a little.

"Heard you were up there at the bombing the other night too."

I nodded.

He scanned the windows of the showroom. "Then if you know I didn't shoot anybody, what the fuck are you doing bringing heat down on me and mine for?"

He already had a lot more heat than he realized, but it wasn't going to be my job, of course, to illuminate him about it.

"Toronto knows somebody you might be doing some business with."

He sniffed loudly. "Is that so?"

"I just wondered if maybe you could put me in touch with the same person."

"Really? Who says you even know what you're talking about?"

I shrugged.

"How does Toronto claim he knows him?"

"Apparently they've done business in the past."

"Uh-huh." He stared out the window. "I don't like the fact you suddenly claim to know so much about my business."

"Word gets around. What can I say?"

"Word gets you killed too."

I stared at him and smiled, feeling the weight of my backup handgun, a Kahr MK9, inside my jacket, hoping I wouldn't have to use it.

"Sheriff's deputy came around here earlier this morning," he said. "He was asking a lot of questions about some veterinarian who got shot up last night."

I didn't like the way the tone of his voice seemed to be modulating. "Nolestar?" I asked.

"You're a goddamn liar, Pavlicek. Probably some kind of nigger lover. Your buddy Toronto's on ice in the Charleston city jail."

I held up my hands in resignation. "It was worth a try, wasn't it?"

"Look, buddy." He reached for the handle on his door. "Get yourself the hell out of here before I really begin to get aggravated."

The MK9 slid easily from its shoulder holster as I put a

hand out to stop him. "Look, *buddy*. All I need is a face. A name."

He eyed the weapon nestled between my fingers. "You know who Tony Warnock is, right? You've been talking to him."

"I know who he is."

"Tony's got more details about who we do business with. He lives in South Hills. Why don't you meet me over at his house later on this evening?"

"Right. So you and your goon army can snuff me out."

"On the level, Frank. None of the rest of my people. No cops. No Feds. No wires." He looked around at his showroom windows again as if he knew he were being watched.

It was a trap, of course. But if I was going to vindicate Toronto and find out what was really going on before the Feds sprang their sting, I just might have to walk into it.

"What time?" I asked.

"Does nine o'clock sound good to you?"

I didn't answer right away. "All right," I said finally. I slid the gun back inside my jacket but still kept my hand on it, like a man holding his broken arm in a sling.

"Great. Now get out of here," he said, shrugging off my grip and turning the handle to push open his door. He climbed out and stood there looking down at me. "And take that fucking mask off your face before somebody else starts calling down the cops again."

Time to take my leave. I sighed, pushing open my own door with my free hand, and began to slide out from behind the steering column. Man, how I hated to have to leave those wheels behind.

27

Climbing the dirt road to Felipe Baldovino's mountaintop cabin in Betty Carew's Buick wasn't anywhere near as easy as it had been the morning before in my truck. For the FBI or anybody else to have come all the way up here in search of evidence must have taken some kind of planning, not to mention information intelligence.

Felipe's Tahoe was still in the driveway beside the house, but instead of the Suburban Toronto had been driving, this time it was flanked by Damon Farraday's old Scout.

Wondering what he might be doing here, I gave the horn a quick honk as I crossed the six-inch hay field that passed for a front lawn, just to let anyone who was inside know I was coming, although I realized that probably wouldn't be necessary. The occupant or occupants most likely would have been able to hear me coming up the mountain long before I actually reached the place.

Felipe stepped out onto the porch as I brought the car to a halt, cut the engine, and climbed out. He appeared to be alone.

I climbed the rickety steps and shook his outstretched weathered hand.

"Frank, good to see you. Where's Jake?"

"He and I had what you might term a tête-à-tête with the FBI last night and they decided they'd like him to keep them company for a while."

"Oh, Jesus." His touched his forehead momentarily before reaching out to the railing to steady himself.

"You all right, old man?"

"I'm okay ... I'm okay. I didn't think it would come to this."

It would come to this? He still seemed wobbly so I took hold of his arm. He leaned heavily on me.

"Isn't that Damon Farraday's Scout?" I asked.

"Yeah. Sure is."

"What's he doing way up here?"

"Came up with that bird of his to do some hunting a couple of hours ago. He's been up here a few times before. They went away over the edge of the ridge and I haven't seen them since. But I expect he'll be headed back this way before too long."

The wind blew a cold swirl up the mountain and it swept across the porch. Felipe wore nothing but faded jeans and a T-shirt covered by a tattered bathrobe. His hair was greasy and disheveled and he smelled of stale bourbon.

"Why don't we get you inside?" I said.

He nodded.

I helped him back across the threshold. Inside there was only one large living space that served as living room, kitchen, and dining room rolled into one. Two small bedrooms and a bath were connected off the back of the cabin. The whole place was warmed by nothing but a woodstove.

"You want to sit down?" I asked.

"That would be good." We moved together toward the wall, where he sat down heavily in a recliner between the stove and a nineteen-inch color television that looked like it had been propped temporarily on a couple of weathered crates, which then by default had become part of the permanent decor. There was a walker with a cane leaning against it propped beside the chair.

I smelled coffee and looked around at the kitchen area. "Can I find you something to eat? You had breakfast?"

He waved his hand dismissively. "Too early for me. If it weren't for that Farraday character showing up I'd have stayed in bed."

"I heard you had visitors after Jake and I left yesterday too."

"Oh, you know about that, do you?"

I nodded.

"Bastards. Comin' up here in those vans with the dark windows. Acted like the damned secret police or something." He sighed heavily, his oversized gut pulling down his skinny arms and shoulders. "I suppose you came because of the rifle they took."

"That, and to find out what else you know."

"What else I know." He laughed, but it turned into a dry hacking cough. For a moment he seemed to have difficulty catching his breath. After a few seconds I stood, but he raised his hand to stop me. A couple more coughs and he was able to breathe.

"Would you like a glass of water?"

"Sure." His voice cracked like dry sandpaper.

I went to the sink across the room, found a clean glass on the shelf above and filled it with cold water from the tap. I brought it back over and handed it to him. He took a long sip.

"Best damned water on the planet," he said. "Right out of my own well."

I waited.

"Okay, let's see. You were asking what I know. One thing I'll say, just like I told those FBI bastards, is that I'm a proud father. I don't care what happens. Jake and me, well … you know how he found me and all, and it sure as hell wasn't like I was deserving of it or anything. But that Jake, he's relentless when he puts his mind to something … but I guess you must know all that."

I said I did.

"There's something going on here," he said, "and it's got something to do with Jake's work."

"His work?"

"Yeah, you know. That security business and stuff. People he goes to work for—clients I suppose you'd call them."

"What makes you say that?"

"Yesterday before you got here, Jake gave me a piece of paper with a phone number on it. He said you fellas still didn't know who shot Chester or why, but he had a pretty good idea that you and he were going to find out for sure, and he said that if anything happened, like you or he got into trouble with the police or something, I should find a telephone, preferably a pay phone, and call this number. He said a man would answer and I should give him a message." It had to be the operative whose name Toronto had refused to divulge, the one who was supposedly working with the Feds, but who—it looked like now—was the one attempting to frame him for the bombings and Chester's murder.

"What was the message?" I asked.

"He said to just tell the man 'The wind blows high.' "

"The wind blows high?"

"Yeah."

It sounded familiar. I thought I remembered the phrase came from an old Scottish tune or something.

"He say to tell the man anything else?"

"Nope. That was it. Just say 'The wind blows high,' and hang up. So that's what I did. After those FBI characters stormed through the place yesterday, I waited a few hours to see if you or Jake came by. When you didn't, I climbed in the Chevy and drove on down to Beckley with a roll of quarters—I figured it was a big enough place and far enough away from here—and I called the number he gave me, told the man what I was supposed to say and just hung up."

"So it was yesterday. About what time?"

"Evening. About six, seven o'clock."

"You didn't tell the man who you were?"

"Nope."

"You didn't stay on the phone long enough for him to have traced the call. You still have the phone number with you?"

"Yeah," he said. "After I got back here, I stuffed it in between the pages of an old cookbook I have on the shelf so nobody else would find it."

There was a shelf full of books in the corner next to the woodstove. "Over here?" I asked, rising and walking to it.

"That's right. The book's about cooking venison and such."

There were a few novels on the shelf, mostly action adventure and crime fiction, another section of books about WWII, and then in the middle of that shelf a book on cooking wild game.

"*Preparing Wild Game,* is that it?"

"That's it. Page one twenty-four. That's the month I was born — January 1924."

I opened the book and turned to the page he'd indicated. A slip of folded notebook paper lay between the pages. I unfolded it and read the number: 202 area code, Washington, D.C.

I dug out my brand-new cell phone, hoping it would work way up here. It did. The screen showed a strong signal, probably from a tower a few mountains away.

"Ah — you got a phone with you," Felipe said. "You going to call him too?"

"I don't know."

What else had Toronto decided not to tell me? What if this wasn't the man he'd talked to me about? For all I knew, I could be calling the chairman of the joint chiefs of staff. But I decided to punch in the number anyway.

"You may have to let it ring a few times. Jake told me that."

He was right. The phone rang exactly ten times before someone picked it up. I pressed the handset closer to my ear.

"Yes?" The deep male voice sounded agitated.

"What does 'The wind blows high' mean?"

"What? Who is this?"

"Who is *this*?"

"You're tying up a secure line."

"So I gathered."

"Who are you?"

"A friend of Jake Toronto's."

I heard him fumble with the phone for a moment. "What do you want?".

Something about the voice was eerily familiar, but I couldn't place it. "I want to know who's trying to set up my friend for a murder he didn't commit, not to mention a

conspiracy to commit acts of terrorism rap," 1 said. "And I
want to know who really did kill Chester Carew. And I want
to know why."

"You want to know a lot."

"Maybe that's my nature."

"How'd you get this number?"

"Immaterial."

There was a long pause, during which I thought I heard
the man on the phone sigh.

"You're on a cell phone, aren't you?" he finally said. "I'll
know in just a minute who you are."

"So you've got a fast trace ... what are you, NSA, CIA?
Why would Jake want me to contact you?"

"You're not the same person who called yesterday."

"No?" I paused just long enough to maybe make him
wonder.

"I'd really like to know who gave you this number," he
said.

"You're the one who killed Chester, aren't you?"

No answer.

"And you're the one who set Jake up for all this."

Still no answer.

"But Jake thinks you're a friendly."

"Frank Pavlicek ... of course."

"Took you long enough. Your high-tech spy equipment
must be slipping."

"Mr. Pavlicek, your questions are amusing, but I'm
afraid the sport you're playing now is a bit over your head."

"Really? I play a mean game of pickup basketball."

"I'm sure you do."

"Numbers can be traced both ways, you know."

He laughed. "Not this one. But please, feel free to talk
all you like."

"So you're in D.C. somewhere."

"Is that the number you called? Well, that's reassuring."

"I'm guessing this is about money. Because if it were
about revenge or betrayal or something else, you probably
would've already tried to kill Jake by now."

"Who says I haven't?"

"Why Chester though? He seemed pretty harmless to me."

He said nothing.

"Well, that land of his certainly started becoming valuable to a lot of people for some reason. Maybe some of these Stonewall Ranger people can tell me. But you don't seem like one of them."

Another chuckle. "No. I put people like that out of business. And I'm sorry, Frank, I know you're a professional and all, and I respect that up to a point, but you really don't have any idea what you're talking about."

"No?"

"No."

"Did Jake do some kind of salvage work for you or something?"

"You might say that."

"You paid him some money."

"Peanuts."

"Compared to what? To the money you're about to make now?"

"You really know how to be entertaining, Frank."

"Well, let's see now, maybe I can do even better. Dr. Winston, the veterinarian? He must represent some other kind of problem. That one was pretty sloppy, by the way. Was that why you decided to betray Toronto? No, wait a minute ... you must've decided that sooner, much sooner. You've been sitting there waiting to set him up all along."

"Incidental expenditures," he said.

Definitely money.

"How long have you known Jake?" I asked.

"Long enough to know what he's capable of."

I smiled. Here I was most likely talking to Chester's murderer, or at least the man who had ordered it done, only to find that whatever his motivation—revenge or money had to be the top two possibilities—he and I shared something in common. Jake Toronto was his wild card, as he was mine. The difference was he'd kept Toronto in the dark about something, and that something had now come under risk, which made Toronto expendable, or maybe even dangerous to him. I wondered if he knew I'd become Agent Grooms's wild card. Or at least I was making a pretty good bid for the position.

"Guess what I'm thinking," I said.

"What?"

"You have cause to worry."

"Yes? And why is that?"

"Because I'm not even sure *I* know what Toronto is really capable of."

I broke the connection, hoping it was true.

Felipe and I watched through the dusty window as Damon Farraday made his way up the hill below the cabin carrying his redtail, Tawny. The plumber moved with an easy grace, like someone long accustomed to moving outdoors over uneven ground. The wind was blowing the trees back and forth up here and the temperature must've been in the high thirties, but the hawk rested comfortably on his gloved fist.

I'd cooked up some eggs for Felipe and he was sitting at his kitchen table eating them slowly with some buttered toast.

"Sounds like I made a mistake, talking to that guy you just talked to," Felipe said.

I shook my head. "No mistake. My guess is Jake's still got a few more tricks up his sleeve."

"Think the Feds'll let you talk to him? Don't he have rights or something?"

I shook my head. "Not at the moment."

"Maybe we should be talking to a lawyer. I got this guy in New York I could call."

"Not yet. I need to get a clearer picture of what exactly is going on."

"Okay, Frank. Whatever you say. But I still say I made a mistake calling that guy."

"You were only following Jake's instructions, right? Besides, what's done is done."

"I suppose."

I stared at him. "Felipe, when I told you about Jake, you said you didn't think *it* would ever come to this. What did you mean? What is if?"

He scraped his plate with his fork. "I ... I don't know. Jake, he's always into something."

"What about you, Felipe. You ever been into something?"

"Ahh." He waved his hand at me. "I'm just an old man who doesn't always know what's good for himself."

Farraday had reached his Scout and was opening the back door to put Tawny inside. When the big bird was settled, he turned and pulled a fat rabbit from his game bag, set the catch on the grass beside the Scout, and kneeled down over it to begin skinning it. If he'd noticed the extra car next to the cabin or it made any difference to him, he didn't seem to show it. I watched as he gutted the creature and removed the organs, discarding most of them except the liver. He then took his bird to the glove again and fed her some more. Felipe took a long sip of hot coffee and bent over the last of his eggs.

A few minutes later, Farraday's boots clomped on the front porch to the cabin. He knocked on the door.

"Hey, Felipe, you in there?"

I went to the door and pulled it open. Farraday stood on the wooden decking, his muddy boots having made a trail from the front of the porch to the stoop. The wind blew cold air in through the opening. His face was red with cold and the exertion of working.

"Frank. What are you doing way out here? Man, you just missed some great hunting. If I'd have known you were going to be here, I'd have given you and Jake a call."

"It was kind of a spur-of-the-moment thing," I said.

"Sure."

"Saw you bagged a nice bunny."

"Yeah, the thing busted out into the open and Tawny was all over that. Where's Jake?"

"You haven't heard?"

"Heard what?"

"He was taken into custody last night. FBI."

"No shit."

"Apparently they're investigating the Stonewall Rangers and they somehow got it into their minds that Jake is the one who shot Chester."

Felipe had edged up behind me with his walker and was crossing to the other side of the room.

"You're kidding."

"I wish I were."

"Jesus, that sucks."

I said nothing.

"What are you going to do?"

"Well, I've just been talking with Felipe here. The Feds were here yesterday serving a search warrant and they claim to have found the rifle that killed Chester."

"Here?"

I nodded.

"Wow. I guess you never know. I mean, what're they gonna do, charge him or something?"

"At this point I have no idea."

He looked over my shoulder at Felipe, who'd now made it back to his recliner to sit down. "You doing okay, old man?"

Felipe waved his hand in agreement. "Fine," he said.

Farraday turned back to me. "Well, I'm sorry, man. Anything more I can do?"

"Not that I can think of."

"You let me know if there is, okay?"

"Thanks, Damon."

"Thanks for the hunting too, old man," he called over my shoulder. "I had a good morning."

Felipe waved at him.

Farraday turned and walked back out to his vehicle, climbed in, and started it up. The engine backfired. He needed a new muffler. He backed the Scout in a circle, and I watched as he burbled off down the mountain.

28

Hercules, Toronto's big retriever, bounded out to meet my
car as I topped the rise to pull up to his house trailer. The
place looked the same as the last time I'd been there a couple
of months before, except that the foliage had disappeared
from the trees, and the grass fields, in their winter dress of
camel and bloodred clay, had lost any remnants of green. I
didn't see Nicole's Subaru wagon, but there was a white
Firebird next to the trailer belonging to Priscilla Thomasen,
Toronto's sometime girlfriend who also happened to be the
local commonwealth's attorney. I climbed out and patted
Herk, who jumped around to the passenger door wondering
where his master was.

I heard a baby cry and looked up to see Priscilla
Thomasen standing on the deck with a dark-skinned infant
cradled in her arms.

"Hello, Priscilla. How are you?"

"Long time no see, Frank."

"Yeah, it's been awhile."

"New car?" she asked.

"Borrowed. You here looking after Jake's birds?"

She nodded.

"Any sign of my daughter, Nicole?"

"No, why?"

"I asked her to meet me here. Thought she might get
here before I did."

She shook her head.

"Cute baby ... yours?"

"Um-hmmm."

"What's her name?"

"Kameesha."

"Pretty." Jake had never said anything about a child.
"Not Jake's too?"

She smiled. "Nope. I was married a little over a year
ago. A surgeon from Roanoke. Things didn't work out

though with him on call all the time and me trying to commute back and forth with the baby and all. He, umm ... well, suffice it to say Kameesha and I finally just had to leave."

"I'm very sorry."

"Didn't Jake tell you?"

"No, he never mentioned it."

She gave a little grunt of disgust. "Figures ... why I could never have a long-term relationship with the man. They must not teach verbal communication with all that security training and whatnot he does."

I thought of stating the obvious, that here she was back in obviously some kind of relationship with Toronto, but figured I'd better keep my own counsel in that regard.

"Why are you here, Frank? And where's Jake?"

I told her what had happened.

She listened, saying little. Finally, she said, "That man's been living his whole life on the edge. Bound to catch up with him sooner or later."

"That's what makes it interesting though, isn't it?"

She said nothing.

"Nicky is supposed to meet me down here. We thought we'd check in on the birds and look through some of Jake's stuff before the FBI decides to come by and tear through everything. Have the Feds been here, or have you heard anything from them?"

She shook her head. "I've been taking a few days off work. You're the first person Kameesha or I have seen or heard from in three days."

Curious, if they were really considering Toronto a potential terrorist. "Well, maybe they just haven't gotten around to serving the warrant yet."

"Maybe," she said, but I could tell she didn't believe it.

"You checked on Jake's babies yet this morning?"

"Yes," she said. "They're all fine. I fed them."

"Good. Don't suppose they'll be doing any hunting for a couple of days."

The sound of another vehicle approaching arose in the

distance. Hercules gave a warning bark and leapt from the deck again.

"Let's hope that's Nicky," I said.

It was. Her station wagon popped into view and she waved when she caught sight of us on the deck.

"There is one more piece of bad news I need to give you though," I said to Priscilla.

"Really? What now?"

"I'll explain it to you and Nicky both inside."

After greeting us and the dog and the appropriate oohing and ahhing over the baby, Nicole followed me and Priscilla and the infant, with Hercules at our heels, into Jake's kitchen area, where we all sat down around the small table. Priscilla laid the little girl down in one of those portable chairs that snap into car seats, where she smiled up at us and cooed softly. Hercules found his bed in the corner and curled into it. I quickly explained about the phone conversation I'd just had with Mr. Spook and about the dead birds Jason and I had discovered in the cave.

"So this man is supposedly working with the FBI, but now you think he may be up to no good, including trying to frame Jake?" Priscilla asked.

"That's the way it looks to me."

"But you have no idea who he is."

I shook my head.

"Who do you think? Some kind of government agent gone bad or something?" Nicole sounded excited to be in on the chase.

"Do you think you could maybe ask around a bit— quietly, I mean—and see if you could find out who he was?" I asked Priscilla.

"I don't know, Frank. I might make a call or two. But you know how the Feds can be sometimes."

"So make up some excuse," I suggested.

When it came to prosecutors, Priscilla Thomasen was about as straightlaced and conservative as anyone could be, a fact that had endeared her to her largely white and rural Virginia constituency.

"We'll see," she said.

"What about right now?" Nicole asked.

"Right now we may not have much time before the Feds decide to show up," I said. "I want to check through Jake's things to see if we can find anything that might help us. Why don't you two check through the rest of the trailer. I want to have a look in the spare bedroom."

Priscilla gave me a serious look. "But it's locked. And that's where Jake keeps some of his — "

"I know. I have an extra key Jake gave me once just in case, and I want to get there before anybody else does."

She nodded.

"What's in there, Dad?" Nicky asked.

"It's just Jake's little office. No time to go into any more detail now. Let's get to it."

I stood and headed toward the back of the trailer. The narrow passageway led past a small half bath and then a padlocked door before ending in the main bedroom in back. I went to the locked door and selected a small key from my key ring. The key popped open the lock. I swung the door open and stepped inside, closing the heavier-than-usual trailer door behind me.

The one window in the room was covered by a heavy drape that I didn't bother opening. A small bit of light cracked into the room from around its edges, but I switched on the overhead ceiling fixture in order to be able to see better. There was a captain's chair and a metal workstation in the center of the room with a computer and a large flat-screen monitor. A satellite linkup attached to an insulated cable on the wall gave Toronto a high-speed connection to the Web and other networks via a dish he had set up at the edge of the woods on the far side of the hill behind the bird barn. Jake did a lot of his work here. The desk was completely free of clutter or disorganization of any kind. There was a small notepad with nothing written on it, a wireless phone housed neatly in its cradle, and a small desk lamp.

In the top desk drawer I found a stack of CD-Rom disks,

one of which was labeled with my name. Toronto had told me to use it in case of his death or incarceration or some other major disaster. The computer was running, although the screen had gone into a darkened power-save mode. I moved the mouse on the pad next to the keyboard and the screen flicked to life to a simple portal-like interface. I took the disk from its case and stuck it into the drive. The light blinked on as the mechanism whirled away.

A message from Toronto immediately appeared on the screen.

Hey, dude. If you're reading this, it must mean I'm dead or in jail or something. I have something important to ask you to do.

I need you to find a secure client-list file on this computer and delete its entire contents. I've made it easy for you. This disk has a utility that will automatically open the correct file. But in order to get there you have to type in your own password, which is the name of that bar on the Upper West Side where you and I used to always go after work when we were first together on the force.

You remember the place. It's the one where the bartenders were all women and I used to drag you there even though it made Camille hysterical. At the bottom of this message, you'll find a password box. Once you're through reading this, you go ahead and type in the name and the program will do the rest for you. It will erase the file in question. In case I'm not already dead, don't worry, I have a backup copy of this file at a more secure location with its own safeguards, so erasing the one here won't do any permanent damage. But if you don't delete it, there are some people on this list who might end up in serious jeopardy if the work I do for them ever comes to light.

Oh, I almost forgot ... if you can't remember the name of the bar or type in the wrong pass code, you'll hear a very loud hissing noise. If that happens, get out and get out fast. There's a Claymore mine wired from the base of this desk to the computer and it's about to explode. The device is on an eight-second timer so I know I don't need to tell you to be careful.

Good luck, Frank. Sayonara. ... And oh, yeah, thanks for taking care of this item for me. Hope you were paying attention. By the way, you probably already knew this disk was encrypted and will only work on this machine.

At the bottom of the message was a small box with the caption FRANK'S PASSWORD. Paying attention? You've got to be kidding. The FBI might show up at any moment and Toronto wants me to break into his private, encrypted files and, oh yeah, by the way, maybe just get myself blown up in the process.

I remembered the name of the bar, Gilheaney's, and typed it into the box. His message didn't say whether it should be upper- or lowercase. Would it make any difference? No time to worry about it. I took a deep breath before hitting the ENTER key.

The hard drive on the computer spun to life and the drive light began to blink rapidly. Thankfully no loud hiss. A brief message appeared then disappeared on the screen: *DELETING ENCRYPTED FILES.* What would have really made things interesting would have been if I could have taken a look at that client list, but obviously Toronto wasn't about to let that happen. Could it mean he was deeply involved in illegalities he didn't want me to know about? The kind the FBI now alleged?

1 pushed the thought from my mind and began checking through the desk. Inside the drawers, which were all much longer and deeper than I'd expected, I found a small cache of weapons: three Glock .45 autos and two Russian-made Saiga semiautomatic shotguns along with ammunition to last a daylong battle. Enough weaponry to arm a small police force. I checked the loads on each of the weapons, emptied all the chambers for the time being, and then carefully placed all the firearms and ammo in an empty suitcase I found in the closet.

That finished I took a final look around the Spartan

room. Not much else to see, except a fine layer of dust on the thin metallic windowsill. The walls were bare. There was nothing else in the desk drawers—no scraps of paper, no stray business cards. Apparently, the truly paperless office had actually made its long-heralded arrival as far as Toronto was concerned. No doubt, the Feds would take his computer apart and find or reconstruct anything they could from his hard drive, but knowing Toronto, they wouldn't find much. Just to be safe, I slipped the disk from the CD drive and wiped down the keyboard, desk, and anything else in the room I'd touched to remove any prints. If they found any fibers or hairs or any of my DNA, I could always claim I was merely here discussing business with Toronto a few days before.

I met Nicole and Priscilla with the baby back down the hall in the kitchen.

"Find anything?" Nicole asked.

I held up the suitcase in my hand. "Enough firepower to help us win a small battle if it comes to that. Let's hope it doesn't. What about you guys?"

"Just some, um, personal stuff I already knew about in the bedroom," Priscilla said. She looked at Nicole and the two of them giggled.

"I won't ask."

"But, Dad, behind some old shirts in the little closet in the living room we also found this." She went to the couch and hoisted something in her hands. It was a twelve-gauge Mossberg, the exact same make and model I'd been struck with in the woods. Not the same weapon, of course, since that had been turned over to the sheriff's department, but there was more. Along with the weapon she held up a dark green ski mask, the exact type worn by my assailant.

"Isn't this the kind of getup the creep you took the gun from the other day was wearing?"

I nodded.

"Are you saying you think Jake might've been involved with that?" Priscilla asked. "Why that's impossible."

"It's a plant," I said. "Same as the rifle the Feds found at

Felipe's. Who else has been here in the last several days besides you and Jake?"

"Like I said, no one."

"Then—"

"Wait a minute. Just before Jake left to head out to Nitro for the funeral, a man stopped by briefly. Another falconer. He said he was on his way back from a trip to Roanoke. Jake showed him some of the birds out in the barn. A young guy."

"What was his name?"

"I'm trying to remember ... Damon something?"

"Damon Farraday," I said.

"That's it."

Farraday. Whom I'd also just seen hunting up at Felipe's. Who'd been present at the bombing that killed Gwen Hallston. Hadn't he gone back to his truck for a while then while we were still in the woods?

"But why, Dad?" Nicky asked. "What would Damon have to gain by trying to frame Jake?"

"I don't know. You said you checked everything out with his background, right?"

"Yes. Like I told you."

"Can you go deeper? Can you try to find out more?"

"I can try."

"What do you need?"

"I've got my laptop, but I could use a broadband connection to speed things up."

"We can't use Jake's connection here—I don't know how he has it wired and he already has the computer booby-trapped to keep anyone from tampering with it." I said.

"How about my apartment?" Priscilla suggested. "It's in town and no one's there right now. I put in a cable modem last year when I was going back and forth with the baby to Roanoke so I could do cases at home."

"Perfect," I said. "After we visit your mom, Nicky, you can get right to work. Whether you find anything or not, you can drive your own car and catch back up with me later out in Charleston."

"What should we do with the shotgun?" Nicole's slender hands were dwarfed by the weapon.

"Take it with us. We need to get out of here in case the Feds do decide to show up."

"Amen to that," Priscilla said. "Obviously, then, from my perspective, you were never here."

"Exactly."

"So we are going to visit Mom next, right?" Nicole asked.

"Right," I said. "But we can only spend a few minutes. We'll head over there now. Priscilla, you feel comfortable with you and the baby being here? I mean with the guy I talked to on the phone and everything. He might decide to make a run at anybody having anything to do with Jake."

"Looks like you're the one he has to worry about for now," she said. "I can take care of Kameesha and myself. And if the FBI shows up, don't worry, I've dealt with them before."

<u>29</u>

Here are what expensive lawyers, a fifteen-thousand-dollar-a-month disability policy from your dead second husband's estate, and a brain almost morphed to mango buy you: A get-out-of-jail-free card (probation leniency of the court since you won't be running around anywhere); a master bedroom decorated with bouffant blue curtains and semifresh flowers; dark silk sheets — better to hide the stains from drool, sweat, and urine; and all sorts of expensive medical equipment and an oversized color television. Not to mention an around-the-clock battery of nurses, the current version of which looked as though she'd made it about half-way through her stack of *People, Time,* and a mixed bag of fashion magazines.

At least, I thought, she knows how to read.

Since most of the money went to my ex-wife Camille's continuing care, Sweetwood Farm looked in the same state of general disrepair as the last time I'd accompanied Nicole on a visit. Her mother still lay in a customized Suntec full electric rehab bed with a permanent bemused crease to her lips, her eyes staring wide and wondering at the world, as if they'd only just discovered it.

More than three years had passed since Camille's addiction to crystal meth, and the legal fallout from her involvement in Dewayne Turner's murder had turned her life to this. The sky outside was gray and the winter cold uninviting.

"How's she doing today?" Nicole plunked herself down in a chair next to Camille's bed opposite the nurse, who occupied the Barcalounger in front of the darkened television.

I hung back in the doorway for a moment. I wanted to see both Camille's and the nurse's response.

"She ate Oreos for breakfast," the nurse said, crossing her arms with a look of disgust on her face. "Wouldn't eat nothing but Oreos."

For maybe just an instant I thought I saw a tiny smile crack across the placid mask of my ex-wife's face. Same old Camille.

"Mom." Nicole reached across the bedsheets and took her mother's hand in her own. "You have to eat. You have to keep up your strength, you know that."

Camille looked on impassively.

"I don't know," I said, stepping into the patient's line of sight. "Oreos sound pretty good to me."

The container with cookies still lay on the bedside stand.

"I fix her a perfectly good breakfast of oatmeal, toast with honey, and orange juice," the nurse said defensively. She looked to be in her thirties, dark brown skin, about fifty pounds overweight but with a proud chin and a determined stare.

"I'm sure you did," said Nicole.

"How you wanna play this, Camille?" I asked. "You going to make your own daughter have to spoon-feed you?" I was remembering an image of Nicole in a high chair in our kitchen in New York and Camille trying to feed her a jar of baby food squash, or maybe it was peas. Nicole had grabbed the glass jar and tossed the entire contents on the floor.

A darker look crossed the patient's face this time, accompanied by a slight shaking of the head.

The nurse roused herself from her chair. "I'll warm up her cereal again."

She disappeared out the door.

Nicole lifted her mother's hand a little and patted it gently. "I've missed you, Mom."

The placidity returned to Camille's face. She reached with her free hand for a small white board with a large felt marker on the bedside stand. Nicole anticipated this move and helped her retrieve the board and uncap the marker. Then we waited while Camille slowly scratched out a barely decipherable message. When finished she shifted the board toward Nicole so she could read.

MIS U 2, it said.

"This is a new daytime nurse. What happened to your old one?"

Camille took the board again and slowly wrote.

MOVE 2 SC

"She moved to South Carolina. Too bad, I know you liked her. Her name was Josephine, wasn't it?"

YES I MIS HER

Another pat of the hand.

The new nurse returned. "Need to get Miss Rhodes set up for her meal," she said.

"We'll just step outside for a minute," I said.

"Dad and I brought you something we thought you might like," Nicole said.

She stood and she and I stepped out into the hall. Along the wall we'd propped a large flat parcel covered in brown wrapping paper.

"You know, Dad," Nicole said. "Wendy told me once that she believes people with severe disabilities who are forced to spend a lot of time in one place develop a kind of sixth sense for people and for things going on in the world around them."

Wendy was the creator of the object beneath the paper, a stunning watercolor painting of a pastoral countryside framed by the Blue Ridge with quarter horses grazing in the foreground. Wendy was also a quadriplegic, a luminous former student of Marcia D'Angelo's, injured when her boyfriend's motorcycle, on the back of which she was riding at the time, skidded beneath a passing eighteen-wheeler. The now ex-boyfriend had walked away without a scratch and had gone on to other more important things in his life a few months later, but rather than turn to bitterness, Wendy had turned to her faith—Marcia and Nicole sat with her at church every Sunday—and her painting. She held the brush with a special rig between her teeth.

"Could be," I said.

We took the package back into the bedroom. The nurse now had Camille sitting upright in bed and taking a bite of oatmeal. The nurse had to help her eat and wipe her mouth. "Thas a whole lot better Miss Rhodes. You should be takin' company more often. Maybe then we could get you to eatin' halfway decent." Camille waved a feeble hand across the sheets at her as if to swat the entire notion away. Her countenance brightened a little, however, at the sight of the package.

The nurse took Camille's bowl away momentarily and gathered up the tray that had been in front of her patient and set it on the dresser. "You see if you can keep that down, Miss Rhodes. I'll just be down in the kitchen doin' up the dishes if you need anything else." She shuffled quickly from the room.

Nicole lifted the parcel onto the bed. "This is something very special, Mom, from a friend of mine. She's bedridden, like you, except she's lost the use of all of her limbs."

Camille scratched at her board again.

PARLYZD

"Yes. Her name's Wendy and she's a quadriplegic. Would you like some help opening this?"

Slow nod.

Nicole and I helped Camille tear away at the paper, beginning carefully at the corner. The watercolor was mounted in a frame of light wood that offset the artist's use of color. The changing textures and brushstrokes would have been striking and unusually appealing, even if you hadn't known how painstakingly the painting had been crafted.

Once it was completely revealed, Camille seemed to look in the direction of the picture for a long time. Was she thinking of the magnificent view down her own driveway, of the wide-open fields, the riding she used to do? Her eyes filled with tears. Nicole moved in to put her arms around her mother.

She scratched out *THNK U SO MCH IS BUTIFUL* on her board.

"You'll always be my mom," Nicole told her.

"You got that right, kiddo," I said. I was proud of her,

proud of the young woman she'd become, about to graduate from the university, a whiz when it came to finance and computers, even if the part-time job she currently held, working for me, wouldn't have been my first choice of things for her to do. But the truth was I was getting used to her prowess around the office and beginning to wonder what I'd ever done without her.

I checked my watch. "Ladies, I hate to have to break up the party, but we've got to get going."

Camille slowly took up her white board and scratched out another message.

WHRE

Nicole looked at me. "Jake's in trouble," she said. "Dad and I need to go help him."

A gust of cold wind shook the windows outside the bedroom.

"Got to be turning up the heat," the nurse, who'd suddenly reappeared in the doorway, said. "S'posed to be getting colder tonight."

Camille had one more message for us.

B CRFL

Then her face became virtually expressionless again. I wondered where her mind must be turning. I wonder now if she'd somehow seen the cemetery on the hill, birds in flight, the last dangerous change in illumination night would bring, how much the future held or didn't.

30

No one answered the phone at Damon Farraday's place. I still didn't have enough evidence to go to Grooms or the police. Hopefully, the ATF had gone through the cave by now, and if the amount of spilled ANFO I suspected was present there turned out to be substantial, somebody's eyebrows should be raised. The Stonewall Rangers' plans Toronto had told me about included nothing to do with a big bomb. Such a device, assuming it had been put together there, could now be headed, or have already been placed, virtually anywhere within a radius of a few hundred miles or more.

My cell phone went off just as I crossed the Kanawha River on I-77 headed back into Charleston. No number was displayed on the caller ID. Thinking it might be Nicole, I punched the answer button and said hello.

"Pavlicek? Where in the hell are you?"

"Agent Grooms. Well, I'm, ah, a bit busy at the moment," I said.

"Busy. You're in a car, right? It sounds like it."

"I have been moving around a little today."

"I want to know where Toronto is."

"Jake?" A stab of fear shot through me. "Aren't you in a better position to be able to know that than I?"

"Don't get cute with me, Pavlicek. Is he there with you right now? I want to talk to him."

"With me? What are you talking about?"

"You mean you want me to believe you haven't seen him?"

"No. Why?"

"Because if you're lying. ..."

"Did you release him or something?"

"Release him? Hell no. He escaped custody."

"Escaped federal custody."

"To add to the growing list of charges against him."

"But how —?"

"Don't ask how. If you're harboring a fugitive, Pavlicek, not only will you never be doing any private investigation work again, you'll be joining your pal out in Leavenworth for a few years."

"I haven't seen him, Grooms. Haven't seem him or heard from him."

He was silent for a moment.

"Did you people check out that cave I sent you to?" I asked.

"Yeah," he said finally. "Still got a team up there."

"I was right, wasn't I? It's ANFO."

He said nothing.

"Was someone building a big device?"

"I want you to drive straight to downtown Charleston to the FBI office," he said. "I want you in here now."

"But what if someone's about to set off a bomb?"

"Pavlicek —"

"What if it's not Toronto and it's not even the Stonewall Rangers?"

"I don't care. You want to stop 'em, you need to get in here. Now. Do you hear?"

"I gotta go, Grooms."

"Listen! You —"

"I gotta go. I'll try to find Toronto for you," I said, and punched the line dead and the power off.

Kara Grayson lived in a third-floor unit of a condo complex near the golf course in South Charleston. Lights glowed from her windows. A couple of stars were beginning to shine overhead. A peaceful setting for a quiet winter Sunday night. I climbed the outside stairs and rang the bell.

A dark spot moved across the peephole before she pulled open the door.

"Frank. Finally come to give me the scoop, huh?" The question was all business but there was a hint of a gleam in her eye.

"Not exactly."

"Not exactly?"

"Well, I, uh, wanted to check and see if you found out anything about that lab company. And I thought I ought to come by and explain a little more."

"You mean about why you and your friend were there."

"Yes. And I wanted to tell you again how sorry I am about what happened to Dr. Winston."

"No, please ... it's okay." She rubbed her shoulders against the cold. She was dressed in a heavy sweater under a bathrobe and blue balletlike slippers, neither of which did much to camouflage her trim, athletic figure. Unlike the night before, she wore no makeup. It gave her a clean, more youthful appearance. "Please come in," she said.

I entered and she shut and locked the door behind me. A fat white tomcat with pearly gray eyes padded across the hallway in front of us.

"Fresco, meet Mr. Pavlicek. ... Oh, it's Frank, isn't it? Is it okay if I call you Frank?"

"You bet."

Fresco narrowed his eyes at me for a moment and arched his back.

"Now, don't you be like that, Fresco. Don't worry, he always does this to strange men. He'll get used to you."

The cat probably still smelled hawk on my jacket or something from the day before. I tried the stare-down technique, but Fresco wasn't about to be budged. Not yet anyway.

"Would you like something warm to drink? I just put on some hot water for tea."

"That would be great, thank you," I said.

She led me into her living room, which had a high ceiling and very tall framed photos of mountains and people skiing. Fresco retreated up a flight of stairs.

"You're into skiing, I see."

"Yes. I used to race."

"Not anymore?"

"No," she said. "I gave it up."

I nodded.

"Have a seat on the couch, if you'd like. I'll be right back with the tea," she said, and disappeared through an archway and around a corner toward what must've been the kitchen.

The living room sofa was one of those huge overstuffed affairs with gargantuan pillows you could sink into. The only other piece of furniture in the room was an oversized furry beanbag that looked like someone had dropped a grizzly bear pelt in the middle of her floor and forgotten to take out some of the bear.

In a few moments she was back carrying a tray with two steaming mugs of hot water.

"I didn't know what kind you liked or what you wanted in it, so I brought a selection."

I picked Twinings English Breakfast tea, no sugar, a little milk, and after she'd put it together she sat down on the edge of the couch a few feet away from me.

"That looks sore," she said.

"Oh, you mean my face." I'd almost forgotten about it.

"You wanted to know about the lab company."

"Yes."

"I talked to Betty Ann—she's my friend the nurse. Everyone's in shock, of course, over what happened. But she said the company the clinic uses is Princeton Medical."

"Okay. Did she give you contact information?"

"Yes. I've got it in the other room. Are the tests Dr. Winston ordered on the blood sample from Chester Carew's bird the reason why you think he was killed?"

"Yes. How well did you know him?"

"Dr. Winston? I knew him from the clinic."

"He have any other friends or family in the area?"

"Greg's main friend was his work ... that and his sports. He was really into biking. I mean really into it."

"Mountain biking?"

"Umm-hm." She swallowed a sip of tea. "Road racing."

"Sure. He was never married then? No children or anything?"

"No. Me either," she added quickly.

"Dating?"

"Dr. Winston? Not that I knew of."

"I meant you."

"Me?"

I nodded.

"No." She looked chastened. "I asked you out, didn't I? How about you?"

"I'm divorced. There was a woman I wanted to ask to marry me, but it looks like that's pretty much over."

"I'm sorry."

"I have a twenty-one-year-old daughter from my marriage."

"Really?"

"She has a boyfriend. Good young guy. Smart. I'm always lecturing her about keeping herself pure for marriage."

"I see." She smiled. "You don't look old enough to have a daughter that age." She crossed her long legs, and when she did her robe slipped back up well above her knee. She made no attempt to straighten it.

I looked around the room at the comfortable furnishings.

"Rumor has it you and your friend are in a lot of trouble."

"No comment."

"Uh-hum."

"Are we going to do the reporter thing again?" I asked.

"Hey, now, it's not that bad. A lot of people are excited to talk to someone in the media."

"Not in my line of work."

She nodded. "I understand. I sometimes feel the same about my work."

"Are you good at it?"

"I'm good at a lot of things," she said matter-of-factly.

"You haven't asked me anything more about what my friend and I were doing there at the vet's office last night."

"I've found it's best to just let people talk about themselves. They usually get around to answering most of my questions."

"Is that so?"

"Anyway, I thought detectives were supposed to be the ones asking the questions."

"Normally."

"Well, here's a question: why did you really come here tonight?" She reached her hands up and ran her fingers through her long hair.

"I don't know."

She smiled again and looked out her tall windows at the gathering darkness. There was a light dusting of snow on the evergreens outside.

"I guess maybe, when people die, and when dangerous things happen, it can either make you want to retreat into yourself or want to reach out to someone," I said.

"Is that what you're doing now, Frank? Reaching out to me?"

"Maybe."

She uncrossed her legs and shifted a little on the edge of the couch. "You know I didn't really get a chance to thank you for saving me last night. I've never been shot at before."

"Doesn't happen to me every day either."

"That's good." She laughed a little and slid over next to me. She reached around behind me and with both hands began massaging my neck. "You're tense as a drum," she said.

A soft growl came from the stairwell.

"What was that, the cat?" I asked.

"Fresco's jealous as the day is long."

"I have to do some things tonight," I said.

"Oh?"

"I have to help out a friend who's in trouble ... and I have to do some things I'm a little afraid to do."

"You don't seem like the kind of a man who scares easily."

"I'm not."

"Then just go ahead and do what you have to. Don't think too much about it. That's what I always told myself in the gate at the top of the mountain."

"Top of the mountain, huh?"

Her fingers felt like a warm balm gently moving back and forth across my shoulders. I turned into her body and then her lips were there, moist and inviting as they melted into mine. She smelled of tangerine and lilac.

"You still haven't asked me what I was doing there last night," I said.

"Ummm."

"Doesn't sound like much of a reporter."

"Maybe I'll have to coax it out of you," she said. But she must have felt my arms tense a little as they raised up to hold her back from our next kiss. She pulled away and sat back on the sofa.

We sat together in silence for a moment.

"This can't happen right now," she said. "Can it?"

"No," I said, as gently as I could. "For a lot of reasons."

She nodded. "I understand."

"You don't want the story?"

"Not if you're not ready to give it to me."

"Maybe sometime," I said.

"Maybe sometime." She rose from the sofa and straightened out her robe. "I'll go get you that information on the lab."

31

A half an hour later, I found myself trolling Charleston's west end looking for the Connors brothers again. Were the two young white supremacists on the run? If Caleb Connors had been sent back up to the site of Chester's murder by Bo Higgins to try to find anything that might tell them who had done the shooting, it meant that Higgins was concerned someone was complicating their own plans. Could it be the same man who was trying to frame Jake? Damon Farraday? Had Caleb Connors seen something or found something that might close the loop on who the real killer or killers were? And where was Toronto and why hadn't he tried to contact me?

I caught a small break. The whore's real name was Beatrice. She was working the bars on Washington Street and said she'd seen Caleb Connors a little earlier in the evening in a different bar down the street and that she'd seen his brother with him too.

"Caleb, he's the one with the firebird tattoo on his shoulder, isn't he?"

"Yeah, that's him."

I put a twenty down on the bar and thanked her.

"Anytime *you're* asking, baby. Anytime."

I drove past the brothers' house again. Nothing—no car in the driveway and the place was locked up tight. It was growing later and I was running out of bars.

I had just walked out the door of the latest when I spotted the bright orange GTO the neighbor had said the brothers drove. It was rounding the corner onto Washington a couple of blocks down and headed in my direction. As the car approached, even though the windows were slightly fogged, I could make out four people inside. One of the brothers drove while the other sat in back and each had a young woman seated beside him. The rear stereo speakers thumped down the street. A front window on the passenger side cracked open, smoke blew out from the opening, and a set of long slender fingers flicked ash onto the pavement as they passed.

Betty's Buick sat just a few spaces away. I kept my eye on their taillights as I unlocked the door, climbed in, fired up the engine, and pulled into a slow-moving line of traffic a few cars behind them.

They were about as hard to follow as a Snoopy blimp. Obviously in party mode, whichever brother was driving cruised casually down Washington for a while, took a right on Pennsylvania beneath the interstate, and only sped up gradually after taking another right and heading into a neighborhood of drab dwellings interspersed with the occasional vacant lot. I kept the Buick back a block or so. When the car turned into the driveway of one of the houses, I pulled into a line of parked vehicles and watched from a distance while the four of them climbed out, the two in the back giggling and clinging to one another like hounds in heat as they extricated themselves from the long two-door and weaved their way with the other two in through the front door of the house.

I checked the cylinder on my .357 as well as the backup pocket 9mm I'd strapped to my ankle before swinging the Mossberg onto the seat next to me. I wore one of Jake's oversized long hunting coats I'd also picked up before leaving his place. The short-stock shotgun slid nicely under one arm and you'd have to look closely to see I was carrying it. I decided to give them a few minutes to let the party swing into high gear before making my grand entrance. A blast of cold wind shook the Buick. I checked my watch and waited.

Twenty minutes later I climbed out and made my way down the sidewalk toward the house. The street was empty and dead quiet. People who were at home on a cold Sunday night had holed up behind the blue halo of their color televisions, eating, drinking, arguing; some, especially the younger ones, making love.

One thing troubled me. If any of my own two pairs of

lovebirds was armed and I didn't happen to catch everyone in the same room, someone could obviously get a jump on me. But a night without risk is like a night without darkness. The house was a small pale ranch with mismatched shutters on the windows. The drapes had been pulled. More loud music beat its hollow noise from inside as I approached across the mud-caked front lawn. Thinking about Chester, I said a silent prayer as I stepped on the front porch.

The front door was unlocked, which almost made it too easy. I pushed through it as quickly and quietly as I could, swinging the shotgun up to waist level as I entered.

"Hey! What the fuck?"

They were all four in the living room, directly in front of me. Each one was naked from the waist up and one of the two girls, who'd been performing a little dance, also had her blue jeans down around her knees. The air was thick with marijuana smoke. The two brothers lay on either end of an L-shaped sofa. Four empty shot glasses, half a six-pack of beer, and a bottle of tequila were strewn about the floor at their feet. The other, nondancing girl gave a sharp scream and removed her fingers from inside the open zipper of one of the brothers, both of whom looked to be too stoned at the moment to do much other than make the aforementioned comment and stare warily at the long barrel of the gun. Lucky for me, the music drowned out the girl's voice. I closed the front door with a soft thud behind me.

"Sorry to have to crash your little party," I said.

The girls rushed to pull their clothes back on or at least hold T-shirts in front of their naked breasts, but the brothers didn't move. Caleb Connors's tattoo was clearly visible and his eyes slowly evolved into recognition as he studied the fading bruise on my face.

"Hey," he said. "You're that fucking guy from up in the woods."

"See what happens when you go pointing shotguns in people's faces, Caleb? Comes back to haunt you."

"Caleb?" The other brother turned on him. "Jesus, man, what'd you do, tell this asshole your name?"

"I didn't tell him jack shit. I had my mask on just like I told you."

"And you let him take the gun away from you."

"I told you, man. I was going to let him go and he sucker punched me."

"Now, boys, let's not quibble over who told whom what. The way you guys parade around town you might as well be wearing neon signs that say Stonewall Rangers."

"Stonewall Rangers?" The girl who'd had her hand down Mart's pants looked at the brothers with anger. "You two don't run with that bunch of nutcases, do you?"

"Uh-oh," I said. "Love is such a fleeting thing."

The muscles in each of the boys' arms flexed involuntarily, and if they hadn't been so wasted I might've been worried they would try something.

"Don't even think about it, gentlemen. Unless you'd like to talk it over and decide which one gets it in the face first."

"Fuck you, man." Still the lack of vocabulary. Caleb's nose was running, but he made no move to wipe it.

"The good news for you all is that I'm only here after information," I said. "Unless, of course, you decide to be difficult. In which case I've got a cell phone and will be more than happy to talk this whole matter over with the Charleston City Police or the Kanawha County Sheriffs Department."

I was bluffing, of course, since heading downtown to the sheriff's department was one of the last things I actually wanted to do at the moment. But they didn't know that. The boys both appeared to be slowly processing whatever options they might have. Their brains, dulled by the smoke and booze and probably not among the quickest to begin with, moved like molasses.

"Sweetie pie," Matt said to the girl who'd spoken. "If you knew what the Rangers was really doing you wouldn't talk like that. We're freedom fighters. You should keep your dumb cunt mouth shut unless you know what y'all are talking about."

"Fuck you," she said. "I let you two jerk offs in here to

party with us and this is what I find out? You're a couple of loonies, that's what you are."

The music mercifully paused for a few seconds between songs.

"Please turn it down," I said. The girl who obviously lived there went to the stereo components piled on a table against the wall and turned off the receiver.

"Thank you. Matt, now that we can finally all hear ourselves think, maybe you can start by telling me what your brother was doing up there on Chester Carew's land."

Matt Connors looked at his older brother, who glared back at him. "I ain't gonna tell you jack shit, mister."

"Oh, no?" I kept the shotgun in one hand and with the other slid the .357 from my inside jacket pocket. Before leaving the car, I'd fitted a silencer onto the end of the barrel. "I'm not going to waste time giving you a bruise or anything like you did to me, Caleb." I raised the handgun and pointed it toward his forehead. "Let's see, if I aim this just right, the exit wound won't make too much of a splatter of your brain matter on the couch."

"Jesus." The young man's lip trembled.

"He's bluffing, man," the younger brother said. "Can't you see that?"

I swung the gun toward his end of the couch and squeezed off a round. Everyone jumped and the other girl screamed. The bullet blew a sizeable hole in the piece of furniture less than two inches from Matt's leg. Little bits of foam exploded into the air and onto the carpet while other finer particles confettied through the air.

"Fuck!"

"I know you're not so concerned with yourself, Matt, so how about I just start with your brother's kneecaps? He won't even bleed to death if you tell me what I want before I have to shoot up the rest of him."

There was a short silence then Matt Connors said, "What do you want to know again, asshole?"

"What Caleb was doing up there."

He looked at his brother.

"Shit," Caleb said. "Go ahead and tell him."

"He was looking to see if the dude who killed that old man and all those cops being up there had screwed up our plans."

"Your plans to fly and track the pigeons with the nerve gas."

His mouth went flat. He said nothing.

"You better not tell him any more, man," his brother cried.

I almost shot out Caleb's kneecap then. But I didn't want to interrupt his brother if he might keep talking.

And the younger brother, either too stoned or too scared, obliged. "Yeah, man. What the hell else you think?"

"Matt! Shut the fuck up!"

"Jesus H. Christ, mister," the girl was saying. "Maybe you should call the FBI or something." She had pulled her blouse completely back on now. "I want you two bastards out of this house, now."

"Who killed Carew?" I asked.

"We don't know."

I squeezed off another round into the couch, coming a little closer to Matt's leg than I'd intended.

"Shit, man! What are you, crazy?"

"I'm calling the cops." The girl made a move toward the kitchen.

"Not yet," I told her. "Who killed Chester Carew?"

"We don't know who killed him and that's the God's truth, ain't it, Caleb?"

Caleb said nothing. I finally turned the long gun toward him.

"You had specific instructions," I said. Higgins was worried about something. "What were they?"

The older brother smiled and shook his head.

"Oh, who gives a fuck anymore, Caleb? Tell the man so we can get the hell out of here before the cops show up. He was looking for that other bird man who was always with the old guy who got shot. The one who's been training us how to track the birds and all."

"You talk too much for your own godamned good. You've always talked too much," his older brother admonished him.

"Another falconer? Which one?" I asked.

"Farraday." So there it was.

"Does Higgins think he's the one who killed Carew?" I suddenly remembered Toronto's theory about a second person being present at Chester's killing.

"Matt," Caleb said.

He ignored him. "Either him or the guy he works for."

"So he works for someone else?"

"Yeah. That's what I heard."

"And who is the guy he works for?"

"Matt!"

"Mister. I'm telling you the truth. I ain't got a clue. Why don't you go ask Higgins or Warnock?"

"But why would Farraday murder Carew? Did Chester know he was helping you people learn to track the birds?"

"No way, man. The old guy showed up with that other guy at a couple of meetings. But we never talk about the shit that is really going on at the meetings. Only a few of us are in on it. We're like a round table—knights."

They were knights all right. Knights of darkness.

"You're blowing our whole operation!" Caleb screamed at him. "We're dead, you keep talking, you little fuck. Don't you know that?"

"Shit," his brother yelled back, "you just talked too. We may be dead already, anyway. I showed you how my hands was shaking." He held up his young hands and they both were trembling—more than just a fear-inspired kind of trembling, these were minor spasms.

"Oh, God, get out!" one of the girls screamed. "You bastards have brought some kind of poison shit into my house."

"Relax," I said. "If they'd brought it here, we'd all be dead or getting ill by now."

"It's not contagious?"

"No." I hoped I was telling the truth, but whether I was

or not, it was a moot point. I looked again at Matt. "You two
have been doing some testing, handling vials of some kind
of chemicals with those pigeons, right?"

"Yeah."

"But you've always worn protective clothing, masks
and everything when you're handling this stuff, right?"

He nodded.

"Will you people please leave my house? I'm gonna call
the cops. This whole thing is scaring me shitless," the girl
said. The second girl, who'd managed to pull up her pants
and rebutton them, was now crying, slumped against the
wall in the corner.

"Okay, fellas," I said. "Time to go. Get your shirts on
and get out of here."

"What, you mean you're just going to let us go?" Matt
Connors looked with wide eyes at his older brother. "I need
help, man. I mean, I'm tired of handling all this toxic shit.
Maybe I'm sick. I want to go to a hospital."

"Then get in your car and drive straight there," I
advised him.

He looked at Caleb as if he didn't quite trust that would
happen.

"C'mon. You heard what I said. Now, move." I gestured
with the Mossberg.

They slowly wrestled their shirts over their heads. Caleb
stared at me with a renewed hatred as he stood and his
younger brother struggled to his feet.

I took a step to the side, swinging the gun directly
toward him. "Don't even think about it," I said.

"What about this grass, man?" He gestured toward their
bong and the other drug paraphernalia. "This shit all
belongs to us."

"Take it, and get out of here."

"Hey, you're just going to let these idiots leave?" the girl
protested.

Caleb smirked at me. "Thanks, asshole."

They scooped up their belongings and headed out the
front door. I watched them down the sidewalk and into the

GTO before I lowered the shotgun. Their back tires bounced over the curb backing up and they burned rubber tearing off down the street.

I'd already committed the plate to memory. The cops and the FBI could figure out the rest. I pulled out my cell phone and dialed 911.

"Like to report a possible DWI," I said.

Snoopy wouldn't get far.

32

"I finally got it, Dad." Nicole's voice, through the cell phone, hovered somewhere between excitement and horror.

"Are you still at Priscilla's?" I was on MacCorkle Avenue headed out of South Charleston toward St. Albans and Farraday's place. It was coming on to nine o'clock and though I might be late for my rendezvous with Higgins and Warnock, I'd decided to focus, for the moment at least, on Farraday.

"Yes. But I'm just about to leave to drive out to you."

"What have you got?"

"Damon Farraday's real name is Drew Slinger."

"Really."

"And get this: he has a criminal record a half a sheet long."

"What is he, some kind of right-wing militia extremist?"

"No! You won't believe it. He spent time in jail for several acts of sabotage against lumber and mining companies. He was also one of the leaders arrested at the protest riots during the finance meetings in Seattle a couple of years ago. Apparently, he subscribes to a more left-wing agenda."

"Why in the world would he be involved with the Stonewall Rangers then?" I asked.

"Good question. Are you sure he's working with them?"

"I just got further confirmation that he is. I'm on my way to try to find him now."

"Be careful, Dad. Priscilla helped me come up with the info on Slinger's record. She also made a couple of phone calls ... and get this, Slinger was let out of jail early with the help of the ATF. Plus, she said to tell you that the ATF and FBI are working in West Virginia with a man named Colonel Goyne—Patrick Goyne. He's ex-CIA and apparently a whole host of other things."

"Gotta be the guy Toronto was talking about. I guess

Priscilla didn't tell you how she came up with all that information."

"She said don't ask."

"No other names? Just Farraday and Patrick Goyne?"

"That's it."

"Great job, honey. This helps close the loop on things. A lot."

"Have you found out any more about Jake's situation?"

"A little, but it's not necessarily good. He escaped federal custody."

"He what? Where is he? Have you talked to him?"

"No. I just talked to Betty Carew awhile ago and he hasn't shown up there either."

"What do you want me to do now?"

"Go to the Carews' in Nitro and wait there until you hear from me. I'm going to try to find Farraday and haul him down to talk to the lead ATF agent on this whole deal. That ought to be interesting."

There was silence on the phone for a moment.

Then Nicole said in a much softer voice, "Dad, maybe you should wait for me to get there. I mean, for backup and everything."

"I'll be all right, Nicky."

"You sure?"

"I'm sure. You go on to Nitro. I'll call you in a couple of hours if not before."

"Okay," she said. "Just be careful."

"Hey, do you remember when you were a little girl, what I used to sing to you when you were scared at night?"

"*Sweet Baby James*, right?"

"Yeah, *Sweet Baby James*. Hang in there, Sweet Baby."

"Sure, Dad ... love you."

The connection clicked off.

I had Stinger's a.k.a. Farraday's address, a house on a quiet residential street backed by fields, but as it turned out, I wouldn't need to go all the way to the residence. His old Scout was just pulling down to the next intersection, a block away from his place, as I rounded the corner by his home.

He turned on to the cross street and I followed.

I shadowed him from a distance for several miles, onto the interstate and all the way back into the city. He seemed in no hurry. We took the 119 Robert Byrd Freeway exit and wound our way up into Charleston's South Hills, a world away from Washington Street and the west end. Tony Warnock's neighborhood. Now wasn't this interesting? Maybe I wouldn't be so late for my appointment with him and Higgins after all.

In a neighborhood of expensive homes, I cut my lights at the curb and watched from around the corner as the Scout drove into the driveway of a stately plantation-style house. Even from a distance I could see it sported brightly lit landscaping, a three-car garage, and an in-ground pool that had been covered over for the winter. And there was another vehicle in the driveway: Warnock's Lincoln Navigator. Farraday climbed out of his vehicle, walked up to the front door, and entered without knocking.

I thought about hauling the shotgun up to the door with me again, but in this neighborhood I decided I was better off sticking with handguns that could be concealed. I left my car and cut across the neighbors' lawns to the back of Warnock's residence. I moved in the shadow of the pool house toward the back patio, beyond which I could see lights blazing in a sunken living room. The room was empty, but I could hear classical music playing from somewhere, Tchaikovsky I thought.

All at once, a side door leading from the kitchen to the driveway flew open and Farraday came out hurrying toward the garage. He went to the side and pushed a button. I could hear one of the heavy garage doors begin to open. A moment later I caught the scent of exhaust smoke, and when the door stopped moving on its rollers, the purring of a car engine's idle floated through the air.

"Oh, Christ," I heard Farraday exclaim. He entered the garage, a car door clicked open, and it sounded as if he were fumbling with something. A few seconds later, he came back out, walking quickly, with a large canvas bag slung over his shoulder. He went to Warnock's Navigator, opened the driver's door, heaved the large bag inside, jumped in, and backed out of the driveway.

As he roared off down the street, I took off running, detouring around the front of the garage on the way back to my car. There was no doubt about what was inside. Tony Warnock's dead body slumped in the seat of a silver Mercedes coupe, its engine still running. A pack of what looked like hundred-dollar bills that must have fallen from the bag Farraday took also lay on the pavement next to the car. I moved in to check on Warnock. No pulse. He'd been dead for some time. I also noticed a contusion the size of a dime behind his left ear.

Suicide? That'd be up to the M.E. to decide.

I needed to stay on Farraday's tail. Leaving Warnock, I raced to my car.

Back in the Buick, I made a quick three-point turn and floored it toward the entrance to the luxury subdivision. I caught sight of the Navigator's taillights ahead, just as they turned onto the highway. I followed, still careful to stay at a distance, although Farraday seemed to be in much more of a hurry now.

I pulled out my cell phone and punched in the number for Agent Grooms. He answered his cell on the third ring.

"Agent Grooms?"

"Ahh, the man of the hour. You know I've just been sitting here twiddling my thumbs since you hung up on me. Got nothing else to do, you know. Have you managed to screw anything else up for us since we last talked, Frank?"

"You and your people must not be too happy with me at the moment," I said.

"That would be the understatement of the decade so far. This is your final warning, Pavlicek. You're interfering with a federal investigation. ..." He went on, but I cut him off.

"Listen, I was just up at Tony Warnock's house in the South Hills. Warnock's dead in his car in the garage. He either committed suicide or someone tried to make it look like he did."

"What? What are you, a shit collector? Dead bodies seem to have a habit of following you around."

"Right now I'm following Damon Farraday, whose real name, as I'm sure you know, is Drew Slinger."

"Where are you? And how do you know about Farraday?"

"How do I know I can trust you, Grooms? Why are you people working with someone like Farraday?"

He said nothing.

"Who is Colonel Patrick Goyne? He's the guy who's helping you sting the Stonewall Rangers, isn't he?"

"You know I can't ... if you would just come down here or tell us where you are we can help each other."

"The way you helped Jake?"

"That's not fair, that's—"

"Do you know where he is?" I asked.

"Who? Toronto? No."

"Me either."

"Maybe, just maybe, Pavlicek, this means you should go back to investigating accident scenes or taping lustful husbands, or whatever it is you're supposed to be doing instead of investigating terrorists."

I said nothing, concentrated on keeping the Navigator in sight.

"We're on top of this situation, believe me. The last thing we need is you going around talking to more people. Pretty soon we'll have some kind of panic on our hands. Don't try to be a cowboy, Pavlicek. You need backup."

"I do have backup." I checked my side mirror as I switched the phone to my other hand and changed lanes. "I just don't know exactly what he's doing right now."

"You're only making things worse for yourself," he said.

"Oh, by the way. When you go to Warnock's, make sure you have your people keep a lookout for any more money. I saw a stray pack of hundreds lying around and Farraday's carrying around an oversized canvas bag I'd just bet is full of cash."

"Oh, that's just great—"

"Sorry, Grooms," I said. "Gotta go."

He was swearing as I hung up on him and turned the phone off for the second time that night.

33

The entrance road leading into the Tri-State Racetrack &
Gaming Center, just over the ridge a couple of miles from
Nitro, glowed in the dark with the faux sense of cleanliness
and prosperity only gambling brought. The Navigator kept
right on moving. We passed a Wal-Mart and other retailers,
a couple of busy fast-food outlets. A race was taking place
under the lights at the greyhound track—sleek muzzled
animals battling in the turns around a man-made lake on a
finely groomed dirt oval. The parking lot was about half full.

A quarter mile beyond the track, the Navigator sped up
a freshly paved roadway that led to the newly opened—at
least according to the sign—Balthazar Hotel. The hotel itself
sat high and fortresslike on its own knoll ringed with huge
white spotlights illuminating the massive building. Fake
stone columns buttressed an impressive arched entryway
whose centerpiece was a fountain tinted in the dark by
smaller, multicolored spots. Clearly a place for would-be
high rollers.

I drove slowly up the hill until I saw Farraday, carrying
the large bag again, enter through the front door. I edged
around the circle as he crossed the lobby and entered an
elevator at the side. As I came around the side of the
building, I noticed the elevator was one of two in an external
glass bank. I quickly pulled into a parking space between a
van and a huge Silverado pickup towing a trailer bearing a
couple of snowmobiles and watched in my side mirror as
Farraday exited the elevator on the top floor.

Penthouse or Presidential Suite, no doubt. Was he
meeting Goyne? I scanned the row of windows along the top
floor, waiting. Sure enough, a few moments later a light
popped on behind the curtains of one of the windows on the
end of the building. Either he himself or someone else was
letting him into the corner suite, but I didn't know which.

Should I wait things out, call for reinforcements, or go

in after him? A hotel room takedown by one man alone was risky. Could I count on Toronto being somewhere here now too? I pulled out the phone again and called Nicole. She'd just arrived at the Carews'. I told her exactly where I was and what I was about to do. She tried to talk me out of my plan. I tried to reassure her and gave her some instructions of her own, but somewhere in the back of my brain another tale was emerging. It hadn't quite taken shape just yet. It spoke of small pieces of a trail missed, elements of risk. At the same time, I realized the time had come. My best shot of taking Farraday was now.

Inside the Balthazar, the lobby was as impressive, in its own gaudy way, as the exterior of the hotel. A massive and modernistic interpretation of a chandelier took up a huge chunk of the ceiling while the floor was a combination of attractively laid tile and thick carpet of a Middle Eastern design. There was an open-air atrium and a restaurant with water burbling through rocks and lots of fake plants everywhere. A few partiers, maybe taking a break from the casino across the way, were laughing at an Eddie Murphy movie on the television at the bar.

I stepped across to the bank of elevators. After a short ride to the top floor, the doors whisked open to reveal an elegant corridor along which were four doors on either side. A panoramic picture window in the hall displayed an impressive view of the casino and racetrack. I casually strolled down to the comer suite and noted the number on the door. Then I returned to the elevator and rode it back downstairs.

Back in the parking lot, I made sure the area was clear, then went and retrieved the Mossberg from the Buick, concealing it as best I could beneath my coat. I searched until I found Warnock's Navigator parked near the back of the building, an old Plymouth Voyager beside it. Pretending I was fiddling with my keys for a few moments, I managed to trip the lock on the Voyager.

The inside smelled like a combination of baby food and dirty diapers, but I climbed in back anyway, sliding the door shut behind me. I waited a few moments and nothing happened. So far so good. I plucked out my cell phone again, punched in the main number of the hotel, and asked to be connected to the suite number Farraday had entered.

"Hello."

It was Farraday's voice.

"Is Damon Farraday there?" I asked.

A pause. "Who's this?"

"This *is* Damon Farraday, isn't it? Or should I say Drew Slinger."

Another pause. "I don't know what you're talking about. Who the hell is this?"

"Frank Pavlicek."

"Frank. I… uh … I mean, what're you calling for?"

"Why don't you come on back outside by the Navigator and we can talk about it," I said.

A pause. "Outside? Sure, okay. That is, uh … I'll be right down."

Three or four minutes later, I watched as he emerged from around the side of the building, walking quickly. I couldn't tell if he was carrying or not, but under the circumstances, I had to assume he was. He kept looking around, as if he were afraid an entire swat team might descend on him at any moment. The parking lot, though full of cars, was still empty of anybody else. I ducked farther down below the window with one hand on the door handle and the other holding the shotgun. I let him come along between the Navigator and the van.

Just as he reached my spot, I jerked open the sliding door and thrust the barrel of the shotgun in his side.

"Howdy, Damon … I mean Drew, that is."

He put his hands in the air. I stepped out of the van, checked again to make sure we weren't being seen, and prodded him to move around into the shadows of a line of pine trees behind the vehicles.

"What do you want, Frank? I think you must be making some kind of mistake."

"Maybe," I admitted. I probed the large lump in his side

with the tip of the Mossberg. "Lose the handgun. With your left hand, two fingers."

He was wearing a hunting jacket similar to my own. He reached inside with his left hand as I'd instructed and pulled out the gun with his fingers. It was a .454 Taurus Raging Bull.

"Nice little cannon," I said. "Toss it lightly, and I mean lightly, into the trees. I want a soft landing and no accidental discharges."

He did as I instructed. The gun made a low thump as it came to rest in among the branches and pine needles.

"Good. Now turn around."

He turned to face me. "Want do you want. Frank? Like I said, this must be some kind of mistake."

"I don't think so."

But I immediately found out how wrong I was when I sensed movement behind and beside me. I turned, but too late, feeling a strong arm pulling the barrel of the shotgun down as the tip of a sound suppressor attached to a Beretta pistol jammed against the side of my head. It hurt. Not as bad as the slugging I'd taken from Caleb Connors's own Mossberg, but I was growing weary of having firearms bashed into my cranium.

I twisted my head to see who had bested me and caught a brief glimpse of none other than Kanawha County's own public information officer, the pipe-smoking Hiram Jackson, minus the pipe now, of course. But that might have just been my imagination. Before the lights went out.

"A little too hot for you back there, Franco?" Farraday asked, raising the rear hatch of the Navigator. I smelled oil and water. My head felt sticky. Apparently I'd vomited as I was waking up. I was lying in my own waste.

"Don't you worry about that. We'll have you in a nice cool place in just a minute," he said and chuckled.

The winter air he jerked me up into was cold enough. The side of my head felt like someone was still pounding it with a hammer. There was another man with him. Not Hiram Jackson, but a short Hispanic-looking young man pointing the shotgun at me, grinning, and saying nothing. He had a bandana tied around his head and a toothpick in his mouth.

We were next to a small warehouse along the bank of the river. A puddle of light illuminated a large dock, and moored to it was a black-and-white-walled tugboat, the kind that pushed the barges up and down the river. Out beyond, the dark Kanawha flowed smooth and silent.

"Not exactly the Balthazar or the Charleston House, but I'm afraid it'll have to do," Farraday continued. He must've felt the need to keep up the chatter. I'd have just as soon he shut up.

They led me onto the dock. A bright array of white lights and steam became visible across the water. One of the area's chemical plants. I wasn't sure which one.

There were no lights on the boat, but there was plenty of noise. A deafening roar came from the stern, where some kind of large engine driving a fan or something — not the boat's diesels, but something else — chunked away in the blackness. Farraday switched on a bright-beam flashlight. We stepped across a gangplank with chain-link railings onto the deck. It smelled of mildew and oil and chlorine.

"He's in the bow," Farraday said to the other man.

They pushed me around the high hurricane deck surrounding the navigating bridge toward the stubby front of the boat, where there was a hatch fastened shut by heavy releases that were padlocked and bolted to the deck. Farraday fished a key from a pocket and unfastened the locks. Then he worked open the latches and pulled open the hatch, shining his light below.

"Hey, Indian brave. Brought you some company," he said. He pulled me roughly forward to the edge of the hatch.

No one answered.

His light searched out a compartment about fifteen feet square. In one corner, the beam caught the edge of a pair of brown cowboy boots, smeared with grease, then climbed upward to reveal the rest of a figure hunched over in a seated position. He stared straight up at us, rather than shielding his eyes from the light, as you might expect. He seemed to want to draw strength from what for him must have been the sudden brightness.

"Howdy, Frank," Jake Toronto said.

34

The hold in the boat was so dark I couldn't even make out the form of my hand when I held it up in front of my face.

"Some dungeon, huh?" Toronto said.

"Yeah." It felt good to see him again and to be temporarily free of our captors, even if my stomach heaved with nausea and it felt like someone was dribbling a basketball in my head.

"And at least it's not too cold in here," I said.

"Right. Be a shame to freeze to death in the dark."

"Be a shame to freeze to death in the light too. Smells like piss though."

"You gotta go, you gotta go. There's a little hole over there goes down into the bilge. Hard to aim when you have to feel for the opening."

I couldn't help snickering. My turn would come.

"You tried yelling, making some noise?"

"For a few hours. Didn't do any good."

"That engine they've got running back there drowns out everything," I said.

"Man, and here I was thinking you were gonna come rescue me like Prince Valiant or something."

"Right," I said. "Don't think I wasn't trying. And where the heck have you been? Grooms called me and said you escaped custody."

"I did."

"And?"

"And I went after the guy I was telling you about and that's how I ended up in here."

"This guy who set you up."

"Yeah."

"Colonel Patrick Goyne."

"That's right. Very good. Feds have helped set him up here as Hiram Jackson."

"He must be very good if he got the jump on you to put

you down here too."

"He *is* very good." There was no shame in his voice, only clinical assessment.

"But you're still alive."

"Still here."

"How'd you first get onto him?"

"Saw him talking on TV and I wondered what he was doing here."

"And Farraday, I mean Slinger, is working for him?"

"You got it, muchacho."

"Who is Goyne working for?"

"*Who* may be too big a question to answer right now."

"But they're planning to do something with a bomb. The whole sting deal with the Feds and the Stonewall Rangers and pigeons and the nerve gas is just a front."

"Yup," he said. "I've been sitting here thinking about it. Goyne's running a false flag operation. I should've known it when I first saw him on the tube. It's the way he likes to work."

I told him all about what I had learned regarding Chester and the ANFO and the cave, and about Tony Warnock and the cash. Then I said, "Tell me more about Goyne."

"Nice little setup, don't you think? With the Feds' help, he must have gotten himself hired by the county here a few months ago just so he could do this job. Colonel Patrick Goyne. Former Navy SEAL, former special ops commander and CIA station chief somewhere in the Far East. I met him about fifteen years ago, soon after you and I were given our walking papers by the NYPD. He was working for the CIA then. I've worked with him a couple of times since. Trusted him almost as much as I trust you … till now, that is. Oh, and one more thing about him. He's a world-class sniper."

"Then he's the one who put the bullet in Chester?"

"Nope. Actually, that was our boy Farraday — what did you say his real name was, Slinger? I got that much out of them before they stuck me down here in this hole. He lured poor Chester into a trap, poisoned Elo."

"Some falconer."

"Right," he said.

"And Elo?"

"The falcon's dead too."

"But we thought there was a second person present at the murder scene."

"I figure Goyne showed up right after to make sure Farraday didn't screw it up."

"And the others that were killed?"

"Farraday had to set the bombs on the trucks."

"That's what I figured too."

"And the vet at the clinic ... I don't know. That was pretty sloppy. I'd probably have to say Farraday there too."

"I can't believe these guys might actually get away with this crap," I said.

He was silent for a moment. Then he said, "You remember that job I told you about, the one up in Canada last year?"

"Yeah. You said you retrieved something, but you wouldn't say what it was."

"Right. Well, they were reinforced cylinders used to store chemical weapons. Empties. They were supposed to have been destroyed in a weapons incinerator in Utah, but I guess these bunnies somehow slipped through the cracks. Don't ask me how they ended up on the bottom of the Straight of Georgia 'cause I don't know."

"You said they were empties. Were they dangerous or something?"

"Not particularly. And they'd been in the water a long time. But we dove in hazardous-materials suits just in case."

"And you did this for Goyne?"

"Right. That and for ten thousand dollars for six hours' work, and what I thought was a legitimate black op."

"Okay. Tell me about it."

"It was like this: I was told the idea had two purposes. Identify potential terrorist cells attempting to acquire chemical weapons by offering to sell them to suspected targets. Provide them with extremely minute amounts —

we're talking almost microscopic — of the genuine article. Not enough to do any real damage. Then set up a big-quantity sale. Pump a bunch of genuine tanks full of a close, toxic but nonlethal chemical relative. Collect the money and either move in for the sting or let the terrorists get frustrated with their worthless weapons. Either dry up their money supply or arrest them or both."

"But wouldn't terrorists be suspicious and run some kind of tests to make sure they were getting the genuine article?"

"That's what *I* said. But I guess most of these ideological types are not all that sophisticated."

"Like Higgins and the white supremacist Stonewall Rangers."

"Brains are not real high on the recruiter's list of attributes. And anyway, contrary to what most people think, when it comes to these chemicals, the stuff is really a lot tougher to deliver effectively than most people realize."

"Yeah?"

"Sure. Weather and wind conditions play a big role. Even with a big bomb or something, you can't always be certain. Tests fail a lot of times or have mixed results. The inexperienced might manage to kill a small animal or something, but that's a long way from wiping out an entire city, or even a crowd of people unless you really know what you're doing. Those terrorists in Japan a few years back got lucky — and that was only because they managed to unleash a fair amount of the stuff in one of the most tightly packed places full of people on earth: a Tokyo subway."

"Sounds like someone's been feeding you the party line," I said.

"Yeah, well, I bought it hook, line, and sinker."

"Don't feel that bad. Looks like the ATF and the FBI bought it too."

"Right."

"Is that why you didn't contact me after you escaped from the Feds — I want to hear that story sometime, by the way — and why you've been acting so secretive?"

"That and one more thing."

"I'm all ears."

"My old man belongs to the Stonewall Rangers."

"Felipe?"

"Um-hum."

"How long?"

"A couple of years. He's always ranted and raved in private, just to me, I used to think, about 'the nigger and Jew problem' he calls it. Says *his* father was with Mussolini. He's actually proud of it."

"But your mother, she was of mixed race, right? And you ..."

"Only makes it worse," he said.

"I can't begin to imagine. Why did you even want to have anything to do with the guy?"

A long pause. Then, in a softer voice I'd never heard him use before, "He's still my father, I guess. Besides, he's mostly harmless. I don't think most of these Ranger yahoos even know what Higgins and his little band are up to, even if they might applaud it. Probably wouldn't have the guts to try to pull it off themselves."

"So we don't know whom, exactly, Goyne is working for, but we know he and Farraday are in it for the money."

"Most likely."

"Anyway," I said, "right now we've got some more immediate concerns. Like how we're going to get out of this tub."

"I've been working on that."

"You got a plan?"

"Yeah, I may. But something else you told me has me even more concerned at the moment. You said Farraday's built a big ANFO bomb, right?"

"That's right," I said.

"I've got a bad feeling."

"What?"

"I think it's sitting on this tug, right here over our heads," he said.

"How do you know?"

"I saw the huge containers and the charges when they brought me down here. It was still light."

"Shit," I said.

"What?"

"There is a chemical plant across the river. They're going to drive this boat into it. I think one of these plants around here — I'm not sure which one — makes the same kind of stuff that killed all those people in India."

"Methyl isocyanate. If a whole lot of it gets released and the cloud passes over Charleston we could be talking major fatalities."

"But I thought you said chemical agents were a lot more difficult to deliver on a population than that."

"I said *could be*. Wouldn't matter if the explosion succeeded in killing a bunch of people or not if all they were after was the panic effect. And guess who ends up with the blame?"

"The Stonewall Rangers."

"And you and me."

"Lovely. And we'll be dead with no way to refute that we weren't involved. ... But I don't get it. Goyne is in this for money, right?"

"Yes."

"And the Feds think Goyne and Farraday are working for them to entrap the Stonewallers."

"They do."

"The Feds know about everything — the birds, the chemicals, the money coming through Warnock — except they don't know about Goyne's plan to bolt with the cash and about this big bomb we're sitting on. Is that right?"

"Yup. Of course the ATF now knows a lot more about the bomb, thanks to you."

"But they're still suspecting the Stonewallers."

"Unfortunately."

"But why would Goyne or Farraday want to incinerate a chemical plant and possibly murder thousands? Why not just take the cash, leave the Stonewallers to be arrested by the Feds, and flee?"

He said nothing for a moment. Then I heard him take in a deep breath. "I can't prove any of this," he said. "But I've got an idea."

I waited.

"I told you about the op in Canada. Well, a few weeks after that, I was talking with one of the other guys involved. He's dealt with Goyne a few times in the past too. He said he'd heard that Goyne was hooked up with a group of insiders, some in government, some who used to be, and that these people came with a pretty screwed-up agenda."

"What do you mean?"

"They have things they want to keep quiet. Such as illegal development of chemical and biological weapons, and deals made with foreign terrorists in order to win elections or advance their platform."

"Which is?"

"This guy didn't know exactly, but apparently they're not too thrilled with the way things are going and the current war on terrorism."

"Party affiliation?" I asked.

"This would be beyond politics, Frank."

"You're saying these folks might employ Goyne and Farraday to stage an actual terrorist attack and attempt to pin the blame on the Stonewallers?"

"I'm saying it's possible."

"Why?"

"Who knows? Maybe they're hoping to stir up criticism of current policy or deflect attention from something else, or maybe there is a score to be settled."

"Well, that might explain Farraday's involvement and why they used the ATF to spring him from jail. If he's some kind of ecoterrorist, blowing up a capitalist chemical plant is right up his alley. Pinning it on the Stone-wallers would just be the icing on the cake."

"Yeah. But I'll bet he's cut in on the money too. This kind of thing takes cash. And here we were thinking poor Damon was just Chester's falconry apprentice, a plumber."

"He must have seen getting involved with falconry as

good cover for what he was doing. And who knows? Maybe the ATF, not recognizing his real motives, even helped him out with that too?"

"Like I said, pretty slick deal if they manage to pull it off."

"Have you told anyone else about what the guy said to you about Goyne?"

"Nah. I didn't think too much about it at the time. You hear these kind of crazy conspiracy theories all the time."

"If there's any truth to it, we might not know what we're up against. There might be FBI and ATF people involved."

"Could be, but I doubt it," he said. "At least not the ones here on the front lines."

"Why is that?"

"Just like the false flag—Goyne's method of operation. He's been pretty much a lone wolf for a long time. Once the directive was given, there would be a hands-off policy and maybe a dozen degrees of separation between him and the people he might actually be working for."

"Easier to stay above any suspicion."

"Uh-huh."

"So we really don't know for sure what the overall agenda is."

"That's right," he said. "We really don't know."

"Welcome to our own little war on terrorism. Shoot first and ask questions later. Because if we don't, we're all liable to end up dead."

"That's the way I figure it."

"How long do you think we have?" I asked.

"Not long. You said they've got their money, right?"

"Right."

He said nothing.

"Nicky's here," I said. "After she heard what happened to you, she insisted on coming. She drove down and met me at your place earlier."

"You went to my place?"

"That's right. Saw Priscilla."

"She and her baby okay?"

"They're fine. She's a little concerned about you though."

"And the birds?"

"Fine."

"So Nicky's here, huh?"

"Yeah, and if she figures out what's happened, hopefully she'll go to the cops and the Feds. I called her when I was outside the hotel to let her know exactly where I was and what my plan was."

"Wait a minute. You told her if something happened to you to go to the cops or the Feds?"

"Right."

"Now I'm really worried."

"You thinking she might try to make a run at this on her own?"

"Got too much of her old man in her."

Neither of us spoke for a minute or two. The roar of the fan motor outside droned on, vibrating through the bulkheads. The darkness felt like a cold hand calling me to sleep, drawing me to places I wasn't ready to go just yet.

"So how are we going to get out of here?" I asked. "You said you'd already been working on something."

"I thought you'd never ask," he said.

35

We were only going to get one shot.

Footsteps reverberated on the deck overhead. At their first sound, I could also hear the soft shuffles and scrapes of Toronto making his move. I could no longer make out the time on the hands of my watch but I was pretty sure I'd been accurate about the timing of their return.

We'd spent a good deal of the last two hours planning and preparing. Everything depended on our captors opening the hatch to the hold again. We were betting that they would, in order to make sure their prisoners were still in their cell before they launched us on what looked like our first and final voyage.

We still didn't know all the details of what they were planning, but if we had at least the rough outline right, checking on us at least one more time would be the smart thing to do. And these folks were nothing if not smart.

Sure enough, the snap of the lock and the clank of metal against metal told us they were opening the hatch. Cooler air rushed down from above as the top was lifted. The sound of the roaring fan motor became even louder and was suddenly backed by a low rumble from the back of the tug as the boat's main engines came to life. The entire vessel shuddered as a bright beam shot into the hold like a laser.

"Time to wake up, little girls. It's party time."

It was Farraday again. I said nothing.

The beam moved along the floor until it reached my arm, then was directed into my face.

"There you are, Frank. Been having a nice time in there, have you? Where's Jake?"

I still said nothing. The beam left me and continued its search along the floor of the hold. "C'mon, Jakie boy. Come out, come out, wherever you are."

The light stopped moving when it came to the bulkhead. A large compressor that had been standing there now lay on its side. The decking underneath had been rotting and after forty-five minutes of pushing and pounding and poking with pieces of the wood that came out, Toronto and I had managed to roll the heavy piece of equipment from its foundation, ripping open a decent-sized gash down into the bilge, almost big enough for one of us to fit through.

"What the hell's that?" The beam ran back to blind me. I stared at the floor.

"What's going on?" Another voice. Goyne's.

More footsteps. The beam of light moved back to the hole in the floor.

"He can't get out through the bilge, can he?" Farraday asked.

"Not unless he's got a welding torch. But he might cause us other problems. Get down there and have a look. Check everything out."

"You got it."

"We're just cranking up the diesels and we've got a schedule to keep. If our friend Toronto wants to die slopping around in the stinking sewer of a bilge, I say let him."

The same rope ladder they had forced me to crawl down before dropped into the hold. Farraday began to climb down carefully, his beam sweeping back and forth, along with the barrel of the weapon he was carrying. He had a little more firepower this time. A sleek black M-16 was cradled beneath his arm.

"So, c'mon, Frank. What's going on? Jake decide to bug out on you?"

"I don't know. You'll have to ask him."

"Oh, yeah." He stood at the bottom of the ladder now. "Where is he then?"

He moved his light all around inside the compartment. No sign of Toronto.

"How come you didn't go too?" he asked.

"I'm not much of a swimmer," I said. Actually, I wasn't too bad, as long as I could stay on or near the surface, as long as I could remember how to find the surface.

"Hey, Colonel! Looks like Toronto decided to try to make a go —"

But the words had barely escaped his lips when Toronto dropped down on him from above, where he'd been concealed behind a bulwark, hanging like a trapeze artist since we'd first heard them opening the hatch. His heavy boots crashed into the young man's skull and Farraday went down in a heap. Toronto was on top of him and had his legs wrapped around Farraday's neck. I pounced on the light and the gun, but Farraday wasn't through. His hand came out from under his jacket with the Taurus, pointing it at me. Jake pushed down hard with his arms and twisted his legs around Farraday's head. Farraday's neck snapped. The gun tumbled to the floor.

"Get up the ladder," Toronto said. "Get up the ladder now!"

I was already climbing, the beam and the gun pointing toward the opening.

"Jesus fucking Christ, Farraday." Goyne's voice again. "Just bring the other one up and let's get moving. I told you —"

Farraday's head and the top half of his body appeared in the beam. He was wearing a gas mask. I squeezed the trigger of the M-16. It shook against my arms, almost causing me to lose my balance, but the masked face dropped away from the opening with a muffled scream.

All at once the boat shuddered even more and began to move out into the river. I could feel Toronto's weight on the ladder beneath me. One more rung and I pulled myself out into the night. A round from an automatic weapon coming from the direction of the bridge struck the side of the hatch. I rolled to my side, squeezing the trigger to spray the area with bullets. There was a cargo container on the front deck and I scrambled behind it. Toronto began to hoist himself through the hatch. I sprayed another round of covering fire at the bridge, but the boat kept moving.

Toronto scrambled to my side. "Confucius say, Watch the firepower around big bomb."

"Just trying to keep you from getting your face shot off," I said.

There'd been no more firing from the darkened bridge, but the boat picked up speed. The tug only had its running lights on. The river all around us was dark, but we were definitely headed in the direction of the bright lights of the chemical plant. We were a little ways downstream, but the river was only about a quarter mile wide at this point. It wouldn't be long before we would reach the other side.

A siren sounded from upstream and behind us. I peeked around the container. A brightly lit Coast Guard patrol boat, its American Flag trailing behind, was closing on us fast. But maybe not fast enough.

Toronto looked too. "What do you know? Here comes the cavalry."

"Good deal. But it's just the river patrol. Unless they're packing a bazooka, they aren't about to stop this guy."

"Whoever's driving this thing must be a kamikaze pilot."

"Not necessarily. They still want their money. They've probably got a raft with an outboard tied off the back or something."

"Yeah … wait a sec. Give me that thing."

He took the M-16 from me and aimed it at the bridge. He fired three precise shots, spreading them evenly across the glass of the bridge, shattering the windshield. The boat kept moving.

The sound of an outboard engine roared to life from out beyond the rear of the vessel.

"Looks like Goyne and whoever else was left just bugged out," he said. "Did you hit him?"

"I think so. Doesn't matter now anyway."

I looked up to see the lights of the huge chemical plant looming before us. It was a sprawling complex of pipe and steam. We were only about three hundred yards out now and would reach the opposite shore in only a couple of minutes. "The bomb must be on some kind of a timer. We haven't got long. You know how to stop this tub?"

I still had the flashlight in my hand. We raced to the bridge and climbed the stairs to the pilothouse. There was no one inside. Toronto scanned the controls.

"See if you can raise the Coast Guard."

I looked upriver at the patrol boat. Even at the rate they were closing, unless we could find a way to stop or slow down, there was no way they'd reach us before we hit the shore. Given what this boat was packing, it was probably just as well.

I found the radio in a panel overhead and turned the dial to switch it on, but it was dead.

"Looks like they've disabled it."

"Figures." He punched a couple of buttons and pulled back on the throttle. The big diesels kept up their steady whine. "Looks like they've done something to these controls too."

The tug was less than a hundred yards out now. I saw a sheriff's patrol car, its beacons blazing, screaming across an access road beside the plant, paralleling us. Too little, too late.

"Wait a minute," Toronto said. He bent down below the captain's chair and ripped a panel from the sidewall to expose a bunch of wires. "Stand back." He raised the M-16. "This'll either stop this thing or blow us to kingdom come."

"Got to be a better kingdom than this," I said.

He fired a burst at the panel. It exploded in a hail of sparks.

We didn't blow up, not yet anyway, and the boat's big diesels suddenly died.

"We're out of here," I said.

"You got that right. How do you feel about ice water?"

The boat had slowed but was still drifting toward the shore. Getting too close for comfort.

We hit the water together. Two explosions washed over us, one on top of the other. The first was the icy blast of water that swallowed me whole, a shock of instant numbness and a powerful current pulling me downward with the weight of my boots and clothes. The second, following soon on the heels of the first, was the concussive wave of the tugboat's detonation on the surface.

The blast slammed me deeper down into the inky current. I bounced against a gravelly bottom and hit my knee against a rock. Something large and solid struck my head.

I was drifting deep underwater, almost like being at the bottom of that pool with the wet suit on again, but this time in utter darkness and with no air. Who knew what had become of Toronto? I thought of a scene from when I was young, my mother and father holding on to me as we looked over the railing of a huge cascade of water. Had it been Niagara Falls?

I swam, but had no idea which way was up or down. I'd lost the bottom after bouncing off it and being pulled along by the current. Panic welled up inside me, but then like a horrific wave passed over me to be replaced by an eerie sort of calm, only to be replaced by the rising panic again.

I'd been underwater for nearly a minute now, I thought. Everything was beginning to go numb. I thought of all the years that had rushed by and all the time I'd wasted in my life, my own parents, Nicole and Camille and Marcia, Toronto's dad. I didn't have much time left.

The blinding light, when it broke through to me in the darkness, might just as well have been the sun. It was pretty far above, but now at least I knew where the surface was. I didn't know if I could reach it, but I had to try.

I kicked and pulled upward as hard as I could. I felt nothing. Rising, I could see more light on the water to my left, more of a glow. But the light directly over me grew brighter and brighter. After what seemed like an eternity, I broke through the surface, gulping cold and smoke.

"Dad!" Nicole was leaning over the rail of the Coast Guard boat. "Dad! Grab the ring."

36

Agent Grooms and Agent Briggs and Nolestar let us watch
the arrests via a grainy black-and-white satellite video feed
from the FBI office in downtown Charleston. It was like
watching ghost cops on an old tape running on a cheap
VCR. Higgins and eight scary-looking Stonewall Rangers
wearing containment suits were captured and taken into
custody while loading what they thought were cylinders of
illegally undestroyed Sarin gas into the back of a van.

Toronto sat chewing a stick of gum with his dirty
booted foot propped up on a chair. His arm lay limp in a
sling from what the paramedics suspected was a cracked
bone in his wrist. Nicole looked as though she were making
a valiant attempt not to bite her fingernails as she watched
the screens.

She'd done an incredible job of surveillance and keeping
her head under pressure. When I didn't call her back within
our agreed-upon time frame, she'd gone to the Balthazar,
where she watched my car for a while and even managed a
discreet walk-by while the vehicle was still in the hotel lot to
make sure I wasn't dead or unconscious inside.

A few hours later, she had trailed Farraday and the
Hispanic man who came to hot-wire it before driving it off
to ditch it in the river. I was going to have to replace Betty's
Buick, but Nicole had done the right thing, staying with the
perps and not worrying about possessions.

After that, she'd alerted the police to the car in the river.
She and Deputy Nolestar and Agent Grooms, along with
several others, trailed Farraday down to the tug at the river.
I couldn't have been more proud of her. I also couldn't help
but notice one of the younger agents in the room making
eyes at her, but she paid him no attention.

Toronto's father, Felipe, looking confused and vaguely
pitiful in his rumpled suit and hat, had also been brought
into the room and sat blankly watching the screens. Like the

rest of us, he was being held as a material witness in the case.

Grooms left for several minutes before coming back into the room.

"Okay. Afraid the show's over for now, folks."

"Thanks for the tickets," I said.

"We've got a lot more to talk with all you people about, but most of it can wait until morning. Hope none of you is planning on going anywhere for a while."

I shook my head.

"I have to admit it. We owe you guys a debt of thanks. None of us realized Goyne and Farraday were playing us like that."

"And now you get to try to find out how and why."

He nodded. "May not be so easy ... Let me ask you one more quick question. How much of all this do you think your friend Carew was privy too?"

"Enough for Farraday to shoot him in the back over it. With Chester's background and sense of what had caused his bird to get sick, he must've suspected the high concentration of the chemicals Farraday was using to build the bomb."

"Which, if Carew reported it and we'd had more time, might have eventually led us to suspect Farraday and Goyne were up to something besides the deal with the Stonewallers. ... And that's why Farraday killed the vet too. We checked with the lab that performed the tests, by the way, and that reporter whose name you gave us. You were right. The tests showed a high concentration of ammonium nitrate and fuel oil derivatives, same as we found in the cave."

"What about Warnock?" I asked.

"M.E. says it could've been suicide, but he's leaning more toward homicide. The carbon monoxide killed him, but he may have been unconscious before he took the big sleep. That mark you noticed behind the ear was made by some kind of blunt object."

"Goyne?"

"He's the prime suspect. Especially given the money. Warnock was not a Stonewaller, but he was close friends with Higgins. When Goyne contacted Higgins about supposedly having chemicals for sale, Higgins went to Warnock asking about sources of money. You know, big donors who might be sympathetic to the cause."

"He found some?"

"Apparently he did. We're still not sure where. We're trying to sort that all out. Looks like somewhere overseas."

"So you think Goyne murdered Warnock in order to steal the money and also get rid of another potential witness?"

"Quite possibly. We had two of our own agents whom the Stonewallers had seen once before actually driving the truck when we moved in to make the arrests."

"But if Goyne murdered Warnock for the money, why did he leave it all behind in Warnock's Mercedes?"

"We knew the money to buy the weapons was coming into the country in the form of bearer bonds. We also knew that Warnock planned to trade them in for cash at three different local banks where he knew officers and could disguise the transactions as a legitimate transfer of funds for various clients. So we set it up with the banks to mark all of the bills with a new type of technology we're using. But we didn't tell Goyne any of that. At least I knew enough not to trust the man completely."

"Goyne must have figured it out though even if Farraday didn't."

"Yeah. He must have sensed a trap."

I glanced at Toronto. "Or he found out the cash was marked another way."

The ATF agent cocked an eyebrow. "You know something we don't?"

"Nothing I'd be willing to stake my word or my PI license on," I said.

Resignation showed in Grooms's face. "Yeah, well something caused my operator to flip on me and the fur is going to fly over this. Most likely my own. We're either dealing with a lunatic genius here or another phenomenon altogether."

Toronto hoisted himself from his seat with his one good arm. "Goyne is no lunatic. I'll vouch for that," he said.

"Mr. Toronto," Grooms said. "I'm not sure yet how we're going to deal with the matter of your escaping custody."

Toronto shrugged and held out his free hand. "You want to arrest me again now?"

Grooms looked at Briggs and Nolestar. "No. Not at the moment I don't."

Toronto shrugged again and dropped his hand.

Grooms looked at Nicole. "If you don't mind my saying so, Pavlicek, this is some daughter you've got here. If it weren't for her, you and Mr. Toronto might still be at the bottom of the river."

I smiled and winked at Nicole, who looked at the floor, embarrassed.

Just as we were about to leave Toronto went over to Felipe's chair. The old man's eyes were still glued on the TV monitor.

"Come on, Dad," he said. "You need to give it up now."

Felipe turned and rested his fingers on his son's arm. "Jake, I ... I thought it was ... I didn't know they was ... I swear ..."

Toronto said nothing.

"My whole life I been trying to do stuff, trying to keep up with things for the family, Jake. I never wanted to hurt you ... never wanted ..." The old man's dry voice trailed off.

Grooms cleared his throat. Someone else scraped a chair on the floor. Almost involuntarily, everyone except Toronto momentarily turned to glance at the screens again to see what might be happening with the ghosts that were being displayed.

It snowed again the next morning. Heavy, moisture-laden flakes stuck to the branches and piled several inches high in the Carews' driveway, the same way they had the night I'd talked with Chester by the fire a couple of years before. Betty Carew cooked up another big breakfast. I sat alone by the window in the dining room, drinking coffee and thinking of nothing for a change.

I was glad to be able to think at all. Both Toronto and I would have some explaining to do, with more to come; but the fact that multiple law enforcement personnel had witnessed the boat drivers' exchanging fire with us and that we'd been able to shut down the boat's engines went a long way toward proving our intentions.

The small television in the kitchen was turned on. I could hear the steady drumbeat of sound vibrating through the walls. The media firestorm over the tugboat laden with explosives that had blown up just outside the chemical plant and the arrests involving the Stonewall Rangers was in full swing now. All the cable news and major networks had descended on Charleston, West Virginia, and the Kanawha River Valley like it was the next ground zero, which, come to think of it, it easily could have become.

The Feds didn't want Jake's, mine, or Nicole's names brought to the media's attention. I was more than happy to oblige. Kara Grayson had left a couple of messages on my office voice mail back in Charlottesville. I hadn't gotten around to calling her back just yet.

Bo Higgins's used-car dealership had been shut down, of course. Cameras were everywhere and eager-looking reporters and anchorpeople were running around looking for employees or customers or someone else to interview. Pictures of the J. Edgar Hoover FBI Building in Washington kept flashing on the screen as well, and there was even a news conference at the White House.

A lot was still being pieced together, but one thing seemed clear: Drew Slinger, the man who'd taken up falconry in order to become a killer, his neck already broken, had been blown to bits by the very bomb he had built. Colonel Patrick Goyne, the mastermind behind the plot to collect millions selling bogus chemical weapons while also conspiring to blow up a chemical plant, had managed to slip through the authorities' fingers for now. And I had sat face-to-face with him only a couple of days before.

I couldn't help replaying the events of the last few days in my mind to see if I might have missed something, if there'd been anything else I could have done.

For his part, Toronto, when I'd seen him out in the bam earlier, was already talking about how we needed to go after Goyne. But we still didn't know if all his accomplices had been arrested or, for that matter, if anyone else in the government was involved, I reminded him. Besides, Goyne's picture was plastered all over the papers, television, and the FBI Web site. The Feds and every other law enforcement agency in the country now had an APB out on the guy. If they couldn't find him, it would be a long time before Toronto or I ever could.

The soft thud of the dining room door roused me from my thoughts. Betty Carew entered the room. She had a portable phone in her hand.

"Marcia's on the phone," she said. "For you."

I thanked her as she stepped out again, put the phone to my ear, and said hello.

"Hello, Frank."

"Hey. Good to hear your voice, Marsh."

"I've been watching what happened on the news. I heard Chester's name mentioned and I just wanted to make sure you and Nicky and Jake were all right."

"We're all okay," I said. "Jake's got a broken wrist, but I think he'll survive."

"So you were there then? You were involved?"

"We were."

"I just can't believe it. Poor Chester. And those other people too ... and a bomb."

"I know."

"You doing okay with everything?"

"I'm sitting here watching it snow."

There was silence on the line for a moment.

"For once, I have to say, I almost wish I could be there with you," she admitted.

"Me too."

I wanted to tell her I missed her and that maybe I loved her. I wanted to tell her a lot of things, but the words just wouldn't come.

"I've got to go now. I've got to get to a class," she said.

"Sure. Thanks for calling."

"I'm glad you're okay," she said.

"I'm glad you called."

We told each other good-bye and hung up.

There was a soft knock on the door.

"Come in," I said.

Jason Carew came scuffing into the dining room wearing his pajamas, his eyes still filled with sleep, his hair a tangled mess.

"Well, hello, pardner," I said.

"Momma said you wanted to talk with me," the boy said softly.

"That's right, I do."

He stood just inside the doorway and stared.

"Come on over and sit down." I patted the seat of the dining room chair next to me.

He shuffled over and climbed into the chair with his back to the wall. We both sat and looked out the window.

"A lot more snow out there this morning," I said.

"Yeah."

"I heard on the TV there's no school today."

"Uh-uh. I haven't been back anyway since Daddy died. But Momma says I have to go tomorrow if they're open."

"Your momma's right."

"Momma says she wants you and Mr. Toronto to have Daddy's birds so you can take better care of them and take them hunting when they need to and all that."

I nodded. "How do you feel about that?"

"I can take them hunting. I know how, I went with Daddy."

"I bet you could. But the law says you have to wait until you're fourteen."

"I know. That's what Momma says."

"Is it okay then if Jake and I take care of them for a

while? Just until you're older, that is?" I asked.

"I don't know," he said. "I guess it'd be all right."

"It won't quite be heaven."

"I know."

"But you wouldn't want them to get sick or die or anything."

"No."

Outside, a squirrel carrying something in its mouth jumped across the lawn and scrambled up a tree looking for the safety of its nest to weather out the storm.

"You heard what happened last night?" I asked.

"Uh-huh." He snuffled, turning to wipe his nose on the sleeve of his pajamas. "Momma told me. And I was watching the television too in the kitchen." He bit his lip, still staring at the oversized flakes outside.

"Did you know a lot of it has to do with your daddy?"

His face went wide with expression and he turned and looked at me. "It does?"

My gaze met his. "You know what a hero is, Jason?"

He stuck out his chin as if insulted by the question. "Yeah. A course. I seen 'em on TV."

"Well, did you know that there are some heroes — a lot, in fact — who never get seen on television?"

"They don't?"

"Nope."

"How come?"

"It's because only a few people know about them. And that has to be enough."

He nodded.

"Your daddy was a great man."

"Yes, sir."

"And I think you should know something. He was a hero, one of those kinds of heroes I was just telling you about."

"He was?"

"That's right. The men you saw getting arrested on the TV were the men wearing the masks you saw up in your woods. If your daddy hadn't started the ball rolling by standing up to them, a whole lot of other people might've died."

The boy nodded some more and his eyes began to tear up.

"And you want to know what else, Jason?"

"What?" he asked, his lip trembling and his voice beginning to crack.

"That makes you a hero too."

"Yes, sir," he said, almost choking on the words.

He began to sob.

I let him at first. Then I held out an arm. He put one thin knee on my leg, wrapped his skinny arms around my neck, and climbed up in my lap in order to bury his face in my chest. I cupped my hand around one of his small shoulders and felt them shake against me. The snow made whispering sounds against the window. A storm was raging somewhere in the clouds above.

ABOUT ANDY STRAKA

Publisher's Weekly has featured Andy Straka as one of a new crop of "rising stars in crime fiction." His books include A WITNESS ABOVE (Anthony, Agatha, and Shamus Award finalist), A KILLING SKY (Anthony Award Finalist), COLD QUARRY (Shamus Award Winner), KITTY HITTER (called a "great read" by Library Journal), and RECORD OF WRONGS, hailed by Mystery Scene magazine as "a first-rate thriller."

Andy has worked as a book editor, movie production accommodation agent, commercial building owner and consulting vice president for a large specialty physician's practice, surgical implant and pharmaceutical sales representative, college textbook sales and manuscript acquisition representative, web offset press paper jogger, laborer on a city road crew, summer recreation youth director, camp counselor, youth basketball coach, assistant parts manager at an auto dealership, assistant manager at a McDonalds restaurant, and even been registered as a private investigator. (Not to mention a longstanding stint as a stay-at-home Dad to six, which makes neurosurgery look like tiddlywinks.)

A licensed falconer and co-founder of the popular Crime Wave at the annual Virginia Festival of the Book, Andy is a native of upstate New York and a graduate of Williams College where, as co-captain of the basketball team, he "double-majored" in English and the crossover dribble. He lives with his family in Virginia.